WOMAN MURDERED

Beri Balistreri

WOMAN MURDERED

Cover photo © Trip B

Copyright © 2018 Beri Balistreri
All rights reserved.

The characters and events portrayed in this book are fictitious. Any similarity to real persons, living or dead, is purely coincidental, and not intended by the author. Names, characters, businesses, places, events, locales, and incidents are either the products of the author's imagination or used in a fictitious manner. Any resemblance to actual persons, living or dead, or actual events is purely coincidental.

Public figures are portrayed fictitiously.

Lyrics by Trip B used with permission.
O. Henry passage, public domain.
Robert Louis Stevenson passage, public domain.
William Carlos Williams poem, public domain.
*Juan Ramon Jimenez, quoted on page 9.

Copyright © 2018 Beri Balistreri
All rights reserved.

Published in association with:
Peace Vision Arts Books
419 Salinas Rd.
San Juan Bautista
California, 95045
   www.peacevision.net

FIRST EDITION

ISBN: 978-1-98-077686-4

Beri Balistreri

For Gracie

WOMAN MURDERED

WOMAN MURDERED

Cody French had never thought about death until now. Graduating high school was as far as his imagination had let him roam. With that behind him, his horizons were all stocking shelves at Bixby's in Carmel, and messing with the junior college girls from Monterey, until he got the text: *Underwater seismic activity at San Gregorio fault! Ghost Trees gone huge!*

The scruffy, good-looking local teen was about to throw away his non-demanding perfect job to catch a wave—the wave of the world. But before he could say *I quit*, his manager, Albert, said, "Get the hell over there, Goomba! Make surf history!"

The blonde-haired, blue-eyed bro didn't need to be told twice. "Thanks, dude! You won't regret this! I'll be back before the lunch crowd!"

Albert slapped Cody on the butt like a coach. "Hey kid …"

"Yeah man?"

"One of us has to live."

Cody shook off the warning. "I said I'll be back. I can shred."

"That's not what I meant," Albert said. The forty-something, Italian-American meat-slicer shook his head at the uncomprehending youth.

WOMAN MURDERED

"Get outta here!"

That was all Cody needed. He was out the door and climbing into his orange Chevy and Hurley surf truck with the 10'2" four-fin board hanging over the tailgate. Pulling on his 4-ply O'Neil, he figured he'd be at Ghost Trees in eight minutes, easily back in time for lunch—a big wave surfer, not just some *quimby frube* who couldn't catch a killer wave to save his soul.

To the unenlightened, the place called Ghost Trees in Pebble Beach is all about golf courses and the superfluous beauty of sunbeams that spin fields of diamonds across the face of the sea. The real Ghost Tree is nothing, but a gnarled wooden remnant of a dead cypress trunk marked No. 17 on the tourist map of the famous Seventeen Mile Drive. Across the road is No. 18, a quaint plot of manicured pathways and stone benches called Pescadero Point, where old ladies walked their dogs and herded tourists arrive in busses and snap selfies.

The place belies a dangerous big wave break a hundred feet below: Ghost Trees, the surfers call it.

When Cody arrived, the sky was petal pink, the swells were big and black, and there was a pervasive white noise that soothed and terrified him as he looked at the gargantuan waves and deep troughs.

Fucking mavericks! How do they work? Cody thought, riffing on Insane Clown Posse's song *Miracles*, where Shaggy2Dope raps *Fucking magnates, how do they work?* That song was the butt of a million jokes—even a Saturday Night Live parody; but, mavericks or magnates, he was about to ride a forty-foot wave, and he recognized a miracle whether he could explain it or not.

The jet-ski driver towed him way out to where the *aggros* were playing, amped. They were executing deep fades into the bowl, taking drops and grabbing cutbacks, bunny-hopping over shallow boils, and searching for that hangar-sized barrel of a lifetime. These guys were no slouchers. They were in peak condition, seeking peak experiences—the kind where everything else falls away.

"Dude!" the driver shouted, as he released the towline.

Cody took his place in the lineup.

Meanwhile, half-a-mile-away, in the spot called the boneyard, a pair of thirty-foot waves flooded into Stillwater Cove and pummeled the Beach Club—that gray-shingled hundred-year-old institution just above the 17th hole of the Pebble Beach Golf Links: that place so reminiscent of old-world East Coast sodalities, where rich, old, young, strong, weak, widowed, orphaned, lost, found, fearful, brave, knowing and unaware, populate the scene.

Straddling his board, Cody watched as guy after guy paddled up, took the drop, and tumbled out. None of the four surfers before him rode their wave. The first one took an injury to the shoulder.

These were the biggest waves anyone had ever seen in California. Dudes were rushing down from Santa Cruz and up from Paso—every top surfer in the state was on his way, but Cody and the other locals had them beat because there was no warning. These mavericks were caused by an underground earthquake—not a storm.

Two photographers with 1300mm lenses channel-paddled on long guns to catch the drama unfolding on this dangerous break that had only been surfed for the last twenty years. A guy from Monterey's On the Beach Surf Shop jetted over to help with water traffic control.

Maybe, I'll make Surf Magazine? Cody thought.

A Coast Guard patrol boat showed up to tell the tow-surfers they were operating illegally. (Someone always called to complain whenever there were jet skis in the Monterey Bay National Marine Sanctuary.)

Staying wide of the boulders that collared and wadded the West Coast's heaviest wave, the Coast Guard vessel checked itself before the *bombora* that was Ghost Trees.

Transfixed by the ascending wall of doom, Cody

positioned himself for the drop—epic, filmic, lethal as fuck.

This is it, killer wave, homicidal, he thought.

An *immemoriam* squeezed his finest nerve. He had a sense of being in a dream where someone was dead.

This ain't no dream. There's only me.

He was clucked.

No way out but through it.

He pushed off.

"Akawww!" His call was shrill as he tried to sound old school entering the backdoor on the wave of the world.

Fading into the bowl of this deadly right-hander, he got worked—wiped out into a fold. Now he was deep under water, tomb-stoned by a two-wave pindown. Yanked up by its buoyancy, held down by its leash, the board stood straight up like a grave marker out of a watery hell. With all that ocean tonnage above him for two times the count, the leg rope snapped and the board split. Flailing cartwheels in the washing machine thirty feet below the level of air, his mind slowed to higher frames per second.

Famous surfers drown here. I'm gonna be one.

His thoughts turned dark.

What if I'm just a Barney, out of my league?

It was time to release the pressure from his lungs; the weight of it all. It was time to open his mouth and take in the frigid sea—find out what's on the other side.

Then, Cody had the thought of a lifetime.

It's sad not to live. It's sad to NOT live.

The eyes of the Coast Guard engineer scanned the horizon-less surface, though he couldn't believe Cody had a chance of surviving the roiling hold-down. Only minutes before, it had been the playground of elite young men and those so-called *men in gray suits*: the great white sharks that play and feed here in one of the coldest, most heavily shark-infested surf breaks in the world.

In a flash-bang, Cody was jolted—rammed hard from

underneath. A bastard shark knocked the remaining bubbles of stale air from his pipes. The boy pressed his lips together. The last experience of his life was about to be death in the jaws of a monster.

Again, he got shoved mightily. Rammed from beneath, he felt himself begin to ascend. He flailed his oxygen-deprived weakened noodles around the beast and held on for life until, most miraculously, he popped to the surface, gasping for air, coughing, sputtering, and at last, breathing.

His body braced itself, still entangled with the beast that had brought him from the depths. He was certain that he was about to get shredded into a car-sized blood stain. He'd seen *foamies* turn pink before.

Nothing happened.

Nothing happens? Or has everything happened, and are we standing now, quietly, in the new life?

He heard random poetry whisper in his ear.

As his brain began to defog, he came to the realization that his savior was not a great white shark, but one of those Pacific dolphins that likes to shoot waves alongside surfers.

The terrifying anticipation of his stone-cold death was instantly morphed into the exhilaration of a near-death experience.

Sick!

At the same time, the terror experienced by the small crowd of onlookers transformed into elation at the sight of Cody's fist pumping the air. In unison, they shifted their attention to the creature that had him entangled. The young surfer's savior was not a dolphin, but an old woman, and she appeared-to-be quite dead.

It took an hour for the personal watercraft to wrangle the body and tow it to the Coast Guard boat. Paramedics pronounced Cody good to live for other days— saved by an anonymous old Jane Doe who died before she could wake, newly privy to the mystery beyond whatever mind may comprehend.

WOMAN MURDERED

CHAPTER 2

Three weeks before, in the middle of the night, Aimee James sat watching her thirteen-year-old son Daniel work the controller of his Sony PlayStation 2, playing the video game he named *Grand Theft Naughty*.

In their tiny furnished rental, there were only three places to look when it was dark outside: at the pine beams that crisscrossed above them; the soot-black maw of the sandstone fireplace that threatened to devour them; or the small-screen tv that sat on the burl-wood coffee table. There was no cable, so it was local news or video games.

Aimee's son Daniel sat on the cold living room floor with his back against the distressed leather sofa where she sat with her legs curled under her. Daniel's avatar wore a black hockey mask, and used an AK47 and a chainsaw, to kill rival gang members, then take their blood-money.

In the game he was playing, a badass drug dealer offered to sell him *something good*. In this on-screen world he could do anything, even buy drugs, without getting in trouble. He didn't want to buy drugs though, so he shot the drug dealer and watched as stacks of cash floated toward him in slow-motion.

"What was that noise? That noise?" Daniel asked his mother.

"It was just my cellphone."

"Kind of late, isn't it?" he said.

How can he hear a single chirp over all the guns and noises? she thought.

Daniel stared at the screen as a shady character popped up and said that he should have sex with a hooker in a stolen car, strangle her, and take his money back. He ignored the guy and continued his virtual killing spree, using a cement truck to bury a bunch of construction workers in *port-o-potties*. The closer he got to the finish line, the bloodier his mission became.

"It's past three. I'm going to bed," his mother said.

"You tired? You tired?" he asked.

"Nope," she said. "But maybe if I read I'll get tired."

"That *Cannery Row* book?"

"It's a good book."

"Sounds lame. Book about canneries sounds lame."

"It's about people from around here. You might like it." She searched his face for a connection.

"I'm going to kill more perps. Kill more perps."

Her face fell. "You should try and go to sleep too, you know. It's hard to sleep in a new place, but tomorrow we're meeting the doctor and her horse. She's going to help you. She's saving you. So, you know what you've gotta do, right?"

"Stay awake?"

His mother frowned.

"Yes, stay awake, but not tonight. Tomorrow."

#

An hour later, Aimee was sitting up in bed in the small, cold master bedroom of the 1950s rental cottage. She was glaring at the sliding glass door of her bedroom, where Michael Mizol had just left. The room opened onto a discreet patio encircled by a deer fence where once there must have been a garden with flowers to protect; otherwise, it couldn't have mattered if the black-tailed deer came and peered inside.

She brushed a stack of twenty-dollar bills into the battered bureau. With the faded red and gold acanthus-leaf comforter failing to comfort her, she shivered.

WOMAN MURDERED

She jumped at the buzzing of her cell phone. It was a Snapchat from Michael; one of those messages you have only seconds to read before it disappears. He refused to use Messenger or text, saying, "Never write anything down if you don't want the whole world to read it."

The Snapchat was a picture of him with the steering wheel of his car superimposed around his head. He wore a Tesla logo like a Triton wreath. He had typed, "Enjoy the tip (smiley face with tongue). You earned it."

A burning sensation crawled over her. She couldn't breathe.

Earned it!? Tip!?

Her eyes began to water.

He said he wanted me to have cash in case of emergency. He called it pocket change.

She looked at her phone to see the message again, but it was gone. She tried to open the application to respond, but she didn't have a comeback anyhow.

It was *pocket change! It* was *a tip!*

She buried her face in her hands.

It was against her better judgment to accept anything from him, especially after he ghosted her last year and then reappeared last night. Still, she hadn't said no. She'd said thank you.

Proof! I'm a bawd!

The thing was, she really missed him, and she was happy when he called, even though it was late.

Look what he thinks of me now!

She'd been hard-pressed financially since the day her house got sealed off with barricade tape, foreclosed on with all its contents, save for a few boxes and an oil painting she squeezed into her old Jeep the night before.

The lawyers got their pound of flesh, didn't they?

She wanted his company, not his money. *Bawd.* The word kept popping into her head from somewhere.

Steinbeck called his madam with a heart of gold a bawd!

A warm buzzing sensation spread over her as she put her hand on her chest and envisioned a literal heart of gold. Her habit of insinuating herself into whatever book she was reading was half envisioning a different world and half longing to make one.

Michael had left her at the hour of the pearl. That's what Steinbeck called the hour of dawn just before the sun broke.

Daniel's dog was panting in the hallway. Aimee crawled out from under the less-than-comforting comforter and let Puppy into her room.

"Come on!" she said, patting the bed for the dog. Puppy wouldn't budge. She'd been trained not to get onto beds. Aimee reached down and lifted the fifteen-pound terrier mutt onto the duvet. She got herself under the cover again and dug her fingers into Puppy's soft coat. "You have a heart of gold, don't you, girl?"

Aimee shoved her foot against a box that had been on the bed since fleeing to the agrestic cottage a month before. So much clutter would have bothered her once, but now she found it served her well. It was insulating. At least she wasn't spending all night sleeping in a chair with the lights blaring.

That's a step toward normal. Not bad. I'm ready to be normal.

Breaking away from Aimee's petting, Puppy explored the satiny cover, pre-shredded in places, and cardboard boxes filled with pleasant-smelling old papers and better-smelling old books. Her nose worked double-time.

"Puppy, what are you doing? Stop!"

Aimee lunged across the bed and rescued a slobbery book from the mouth of the gentle dog. "Bad dog," she said, then froze.

"Wait. You're not a bad dog."

She pulled Puppy to her chest and buried her face in the dog's fur. "You're the best dog in the whole world."

WOMAN MURDERED

Puppy jumped off the bed and scratched at the slider.

"Do you have to go? You just want to bark at raccoons, don't you?"

Puppy cocked her head.

Aimee let the dog outside and watched her trot off into the darkness. She wondered what really lurked outside that deer-fence that kept her close. Beyond its flimsy barrier, the property sloped in all directions, shrouded by giant trees, dead and alive. Were there predators that would harm an innocent creature just trying to be brave outside of its element?

Predators of the animal sort.

Michael entered her life before the maelstrom that was the sudden death of her ex-husband, and the trial of her son for killing him; but he flew out of San Francisco on business before the trial was over, and stayed away. Maybe that was because he saw it was becoming an auto da fé, and he didn't want to be associated with the damned.

People put the trash out, or creep out to fish at this hour.

Crawling back under the duvet that seemed like something from a bed in the Palace of Versailles, she thought about coming here to this beautiful but lonely place with her boy, who'd survived so much.

Her mission was to help him recover from the curves that life had thrown him: the traumatic death of his father, and his own conviction of manslaughter for patricide. She'd read everything about Asperger's Syndrome, but even the experts didn't agree. She had to follow her own instincts. Daniel didn't put out a lot of spoor. She was a tracker in a desolate landscape.

Nothing ever happens now except endings…

Pulling the bureau drawer open, she sifted the stack of twenties that Michael left. The extra money meant that she could take Daniel on the recommended outings.

Michael's ATM limit must be five hundred.

Beri Balistreri

He never gave his all, no matter what; time, money, or love. He always held back at least thirty-three and a third percent. A corporate attorney who billed a grand an hour, setting antes and stacking decks was his game.

It must have given him a thrill to see me take that.

She couldn't figure any other reason he drove two hours from San Francisco to be with her.

I'm not exciting, I'm not convenient, and now I'm not even free. Not free.

Freedom had been her unwavering focus for the past year and she'd received a miracle. Her son wasn't locked up for the murder of his father. He was with her, starting over in a new place where they wouldn't be scrutinized under a microscope by scientists or with a magnifying glass by snoops. She was aware that his Asperger's Syndrome made people believe that he was capable of murder. They said he lacked empathy and was obsessed with violence.

It would be better if nobody knew anything about him, except Dr. Peletier, of course. She was going to be their savior.

... and beginnings, maybe.

Aimee and Daniel left San Francisco for the dilapidated cottage in the Del Monte Forest. They had to be close to the equestrian center and its new psychiatrist-in-residence.

Hitching a U-Haul to their vintage J40 jeep, they drove two hours south to the most beautiful place on earth. Aimee was certain that in this new place she would connect with other people who loved the natural beauty of California's Central Coast. She felt ready to be alive again. According to a GoToQuiz, she had "a big empathetic heart" and "an authenticity" that almost guaranteed making new friends.

Dreaming. That's what can happen at this hour.

Holding the dog-slobbered book in one hand, Aimee blotted the eyes that Michael called her big browns, even though they weren't really. She opened the green clothbound volume of O. Henry to page forty-seven.

WOMAN MURDERED

In New York City in the early 1900s a young woman was carrying a typewriter, looking for a room to rent, but she couldn't afford the twelve-dollar room or even the eight-dollar room. She had to rent the attic. With little money, she was slowly starving to death.
Maybe, this isn't a good story to go to sleep with.
Aimee tugged at the majestic bedspread. She read on, shut the book, then opened it again, skipping ahead.
Rescued by an ambulance doctor!?
She was glad the woman hadn't died, but felt sorry, thinking that such romantic rescues are, in reality, totally absurd.
Why does a woman have to be rescued, anyhow?
It was a tiring question. She went to sleep.

#

Daniel was shredding people with a lawnmower in his video game, but his thumbs were sore. He saved his position to a memory chip and switched off the PlayStation.
Moving from their apartment in San Francisco to this crappy cabin a hundred miles away was keeping him out of jail, and he knew it. The judge told him that he was lucky to be doing time with horses instead of other violent offenders. He wondered if the Columbine Kids and the Newtown Kid had to have horse therapy.
Get to. he reminded himself.
"Get to," he repeated in a whisper.
I get to have horse therapy.
When the game was off, and the ambient sound returned, he heard a noise coming from outside.
Clowns, he thought. *Why'd it have to be clowns?*
It was illegal to be outside dressed like a clown in some places, but evil clowns had been spotted in some woods, somewhere. He steeled himself to take care of what he had to.

Beri Balistreri

When he was very little, a birthday party clown made a balloon animal for him. An older kid called him weird and told him the clown was John Wayne Gacy. He eventually found out who Gacy was and grew up believing that a murderer wearing face paint had made him a pink giraffe.

An hour earlier, Daniel thought he saw someone moving in the backyard, but he couldn't stop playing *Grand Theft Naughty* long enough to go see. Now he knew someone was out there.

His heart pounded so hard it hurt. His skin crawled with prickly heat. There was ringing in his ears.

He wished he'd never gotten PTSD from seeing his dad dead.

Hyperarousal, it's called. I got hyperarousal.

He wished his dad hadn't deserved to die. He wished he was a normal kid.

I got a dog to protect me, but now I've got to protect my dog.

He felt like he was about to cry, but he didn't. He'd never really cried before, and he didn't actually know what it would feel like.

Maybe, like throwing up, he thought. *I do that a lot. A lot.*

He stepped into the darkness with his pulse racing. The thickness of the trees wouldn't let the moonlight reach him. He struggled to focus on anything. He couldn't see, but he could hear sharply.

They're trying to get me.

His thoughts raced, his heart pounded, sweat poured down his face.

There *was* a sound coming at him, and it *was* inhuman.

Daniel grabbed a rotten paintbrush from a forsaken project and willed himself toward the noise. Pinned by fear, the sound of his own breathing terrified him.

It's always the same. Kill or be killed.

He broke the splintered paintbrush, and its dull wood

became a shank in his hand. With fear and will bundled together, he lunged at the moving shape. He felt the stick penetrate. He pried it. There was no give. Silence returned to the darkness.

Puppy, with her dangerous wanderlust, came crawling back under the deer-fence and emerged from a forest hardly ever seen by human eyes, none the worse for wear.

"Come on Puppy. On Puppy," She trotted to her boy. "Good Puppy—good Puppy."

She followed him into the house, and to his bedroom. The little black dog stayed at heel.

"You sleep there." Daniel pointed to a pillow on the floor. Stepping onto it, she turned three circles and plopped herself down. He knew that if he yelled in his sleep she would come and lick his hand until he stopped.

#

The next morning, Daniel was sitting at the kitchen counter watching his mother stir three spoons of instant coffee into a mug of hot water.

"Was Michael here last night? Last night?" he asked.

"What makes you wonder that?" she asked.

"Smells like Michael. Like Michael."

"Yes. He was. I needed to talk to him."

"Does he want to marry you? Marry you?"

"I don't know. I don't think so."

"Good. I hate how he talks to you," Daniel said.

"How is that?" she asked.

"He always says something he doesn't mean, and then you're dumb if you don't know he doesn't mean it. If you don't know he doesn't mean it."

"You mean sarcasm?" she asked. "I don't like sarcasm either."

When Daniel was in the first grade, he asked his teacher if they were going outside for recess on a rainy day. She said they would go outside in the rain in their pajamas and roast marshmallows by a campfire.

Daniel got put in *time-out* several times that day and had to skip his snack for being disruptive. It turned out the teacher punished him for being a smart-aleck because he kept asking about the marshmallows, and pajamas, and campfire.

"Come to think of it, I hate sarcasm," his mother said.

"It's not funny. Not funny. Jokes are funny. Riddles are funny. You know what's black and white and red all over?"

"A newspaper?"

"Nope."

"A sunburned zebra?"

"Nope. Nope."

She sipped her instant coffee and glanced out the window. Her eyes fell on a thing.

Oh. My. God.

She was looking at the fresh entrails of a dead raccoon.

Black and white and red all over.

WOMAN MURDERED

CHAPTER 3

Dr. Bridgette Peletier strained her eyes down the dusty road where she expected her youthful subject to appear. She was champing at the bit to assess him in person for the first time and begin working with him as the equine therapist studying Post Traumatic Stress Disorder in children on the autism spectrum.

That's what the court had ordered for this adolescent boy, but she had more planned. Within this ten-acre clearing surrounded by a dark boscage, more than one future would be determined.

It's a true crime story and I'm going to write it. That's all there is, she thought.

She held her thumb to the iPhone, while she ground her Hermès riding boot into the dust until a flower-crown filter appeared on the screen. She puffed out her lips and pressed the white circle to take a SnapChat photo of herself. For a second, she felt like a girl—not serious, professional or important; and, like a girl, self-conscious.

Thank God it doesn't last!

She wouldn't want that picture swirling around the internet. She was going to build a stunning reputation for herself, here, by the famed golf links of Pebble Beach, Spyglass, and hallowed Cypress Point. From inside this rawboned white fence that served to organize the in-and-outs of the Pebble Beach Stable, an outré era compound where Secretariat himself once visited but was upstaged by the simultaneous appearance of Clint Eastwood and Arnold Palmer—she will rise.

Waiting is a bitch, she thought.

Beri Balistreri

She waited within the skeletal arms of the equestrian center, currycombing the thinning coat of a piebald mare. Califia was the creature that would, ostensibly, spare the boy's life and give her the life she dreamed of.

She had received the horse as a gift for her sixteenth birthday instead of the white Beemer she was promised. The Canadian psychiatrist, ersatz equine therapist, chose this yin place—with its handful of hippodrome has-beens amongst the rust-coated oil-drums that marked barrel races never to be run—for her coming out.

Hearing the death rattle of a four-stroke diesel, she looked up. In every direction, the skyline was cut with jagged pines towering in eerie presage. She saw the mom, Aimee James, steering her rickety blue Toyota jeep with one hand while twisting her Ash-Brown No. 5 hair into a messy bun.

The glorious subject who would change everything was seated next to a small black dog.

There he goes, she thought.

Daniel James was given a chance to change his fate. A month earlier he was headed to the San Francisco jail, convicted of voluntary manslaughter in the death of his father. The prosecutor compared him to the Newtown Killer, whose own father said that his son would have killed him in a heartbeat.

Too weird. Too rare, she thought.

This kid fixated on death every day of his life, according to court documents—several times a day, by his own admission. In the best of light, he was regarded as a precocious misfit or an idiot savant; but he listened to the horror-rap music of the Insane Clown Posse and Trip B, and played disturbing video games from the franchise known as *Grand Theft Auto.*

One of the Devil's own prototypes.

Her thoughts flowed in Hunter Thompson prose as she fastened the royal blue standing wraps and left the horse to go meet the kid in the dirt parking lot. Damp cinder-block fragrance mixed with the scent of ocean breeze, pine, and horse-related perfumery charged the dusty air. A ceiling of high fog diffused the light and washed away the shadows.

Finally, the beginning.

Dr. Peletier's classically wheat-colored shoulder length hair was pulled into a black velvet bow at the base of her neck. Her English-khaki jodhpurs smoothed as she rose to meet her marked-down quarry. With each step, Daniel's chin-length dark hair lifted in the breeze. Her heart fluttered, seeing the lanky teen with the awkward gait, closed smile, small brown eyes, and one deep asymmetric dimple on his left cheek.

He was everything she hoped for. Her thoughts shifted from Thompson to Tennyson.

Ours but to do or die, Daniel.

Daniel James was to be the subject of her research project entitled: *Equine Therapy Treatment with Asperger's Syndrome and PTSD in a Juvenile Offender.* She'd been languishing in the hinterlands of research for ten years. If she didn't find success soon, she'd be relegated to the status of a never-was. With the right subject, though, she could break into the tight world of publication.

Screw the academics.

Fortunately for her, James showed up like Dahl's golden ticket in a candy wrapper. An admirer alerted her about the young Asperger's killer during his trial and pointed out what he could mean for her career. Now she would be making her mark using this single horse and this troubled autistic.

"You must be Daniel," she said.

Aimee James extended her hand. "Hi. I'm the mom."

Dr. Peletier looked at the outstretched hand.

"Ah-ah. No shaking hands. That's sensory invasive."

How does the mom of an Asperger's child not know that? she wondered.

"It's nice to finally meet you anyhow," Aimee said, as she dropped her hand to her side. Dr. Peletier looked at the small dog at Daniel's feet and the book in the other woman's hand.

"Look at you. You brought your friend and your reading," she said.

A bodice ripper? she thought. The doctor smirked at the library book Aimee held, with its 1970s-style illustration of a swashbuckler in a white shirt slashed to the navel. It could have been Fabio.

"You won't be doing much reading here, Mrs. James. I prefer you not be on the grounds for our sessions."

"Oh. Okay." She looked surprised. "Call me Aimee, at least."

"Okay, Aimee. Feel free to go read your book now. I've got Daniel."

"This is Daniel's book," Aimee said, looking at the tome in her hand. "Or at least, I hope he'll read it. I picked it out for him at the library."

"You picked that for Daniel?" Dr. Peletier laughed.

"You don't think it could be wrong, do you?"

Dr. Peletier looked closer and saw that it was *Treasure Island*. "Ah. That's supposed to be a pirate. Long John Silver or someone."

"Not exactly Mr. D'Arcy, is he?" Aimee said, searching for a connection.

What's her game? the doctor thought.

"Oh, right. The misjudged noblesse," she said.

"Isn't every woman in love with him?" Aimee asked.

This woman believes it's all about her, the doc thought.

"Fun, isn't it?" the doc said.

"Hey, did you know that according to our guidebook Robert Louis Stevenson wrote part of *Treasure Island* here in Pebble Beach?" Aimee said.

"Really? A+ in literature," Dr. Peletier said, turning away.

"Daniel, I'm Dr. Peletier. You and I are going to get to know each other really well between now and New Year's."

Daniel looked to his mother.

"If we can't make that happen you won't be able to stay here. If you can't stay here you'll have to go back to San Francisco to jail, then prison when you turn eighteen."

"He's terrified of that," Aimee said.

The sound of her voice convinced the doctor that she was the one who was terrified.

"It sounds harsh, Daniel, but it's a good sentence. You're very lucky the judge gave it to you. We can make this work, can't we?"

Daniel didn't answer. One hand clenched and unclenched.

"Of course, we can," his mom said.

Dr. Peletier wondered just how dangerous this silly-looking youth in color block zip-off shorts was. He had killed his father, after all.

Would he kill me? Would he kill my horse?

"I explained it to him," Aimee said. "I explained that he has to make friends with your horse. I explained everything."

"That must have been quite a feat," the doctor said. Aimee's face fell.

Daniel shuffled his feet in the powdery dust.

"Feet," he said. "Feet."

"Daniel are you going to trust me?" the doctor asked.

"Trust is a hard thing for him after all he's been through. You know all about it I think," the mom said.

"Daniel, can you learn to trust me?" the doctor asked again.

"Can I?" Daniel said in a loud voice. "Or will I? Will I?"

"Okay then," Dr. Peletier said, pressing her palms together.

She started toward the corral and motioned for Daniel to

follow. Seeing Puppy at Daniel's heel, she turned back.
"You'll have to leave the dog with your mother."
"Can't do that. Can't do that."
Dr. Peletier took a light-weight lead from a hitching post and slipped it around the dog's neck.
"Noooo!" Daniel wailed in a high voice. "Noooo!"
He grabbed the rope from around the dog's neck and threw it to the ground.
"What's the matter?" the doctor asked.
Daniel started yelling in a high sing-song voice.
"What's the matter are you scared? What's the matter? what's the matter..."
Daniel held his hands inches from the doctor's eyes and clapped. She flinched away. He continued to sing, *"...tell me are you fearless?"*
Bridgette Peletier's body shuddered and she rubbed her face with both hands.
Aimee scooped the dog up.
"I'm sorry. He didn't mean to scare you. Those are song lyrics. He does that to me too."
"Well he shouldn't," the doctor said, smoothing her pony tail.
"Don't do that again," she said, glaring at Daniel.
"No noose!" he yelled. "No noose!"
"There's no noose," his mom said. "See, it's a leash."
"It's just to keep the dog out of the way," Dr. Peletier said, picking it up off the ground.
"We never put a leash on Puppy," Aimee said. "It's a trigger." She took a few steps back until she could feel the fence behind her.
"I think I know what a trigger is!" Dr. Peletier snapped.
"I'm sure you do," Aimee replied, in a placating tone.
"Was that actually a song you were singing, Daniel?"
"Without music, life would be a mistake—a mistake," he said, quoting Nietzsche. "That's an ICP rap—That's an ICP rap."

"Ah. The Insane Clown Posse I've heard so much about," she said. "Okay then. We need to move on. Let's get started with the horse."

Bridgette Peletier removed a heavy bridle from a rustic hitching post. Daniel winced at the sound of clanking metal.

"Come on Daniel, there's someone I want you to meet."

He followed her and the noisy bridle.

"Daniel, this is Califia. She's been waiting a long time for you."

Califia was the same age as Daniel, old for a horse. She suffered from thinning cartilage, a constant discomfort that made her gentle with people, especially frail ones. She tolerated their limitations, aware of her own.

"Do you know what this is?" Dr. Peletier asked, holding the harness high.

"No."

"It's called a bridle. It's used for control. Can you guess how it works?"

"It marries you? Marries you?"

"That's not funny, Daniel. I won't engage with sarcasm."

"Ha. Engage," he said.

She looked at him sideways.

"This little piece here is called a bit. It goes into the horse's mouth. These straps are called reins. You see, they move the bit. Everything the horse does can be controlled by moving this little piece of metal with these straps. It's really quite wonderful when you see how it works. You'll be able to do that."

"Why doesn't the horse spit it out? Spit it out?"

"Because she can't," the doctor said. "It's held in by the reins."

"Like me," Daniel said, "Like me."

"Is that supposed to be clever?" she asked.

"It's supposed to be a metaphor," he said. "A

metaphor."

"You *are* clever," she said, raising an eyebrow.

"What's clever?" Daniel said.

"You are."

"Is clever good?"

She fixed the bit in Califia's mouth.

"That's a bit—a bit," Daniel said. "Not clever—a bit."

The doctor motioned him forward. Stopping a few feet from the horse Daniel watched Califia throw her head back and shake her mane. She whinnied. Daniel stepped closer. Califia stepped closer. He repeated. They were equable.

This is going to work.

Dr. Peletier's heart fluttered.

She moved Califia's head side to side using the rein. She turned to see if Daniel was paying attention. He wasn't. She glared at his mother who was sitting on the fence.

"Daniel, go give the dog to your mother, please."

Daniel didn't budge.

"Mom come get this dog," the doctor called.

Aimee slid off the fence to get the dog.

"I think maybe he needs Puppy to be with him while he adjusts …"

"He doesn't," Dr. Peletier said. "Trust me. I know what he needs to adjust."

Aimee's face grew pink.

Daniel turned to his mother.

"You promised—you promised," he said.

"It's true, I promised," Aimee said.

"You really shouldn't have."

"I guess I'm gonna have to break it, huh?"

"It's not in your hands anymore. Really. You need to let go."

Aimee looked down at her empty hands.

"I'm sorry Daniel, it's my bad. Please go along with whatever the doctor asks. She's on your side."

Daniel gave the dog to his mom and went back to stand

near the horse.

"Good. You need to be able to focus on what we're doing here with Califia. See how I've put the bridle over her head and the bit into her mouth. See how she moves," the doctor said.

After another fifteen minutes of distracted attention from Daniel, she called time.

"Let's walk back to my trailer."

She stopped in front of Aimee and made a throat clearing sound.

"Excuse me."

Aimee, absorbed in her reading, looked up with a start. Puppy jumped from her lap and the book fell to the ground.

"Oh, shoot!" she said, as it disappeared in the fine dust.

"Maybe you should save your reading for work," said Dr. Peletier, stooping to retrieve it.

"You mean my work with Daniel?" Aimee asked.

"No. I hear you're quite a reader for the job you do."

"I hadn't thought of it that way. Summarizing depositions is pretty artificial. Novels seem a lot more real."

The doctor raised an eyebrow.

This woman's never going to be able to grasp reality. She thought.

"Isn't it the other way around? Depositions are real. Novels are fiction?" she said.

"That's one way to look at it." Aimee closed her eyes to think, then opened them to answer. "It seems to me that most self-disclosure is a lot of fiction, and most fiction is a lot of self-disclosure."

"Would you mind repeating that," the doctor said.

"I guess it sounds like I'm talking a lot of gibberish."

"Did you tell that to the judge?" she asked, handing Aimee James the dirty library copy of *Treasure Island*.

"I didn't think of it," Aimee said, accepting the retrieved book. "Should I have?"

She tried to shake the dust from inside the book's spine.

"You're kidding right?" the doctor said, with a laugh. "You should try curbing your imagination. Read less. Live in the real world—this century at least. Try reading magazines instead of novels."

Aimee's face flushed.

"Maybe we could grab a cup of coffee some time."

"You and me?" the doctor said.

"It looks like Carmel has some cute cafes. I don't know a soul here except for you. We already have at least one thing in common."

I highly doubt that, the doctor thought.

"We have Daniel," Aimee said.

"Yes. We do," Bridgette said, curtly. "But look, you didn't come here to make friends. You know, professional boundaries."

Slipping down from the fence, Aimee landed in a small pile of horse manure.

"Oh, crap!" she exclaimed, as the book fell again.

"What it is. What it is," Daniel said, covering his nose.

Puppy freed herself to run circles around the disaster.

Aimee wiped her feet on a patch of dry grass while the doctor described what Daniel would do. "He'll groom the horse, walk her on woodland paths and beach trails, and sometimes see to her feeding." She pulled a tissue from her pocked and handed it to Aimee.

Embarrassed, Aimee worked at wiping the manure from her knock-off Frye boots, the tissue moist with ammonia and pilling into paper worms.

"That's how he built trust with his dog," she said.

Dr. Peletier glanced at Daniel and the mutt, both sniffing at the mess.

"He needs to build trust with *me*," she said.

"He's already showing a lot of improvement with his therapy dog," Aimee said, working the disintegrating tissue.

Dr. Peletier produced a second Kleenex.

"But that's not a therapeutically trained animal. It's a pet."

Aimee accepted the new tissue and dusted the cover of the library book with it.

"But he was non-verbal after his father's death, and *Puppy* was the first word he spoke in six months."

"The court appointed psychiatrist from his trial wrote that he has functional speech, save for some echo-like iterations common in Tourette's."

Aimee shook her head at the Naugahyde harness boots, still caked with manure and not improved by her efforts with the tissue.

"He says a sentence and then repeats the last few words. It drives people crazy."

"Does it drive you crazy?"

Aimee froze. "He's what they call selectively mute," she said, before sitting to take off her boots.

"That's a very uncommon phenomenon," the doctor said. "He's capable of speech, but only talks in certain situations, to certain people."

"That's how it seems."

"Then I really hope he makes the right choices."

"I'm sure he'll talk to you," Aimee said. "He talks to me all the time now. He might even talk your ear off. I'd feel totally guilty if he did that."

She was using her socks now to finish wiping her boots.

"Would you really?" Dr. Peletier asked. "I don't feel guilty about anything. I feel sorry for people who experience guilt."

Aimee put her boots back onto her bare feet. Holding the smeared socks and disintegrating tissues in her left hand and *Treasure Island* in her right, she headed to a nearby garbage can.

"The consequences of selective mutism can be grave," Dr. Peletier warned.

"Should I try to explain that to him?" the mother asked.

The doctor shot her a look. "Don't explain anything to him. He knows the stakes."

Aimee's eyes fell to the ground. "I wish he could understand how it all really works." She tossed the tissues in the garbage, and then, as an afterthought, the socks.

"It's part of the therapy," Bridgette said. She wondered how deluded the mother of a murderer could be; and, though the court never established it, whether this mother pushed her son to do the killing for her.

"Trust the doctor," she said, awkwardly patting Aimee's shoulder.

"You're serious?" Aimee clenched and unclenched her hands.

"As a heart attack."

Daniel was halfway between them and Califia when they heard him whinny like a horse and bark like a dog.

"You really think you understand him?" Aimee asked.

"Neigh, hay hay. Ruff, rrrrrruff," Daniel screeched.

Dr. Peletier twisted her brow into a knot that gave way to a grin.

"He's going to be fine. He's going to be more than that. He's going to be perfect."

"Come here Daniel," she called. "You know, Califia was my horse when I was your age. I had to leave her when I went off to school, but now that we're back together we're going to make a great trio, don't you think?"

"A quartet," Daniel said. "A quartet."

Dr. Peletier looked to Aimee.

"Danny, I have to stay back at the house and work while you spend your days here with Califia. Those depositions won't summarize themselves and you know how slow I am."

"But why? Why?"

"I have to think about the words," his mother said.

Daniel dropped to his knees and ran his fingers through

WOMAN MURDERED

the dust.

"Puppy makes four. Puppy makes four."

Puppy nudged the boy's hand.

"I'm sorry, Daniel, but your dog can't be here for the therapy. It's Califia and me that can help you make a good impression on the judge."

Daniel didn't budge.

"Please take your dog to the car while I see your mother into my office. It's time for her to sign some papers."

Covered in dust, Daniel walked Puppy to the J40 to wait.

In the newly anointed office of legerdemain, Aimee James, with horseshit-stained hands, signed the release forms, privacy notifications, court documents, plan of care, scope of services, parental instructions, and dissembled publication rights.

Bridgette Peletier looked out through the gray venetian blinds. She would not be relegated to the life unobserved. The sun was low, and the fog filtered in from the ocean, spreading across the ground like steaming bath water.

Beri Balistreri

CHAPTER 4

Roberta Wagner was fulminating at 3 a.m., pacing the buffed parquet floor of her grand belvedere overlooking the Cypress Point Club, a private golf course with only 275 members, and only 30 of them local. She pulled her pink quilted satin robe more snugly around herself.

Damn it! God knows how desperate I am.

She squeezed out a profane prayer, wringing her hands.

An animal was robbing her of sleep. It wasn't the usual succubus seals caterwauling in the cove or the bullfrogs squalling in the puddles. It was a dog barking in the night.

The offensive cur must belong to the new renters of that ramshackle bungalow on the adjacent property; vacant for years while the owner waited for it to fall down so he could build a faux Tuscan villa for some nouveau riche pretender.

Fuming, she imagined her hair spontaneously combusting.

My God! I have to look my best tomorrow, she thought.

She was meeting her friend Judith Rodewald for lunch at Casablanca. Judith, her bosom buddy, was her coeval but aging better. She had less trouble with simple things, like keeping track of the time.

Roberta loathed anything that made her feel senescent. When her doctor suggested that she use an aluminum walker, she found a new doctor.

Kip is the only walker I'll ever need.

She could hear Kip's breathing from all the way down the hall.

He sleeps like a man with nothing on his conscience.

Roberta stopped pacing and went to the kitchen to take a

soporific. She shuffled back to the bedroom and stared at her sleeping husband, curled on his side with one arm resting on the French bulldog he called Stubby.

She sat on the edge of the bed, removed her slippers, and climbed in. Stubby rolled over and stretched his little white paws. He yawned and stuck out his curling tongue. She rolled the other way.

As she pulled her satin sleep mask over her eyes she felt a gentle kiss on the ear. Kip was no longer snoring, but she wanted to be rested for her lunch with Judith. She told herself it was just Stubby.

Kip will understand. He always does.

#

The next day, at the fairytale-cottage bistro, Roberta brushed past the Portuguese *azulejos* and Mexican *retablos* that dotted the pale-yellow walls. She maneuvered around the fountain burbling in the center of the greenhouse room, spotting Judith Rodewald's preternaturally thick platinum bouffant.

"How late am I this time?" Roberta asked.

Judith, a soigné septuagenarian whose high cheek-bones and deep-set eyes were magnified by heavy glasses, was already on her second cocktail when she extended her Lady Rolex to show her friend the time.

"Damn it to blue blazes!" Roberta exclaimed. "Fifteen minutes!"

She tapped the face of her own jeweled timepiece.

"I'm tired of being late because of a damn watch. I swear Kip is going to take this thing to Hesselbein's if it's the last thing he does."

Asking Kip to have her watch repaired would lead to a pettifog. He'd say there was nothing wrong with it and refuse to take it to the jeweler. Feeling ill-attended, she would blame him for causing the rub in her friendship with

Beri Balistreri

Judith.

She'd had words with him just before leaving the house:
If Judith has to wait for me it's your fault, she said.
What on Earth are you talking about? he said.
She gets fractious when I'm late.
How is that my fault?
You don't pay attention to me.
Woman, you don't know the half of it.
Take that barking dog; I think you want it to drive me crazy.
I've had just about enough! he said.
Why can't you be on my side, for once? she answered.

Kip had turned his good ear away from her and she had raised her voice at him.

She couldn't remember when she first started growling at her husband. She attributed it to his being hard of hearing but eventually acknowledged she took pleasure in it.

"Are you going to take your seat anytime soon?" the waiter asked from between clenched teeth, as he squeezed behind Roberta while attempting to deliver a Caprése salad to the next table.

Strange looking people, Roberta thought.

She stared at the homely dark-haired boy and the woman in the pea coat with hair pulled into a pony tail too high for anyone over thirty.

At least she didn't put a bow on it.

Easing herself into the chair across from her friend she called for a vodka gimlet.

The waiter shot her a poisoned look.

She glanced around the room to make certain they had the best table.

"If this was evening and we were with our husbands we'd be seated in the Cézanne Room," she said, referring to the private room with a table, reputedly used by the French impressionist whenever he dined at a certain café in Aix-en-Provence.

Judith shot daggers from her eyes.

"I'm not senile," Roberta said. "I know that Lang's no longer with us; but, if he were, and we were still a foursome…"

"Just stop talking and decide what you're going to eat so we can order. You're very late again. Is it that damned watch?"

"Yes! Kip doesn't believe me. I keep telling him that my watch needs fixing and he keeps telling me that it doesn't. I feel like I'm Ingrid Bergman and he's Charles Boyer in that movie where the man keeps trying to make his wife think she's crazy. You know the one."

"Gaslight?"

"That's it. That's just what he's like. You have no idea," Roberta said.

"You look tired, dear."

Wondering what about her looked tired, Roberta wanted it fixed, and now.

"I *am* tired. I'm *so* tired. You don't know how tired I am. I'm scared that I'll never not be tired."

"What on earth is the problem?" Judith asked.

"The problem is a d-o-g!" Roberta said, spitting out the letters.

"You're jealous of Honey?"

"Honey?"

"Kip's little dog."

"No. I'm not jealous of Stubby. It's that damn dog next door barking like hell at all hours. It's driving me bonkers."

"Is it driving Kip bonkers too?"

"No. He sleeps through it. Doesn't even hear it. Won't believe me. Says I'm exaggerating. Damned gas-lighter."

"Have you called the sheriff? Have you left an angry note?"

"Everyone in Pebble has a dog," Roberta said. "The sheriff is useless and for God's sake you never talk to *renters*." She snarled as she pronounced the word.

"A barking dog can drive a person out of their mind," Judith said.

"Kip could get ahold of the property owner, but he won't even try. He makes me so angry I could shoot him."

"I can't believe he won't deal with this for you. Tell him I said so."

"Why would he listen to you?"

"You know, there's a way you can take care of it yourself if you've got the stomach for it."

The waiter brought Roberta's gimlet. Judith grabbed his pen and a cocktail napkin. She wrote an apothegm on the square and passed it across the table.

Roberta read it and tucked it into her décolletage.

#

Aimee James and her son Daniel were seated in a restaurant they had selected from a tourist guidebook. They were there to have the socialization experience recommended for Asperger's Syndrome.

It was a cozy spot on this overcast September Monday, with its twinkling lights and heat lamps in the open-air greenhouse room.

"What are we supposed to do? Supposed to do?" Daniel asked.

"Whatever we want, I guess," she said.

"What do we want?"

We want to keep you from dying in prison and me from dying of loneliness, she thought.

"I don't know. Just be friendly," she said.

Aimee's eyes darted around the room. She overheard the waiter complaining to the bartender.

"I can't stand those two old bitches. They reserve a table for Tuesdays at noon. The tall one shows up fifteen minutes early, demands to be seated and served a drink right away. Then her friend shows up at noon like a lumbering ox, complaining that we hurry her too much."

"What's the rush at that age? They got somewhere to go? The short one looks like she has a date with death already. Jesus please before they rub off. Just look at them! Ew," the bartender said.

Aimee stopped her accidental eavesdropping.

"Let's make this beautiful," she said.

Daniel sat up, observing a jocund party of four. "That's how we'd be if we had friends. If we had friends," he said.

"That's the truth," his mother said.

Daniel glanced at the two men and women drinking wine from what looked like fishbowls. They were laughing loudly.

"But if we did, we'd use our restaurant voices. Restaurant voices," he said.

"We would. We will."

"Can I have the book now? Book now?" Daniel asked, reaching for the paperback guidebook that his mother had checked out of the stucco library on the corner of Ocean Avenue and Lincoln.

"We're gonna have friends, Daniel. Just wait and see."

Rounding her small shoulders, Aimee wondered if she'd ever set a good example for her son.

Loners have children who are loners, don't they? But isn't having a child an act of defiance against loner-ism?

"Do you think loner-ism is a word?" she asked.

"Yeah. It's the opposite of borrower-ism. Borrower-ism."

"That's a funny one, but I don't mean loaner like loaning money. I mean loner like being lonely."

"What's the opposite of lonely? Opposite of lonely?"

"I don't know," she said. "I mean, we say *don't be sad, be happy* and *don't be mad, be glad*. But we don't say *be un-lonely*. It doesn't work."

How can you fix a thing when you can't say what it is?

"Un-lonely. That's another made-up word. Made-up

word. There's no such thing as un-lonely. I'm getting good at this. Good at this."

"You are."

She smiled at her only child.

"Do you need help?" The waiter with the hipster vibe asked. "I can probably answer any questions you have."

Aimee cocked her head.

"About the menu, I mean. I couldn't tell you the meaning of life or anything like that."

"What about death?" Daniel said. "What about death?"

Aimee lost her grip on a water glass. The waiter rescued it.

"Can you tell me if you have a Caprése salad?"

"I can. We do. Anything else?"

"Can you tell me why *I will be alone again tonight my dear*?"

He puzzled, then caught her drift. She was quoting a lyric from the song playing on the restaurant's sound system.

"That's *Calexico*. Some cool Latin stuff," he said.

"It's my jam," she said, trying to be ironic.

People are the greatest fun, and I will be alone again tonight my dear.

The waiter wandered off, and she stopped daydreaming about flamenco dancing.

I hope he didn't think... Of course, he didn't.

Flipping through the guidebook Daniel said, "No baseball here. No baseball here. Didn't think they'd have it, but they don't. They don't."

Life in San Francisco was rhythmic. They had baseball. The only crowded place Daniel enjoyed going was a Giants game. They went whenever they could. Barry Zito would touch his cap toward Daniel each game before retiring. Aimee thought it made her son feel special and normal.

"This book says that famous people live here. Famous people are living in Pebble Beach and Carmel-by-the-Sea right now. I wonder if Barry Zito lives here. Lives here."

"I don't think that's very likely."

"Why not? Why not?"

"Well, he's just not that old, I guess."

"There's a lot of old people here, hmm? They never like me. Never like me."

Aimee wondered what his grandparents would have thought of her boy.

"There was that lady who walked her dog on Potrero Hill who always said hi to you. I'm pretty sure she liked you."

Their hegira to Pebble Beach severed the thin-as-spider's-thread connections they had.

"The book says according to local lore nefarious types and celebrities find anonymity here. The houses don't have addresses and the streets don't have lights; so, it's really hard to get found."

"You see, we fit," she said.

The waiter set the Caprése salad in front of her.

"Is this what you had in mind?" he asked.

"Yes. It's beautiful."

Aimee had a Caprése salad just like it at the Caffe Florian on St. Mark's Square in Venice where an Austrian couple struck up a conversation while a string quartet played Strauss waltzes, and for three hours they talked about art, film, literature, and love.

Life is like that. Sometimes you see someone, and you know they're meant for you, even if just for a conversation.

Daniel feared conversation, especially with strangers. He hated restaurants unless they were empty. She was making him try this because it was part of saving his life.

Maybe mine too.

Just then the older woman next to Daniel lost her balance as she was getting up. Daniel reached out to steady her, but she jerked her arm away.

"Don't touch me," she said.

Daniel dropped his hand.

"Not friendly. Not friendly," he said.

"You have no idea who you're dealing with," the woman said.

Neither do you, Aimee thought. *Neither do you.*

Daniel finished up the last morsel of bacon avocado burger with a side of sweet potato fries. His eyes wandered to the big-busted woman at the table of four.

"You can stop staring at my wife now," said the well-liquored man in the pink golf shirt.

Aimee's stomach tightened.

"I'm sure he just thinks your wife looks very nice."

The man ignored her.

"You're a sick kid, you know that."

"I'm not sick! Not sick!"

Daniel looked to his mother, who felt sick.

"Puppy cured me. Cured me."

Standing up from the table, the man bumped an elbow into Daniel's shoulder.

Aimee looked to see if they needed to leave in a hurry.

"Bad manners. Bad manners," Daniel said.

Aimee was relieved that was all.

He's making progress, she thought.

"I'll show you bad manners, you little freak," the man said. He made an ugly gesture and left.

Daniel shook his head repeatedly. "Not nice. Not nice."

Aimee's shoulders tensed.

"Puppy cured me. Cured me!" Daniel repeated.

"She did. You're doing beautifully."

Seeing her son using his words and his manners, but still be shunned, made her heart ache.

What more can I do?

"This was a bad idea. I'm sorry. I feel like I wreck everything."

"You do," he said. "You do."

"I do?" she asked.

"Feel like you wreck everything. You feel like you wreck everything."

"Oh, yeah. I do."

She reached out to touch her son's hand, but he pulled it away. "I want to see Puppy. Want to see Puppy."

"She's a good dog," his mother said. "Guess what? We're going to start taking her to visit folks who live in a nursing home."

Daniel's face was blank.

"You'll be sharing Puppy with other people who need a dog to pet."

Daniel's lip curled.

"Can't do that. Can't do that."

"You've got to try, Sweetie, or else."

"No. I can't."

"You can. We can. We'll do it together. We're gonna be so badass helping old people and s*h*i*t."

"You said a bad word. Bad word."

"No, I didn't."

"You spelled it. Spelled it."

"That's just bad spelling then."

"Good spelling. Bad word."

"You win." A smile crossed her face.

"It stinks."

Daniel plugged his nose.

"The judge ordered you to complete a thousand hours of community service. He said you have to prove that you have empathy. Puppy is already registered as a service dog; and, this way I can help. It's all I could think of with your special needs."

"Why do old people need to pet Puppy? Can't they pet their own dogs?"

"They aren't allowed to have their own dogs in nursing homes."

"Dogs go everywhere in Carmel-by-the-Sea."

"It seems like it."

"Stores that sell clothes for dogs. Dogs on the beach with no leashes. Dogs on the beach with no leashes."

"I know. They can even go to restaurants, but they can't live in nursing homes. People have to leave their things behind when they go to live in those places," she said.

"Sounds like jail. Like jail," he said.

"I guess it is."

"Wait. Dogs can go to restaurants? To restaurants?"

"Yes, to lots of them," she said.

"Next time can we bring Puppy? Bring Puppy?"

"She'd get all the attention. We're supposed to be interacting with people."

"I don't need no stinking people," he said.

"You sure about that?"

He folded his arms.

"I got a dog," he said.

WOMAN MURDERED

CHAPTER 5

Returning from his morning jaunt at Cypress Point, Kip Wagner paused beside the gate with *Heaven's Edge* in scrollwork across the top. He took a handkerchief from his pocket, wiped the perspiration from his suntanned face, smoothed his silver widow's peak, and re-tucked his shirt. Opening the foot gate to his pristine estate, he began his ascent of the long, curved driveway.

His best friend, a tawny French bulldog named Sergeant Stubby, was at his side. His wife Roberta swore that he named the dog to spite her. She said to name it Honey because of its color, but he reminded her that when they first married he called her Honey and she hated it. She banished the sobriquet his parents lovingly called each other, until his diminishing years when she, at last, deigned it acceptable, but only for a dog. No, he only had one Honey, whether he could call her that or not.

"Here, boy!" Kip whistled for the dog. Stubby came trotting on bowed legs. "Here we go. Up-up now. Just a tad more. There's a good boy."

"Thirsty, boy? Let's get you some water." Kip looked the picture of health, even if he did have to stop to catch his breath at the incline. Stubby sat in a patch of mulch. "Look here, you're getting soiled. Roberta wouldn't like that."

Inside the single-story manor house, with its French doors and Italian porticos, Kip poured refrigerated water for man and beast. The retired naval officer cum real estate investor set Stubby's bowl on the floor and carried his glass to the den, where *his and hers* white wing-back chairs faced the window. Pinned to his chair was a note from

Beri Balistreri

Roberta: "Do something about that dog."

"What dog?" he said to Stubby. "I heard no barking, did you?" Stubby cocked his head. "She's an absolute harridan." Kip sat with a groan.

"Stubby come here." The dog trotted to him. Kip patted the seat of her chair. "Come on boy, sit here." He held his glass of water for the dog to take several long slurps, watching, amused.

"Where have forty years gone? Where has Roberta gone?"

Stubby turned three circles on the silk cushion and plopped down.

"It's been a long time since I made her happy." Kip lifted Stubby from Roberta's chair and held him on his lap. "She keeps herself busy enough at the benefit shops, auxiliaries, always some kind of charity or other.

"Did you get enough water, Sarge? It gives her somewhere to go, a title, and a little cachet. I'm still parched I'm afraid. Poor old gal in all her glory as head of the volunteers of The Whispering Cypress Sniff."

Kip squeezed Stubby too hard.

"What would I do without you? What would you do without me?"

He stared out of the picture window through eyes the color of earth from space.

Distant breakers collapsed into plumes of silent spray. The fog drifted from the southwest. Some trees had already disappeared from view.

#

Roberta Wagner was dressed in a teal-blue St. John knit pantsuit and russet-brown Tod flats as she waited for her appointment with the new trainees. She stood inside the double-doors of the Whispering Cypress Skilled Nursing Facility, a 1950s-era rest home with the original green linoleum floors.

The smell of microwaved gravy and rubbing alcohol permeated the air as the volunteer coordinator fussed with a pen on the chain of a clipboard.

She looked up to see the arrival of Aimee and Daniel James and their small black dog.

Oh God no! she thought.

Roberta shook her fluffy white pageboy.

They're the volunteers? I should have known! Look how they dress, she thought.

The mother wore black pants and a blue shirt and carried a pea coat under her arm. The son was wearing jeans and a black t-shirt.

A teenaged boy? What's next, the apocalypse? Roberta thought.

She shook Aimee's hand but was rejected by the boy.

"Remember what the doctor said," his mother said, advising.

"Is he ill?" Roberta asked.

"I'd never bring him here if he were sick. We wouldn't bring germs to a SNIF. It's just over-stimulation. There's something about handshakes. Please don't worry."

Who are you to tell me whether to worry? Roberta thought.

"This is not a SNIF. It's a Skilled Nursing Facility."

She didn't receive a response.

"A sniff requires a tissue. I can't have a teenaged boy here. When you said your son was not in school I assumed you meant he was an adult."

Aimee slumped.

"Please let him stay. He has to stay," she begged.

"What do you mean he has to?"

"I mean it would be so wonderful for him to work with seniors."

"It's out of the question," Roberta said. She yanked her chained pen to cross their name from the list.

Beri Balistreri

Aimee James moved closer and tried to make eye contact with the woman who was Roberta Wagner.

"Please. It's the only thing he can do. We'll do it together. I'll watch over him."

"This place does not exist for the benefit of your child," she said.

Does anyone ever do anything unless it's for themselves? she thought.

Roberta thought the matter was settled, until the James woman blurted out—begged—one last thing.

"My child never knew his grandparents," Aimee James said.

Roberta Wagner took a deep breath and pushed it out slowly between pursed lips.

"Why do you want to volunteer here?" she said to Daniel.

Daniel didn't take his eyes off Puppy.

"Look at me when I'm speaking to you," the coordinator said, her face reddening.

Daniel didn't move.

"For God's sake, speak when you're spoken to!"

My teenaged daughter would have known better, she thought.

Aimee James interjected on behalf of her son, as she'd done a million times before.

"He can't always speak. I was hoping that the interacting with seniors would feel less threatening to him."

Roberta Wagner practically spit onto the timid mother.

"Nonsense! It's the seniors who will feel threatened by him!"

Aimee's eyes watered slightly.

Roberta showed no sign of being moved.

"I can't have him here! You're just doing this for yourself."

Now it was Aimee's face that turned red.

"You're wrong!" she said.

"Excuse me?"

Au contraire. It's you who will never be right, Roberta thought.

In the moment it took for Roberta to think the thought, the mother's demeanor became meek. Her shoulders shrank, and her voice hushed.

"I'm sorry. You're right. What you said is true. I'm a mother who can't separate myself from my only child. Everything I do is for myself."

"Damn it to blue blazes!" the older woman muttered before handing over the clipboard, its chained pen tangled around the spring that held a stack of printed sheets.

"The rooms listed are residents who want a pet visit. A knock on the door before opening it will suffice. Don't wait for an answer. If they are asleep, move on. Be sure to write a note about each visit."

No one would ever read the notes, but it was her way of keeping control. She gave Daniel the once-over again.

"Why isn't your dog on a leash?"

These people believe they're above the rules, Roberta thought.

"No noose," Daniel said. "No noose."

They were the only words he spoke to Mrs. Kip Wagner, Volunteer Coordinator of the Whispering Cypress Skilled Nursing Facility.

Lord he's strange.

"Keep him under control at all times," she said.

"Thank you," Aimee said.

"And for God's sake, no barking. I will not have anyone's sleep ruined by that God-awful noise."

"She only barks at raccoons."

"Do you understand me?"

"No barking."

Of all the different volunteering people did, Roberta thought visiting with dogs was the most ridiculous.

Why some people think dogs are the end-all, I'll never

understand.

Roberta turned the corridor and nearly tripped over Puppy. Daniel reached out to steady the woman.

"Don't touch me!" she barked.

God, he scares me.

"We'll just go start knocking on doors, then?" Aimee asked.

Stupid woman, Roberta thought.

#

Aimee James knocked and opened the first door as instructed.

"Doggie visit. Who wants to see Puppy?" she said.

The patient listed on the clipboard as Bob M. was sitting up in his wheelchair, finishing the last spoonful of pink Jello from a plastic cup.

"I do," he said.

When Aimee, Daniel, and Puppy came in, the old man reached out for the black terrier mix with a white spot on her chest. Puppy climbed into his lap. He laughed.

"This is a cute one," he said.

Puppy licked his face for Jello.

"You can't fool me," he said, giving her a frisking.

He noticed Daniel looking at the baseball cap left upside down on the nightstand.

"What's the 'W' for? 'W' for?" Daniel asked.

"Is it 'W' or 'M'?" Bob answered.

Aimee held her breath. Daniel's responses could get complicated.

"Just kidding. It's the Washington Senators. You like baseball?" Bob said.

"I got Barry Zito's autograph. Zito's autograph," Daniel said.

"Cool. One time when I was about your age I chased Whitey Ford down a New York City street and jumped into a taxi with him. I got his autograph on my Cub Scout card. I still have it somewhere. *To Bob, best wishes, Whitey Ford.* That's what he wrote."

"Cool," Daniel said. "Cool." Aimee felt a surge of pride at this simple – yet extraordinary for her son – exchange of conversation. *Maybe this* was *a good idea.*

The next room they went into was Mrs. Collier's. She was a fifty-something woman debilitated by a stroke. Docile Puppy wasn't frightened by her jerking motions and the noises she made. Daniel watched his mother place the woman's hand on Puppy's soft wavy fur.

After a few more rooms, they crossed a large central hall to the wing on the north side of the building. The name on the clipboard was LaTorella. Aimee was about to knock when she heard Roberta Wagner's booming voice.

"Not that one!" she said, turning away from the nurses' station.

"It's on the list," Aimee said.

"Then the list is wrong! Cross it off, and you're done for the day."

Aimee scratched the name from the clipboard and handed it over.

"Next time avoid the north wing. It's not your territory."

Daniel froze, but Aimee smiled. "I feel like Belle," she whispered to him.

"Do you have any questions?" the volunteer coordinator asked.

"I do!" a man yelled from a wheelchair. "How the hell do I get out of here?"

Everyone looked, but no one spoke.

"Nobody likes that one," Roberta said.

#

As they made their way back through the Del Monte Forest after their Whispering Cypress initiation, Aimee watched her son stare out the passenger window.

The fog slipped between the trees and floated over the asphalt, indifferent to the jeep slicing through it. Little Puppy slept at Daniel's feet, worn out from her first day on her second job.

"He has to die," Daniel said.

A chill ran up Aimee's spine.

There's an observation, she thought.

She scanned responses in her mind.

"Who?" she said.

"That man. He has to die. Has to die."

"Why?" she asked. Her hands trembled on the steering wheel.

"To get out of that place."

"Oh." She remembered the man in the wheelchair.

"I guess he does," she said, then laughed.

"That's funny? That's funny?" Daniel asked.

"It's called irony," she said, still laughing.

Daniel stayed expressionless.

"Is it wrinkled?" he asked.

"What do you mean?"

"Irony. Irony," he said.

"Ha! I get it."

The real irony is that you're the one almost locked up, she thought.

Picking up the pieces of Daniel's life and trying to put them back together was her own Sisyphean task.

Everyone had said that Aimee was the luckiest mom in the world with a husband so involved as a father. Sometimes Todd took over Daniel's care completely and sent her away to a retreat or something.

See how he loves me! Doesn't he love me? He loves me. Doesn't he? she'd asked herself a million times.

The endless question was dizzying.

I'm lucky. See how lucky I am.

It was at Daniel's well-check for kindergarten that

Aimee's luck began to unravel.

"I want to run some tests," the pediatrician said.

"I don't understand," Aimee said.

"I'd like to rule out lead poisoning."

"You think he was exposed to lead?"

"Haven't you noticed anything different?" the doctor asked.

"Well, he hasn't… he doesn't…"

"He rarely makes eye contact?" the doctor asked.

"He's never made eye contact. He stares, studies, and looks past people. He looks past me. I rock him, coo at him, sing for him, but our eyes never meet. Is that normal?" She began to cry.

Dr. Moriarty wrapped her arms around the mother's trembling frame while little Daniel sat lining up tongue depressors end-to-end.

With an Asperger's diagnosis there was no daycare willing to take the boy who got upset, repeated every last word, and hit himself. So, she stayed home, to care for his needs and to teach him.

Now her son seemed threatening to people just because he was a teenaged boy and he didn't make eye contact. The volunteer coordinator didn't even know that he had a record.

We have to make things work with Dr. Peletier or we're already dead.

The judge might let Daniel stay in Monterey County until he was eighteen, when his juvenile record would be sealed, but a sealed record was no guarantee that nothing bad would happen.

It's all up to me, she thought.

Beri Balistreri

CHAPTER 6

At the Whispering Cypress Skilled Nursing Facility, in the wing reserved for long-term residents, Detective Frank LaTorella held a pamphlet and read to his son.

"A wealthy woman died alone in a Mount Pellegrino cave. In her honor, four hundred years later, a sanctuary was built in that same cave. They built it because the smallpox plague that hit Palermo Italy during the middle ages was lifted after the town's people had a procession carrying her remains. The fatal suffering ended miraculously."

"We're gonna see the fishermen's procession tomorrow, so rest up. The Mass at San Carlos Cathedral is at 10:30 and the opening ceremony is at 12:30 at the Custom House Plaza. From there, we go to the Santa Rosalia statue to watch the blessing of the fishing boats. We gotta get started early."

The father stood up and wiped his son's face with a napkin as he looked out onto the forest of pointy needles, twisted branches, and broken shanks. The young man grunted and moved his head involuntarily.

"It's on then. I'll pick you up at 8:30 in the morning. Be ready."

Frankie Jr. was born prematurely. He was deprived of oxygen at birth, and it resulted in cerebral palsy. He was cared for at home, then in a regional facility. When he became an adult, his father moved him to the Whispering Cypress. In his room on the long-term wing, there was a curtain, a bed, a tray, a Formica nightstand, a guest chair, A tv, a video game system, and a call button.

"Don't give me that look. You haven't been outside for months. Fresh air is good for you."

"Your mama was named for Santa Rosalia, and your Nonno was a fisherman. C'mon! You gotta go. It's tradition."

Frank Sr. raised his arms like Tevya from *Fiddler on the Roof*. He took Frankie Jr. to see that musical at the outdoor Forest Theater in Carmel-By-The-Sea a long time ago when his wheelchair could sit near the blazing fire-pit during a fog-chilled summer evening.

An aide came in to take Frankie's tray away.

"I hear you're going out tomorrow," she said. "You're gonna have a good time with your daddy. It's nice being away from here."

"That's right," Frank Sr. said. "Tell Maria Madelena where we're going."

"Fest—Fest—Festa Ital—Italia," he said. He could speak, but it wasn't always easy. He preferred playing video games with a specially adapted controller, or sometimes he would listen to music.

"More story," Frankie Jr. said.

"How about I read from *Treasure Island*?"

"Arrrrrg," the boy said. The dad reached for the library book, found his place with the pirate bookmark, and read aloud to his son.

"His stories were what frightened people worst of all. Dreadful stories they were—about hanging, and walking the plank, and storms at sea, and the Dry Tortugas, and wild deeds and places on the Spanish Main. By his own account he must have lived his life among some of the wickedest men that God ever allowed upon the sea, and the language in which he told these stories shocked our plain country people almost as much as the crimes he described."

"My father was always saying the inn would be ruined, for people would soon cease coming there to be tyrannized

over and put down and sent shivering to their beds; but I really believe his presence did us good. People were frightened at the time, but on looking back they rather liked it; it was a fine excitement in a quiet country life, and there was even a party of the younger men who pretended to admire him, calling him a 'true sea-dog' and a 'real old salt' and such like names, and saying there was the sort of man that made England terrible at sea."

#

It was morning and Aimee was putting a mug of water into the microwave when Daniel, all dressed and ready to go see Califia, came bounding into the kitchen. He opened the fridge and rummaged around.

"I need an apple—need an apple," he said.

"I already packed your lunch, but there's no apple in it."

"Dr. P. said I can feed Califia an apple if I got one. If I got one."

"Well you don't get one," his mother said. "Why don't you bring her a lump of sugar instead? Horses like that."

"Lump of sugar? What's that?" Daniel laughed. "Is that irony? Lumpy sugar—lumpy sugar?"

Aimee reached into the cupboard and handed him a sugar cube. "It's not irony. It's a misnomer. That means it's misnamed. It's a cube, but it's called a lump. Maybe, they used to be lumps before they made cubes. Things change."

"That's wrong. Wrong," Daniel said.

"That's language," she said. "It changes."

"No. I mean it isn't fair. You never let me eat sugar lumps. Sugar lumps."

"That's life. It's not fair, and it never will be."

She immediately hated what she had said to him.

Of all people to say that to! What's wrong with me? she thought.

Grabbing the sugar cubes, Daniel plopped one into his

mouth and shoved another one into his pocket.

He ran out the door but returned an instant later.

"You want more?" his mother said.

"I forgot to wave Goodbye." He waved and left.

Things are getting normal, she thought.

She watched through the window as he skipped down the hill. A warm feeling spread across her chest.

#

Dr. Bridgette Peletier was already at Spyglass Hill with Califia saddled and ready to ride when she saw Daniel running toward her at full speed on the bridle path, traversing upward to the crest and down toward the roiling sea.

"What happened to you? You're late," she said.

"My mom had to explain sugar cubes," he said. "Sugar cubes."

She keeps a rein on him, the doctor thought.

"I brought one for Califia," he said, holding out a single sugar cube.

"I said you can feed her an apple, not sugar," the doctor said. "She can't have that."

Daniel held his palm flat and stared at the grainy white treat.

"You know what?" she said. "Califia has taken a liking to you, Daniel and so have I. Cal and I knew we would have a special friendship with you from the minute you came here."

Daniel moved his hand closer to the horse, who licked the sugar off his palm with her slobbery tongue.

"Our paths were destined to cross," the doctor said.

Daniel grimaced, smelled his hand, and wiped it on his jeans.

"Horseback riding is more than a character-building sport, Dan."

"Sports. Not good at sports," he said. "Not good at sports."

Dr. Peletier laughed. "You'd be surprised how much we have in common, Danny Boy."

"Like what—like what?" he said.

"Well, I'm not that good at sports either." She watched his face. "And my dad also died when I was a kid, like you." Daniel's face changed, but he said nothing.

"Here, put your foot in the stirrup and boost yourself up. Swing your leg over like I showed you yesterday."

Daniel did it. He got into the saddle with ease.

"You know, the vibrations created by a horse while it's being ridden activate an area of the brain called the sympathetic nervous system."

"Califia will make me sympathetic?" he asked.

The doctor led the horse along the natural bridle path toward the beach.

"A study by researchers from the Tokyo University of Agriculture published in *Frontiers in Public Health* shows that riding horses improves children's ability to perform behavioral tasks leading to better memory and problem solving before and after riding a horse."

"I can solve problems after I ride Califia?" he asked.

"Their steps produce a three-dimensional acceleration," the doctor said. "It's a motor and sensory input you can't get from other sports."

Daniel felt the motion of the horse under him and listened to the rhythmic white noise of waves crashing on the shore.

"Like being carried by your mom? Carried by your mom?"

Dr. Peletier looked sharply at the strange boy.

"Your mom can't do what Califia will do for you."

"She can't carry me anymore. Can't carry me anymore."

Califia stumbled, and Dr. Peletier kicked a rock out of

the way.

"Did you kill your dad?" Daniel asked. "Kill your dad?"

The doctor hid her surprise.

"No. I guess I didn't," she said.

He looks disappointed, she thought.

"Do you believe you're responsible for your father's death?" she asked.

After a moment of silence, she rephrased the question.

"Do you think it's your fault?"

"They say I am."

"Say you are what?"

"Responsible."

"Who *is* responsible?"

"I know who," Daniel said.

Dr. Peletier sidled in to Califia and looked Daniel square in the face.

"Who?"

"He is," Daniel said. "He is."

Damn it!

"Are you sure? Don't you think your mom has responsibility?"

Daniel's expression didn't change.

The doctor backed away toward a dead Cypress.

"When you love someone, sometimes you'll do anything for that person," she said.

She picked up a piece of bark and broke it.

"You mean kill? Kill for love?"

"A person you really love might convince you that someone else deserves to die."

"Or someone that really loves you kills to keep you safe?" he asked.

Dr. Peletier dropped the bark and took the rein from his hands.

"Is it your job to keep your mother safe?"

"It's my job to keep Puppy safe. I keep Puppy safe."

"Like I keep Califia safe; but, what about your mom?

It's no secret she hated your dad."

"I hated my dad," Daniel said.

"Well, I didn't like my dad all that much either, Danny."

"Did he take pictures of you?" he asked.

Dr. Peletier paused to choose her tack.

"Sure. Don't all parents?"

"Whatever," Daniel said, turning away.

"Would you kill for your mom to protect her?"

"I'd kill for my dog. I'd kill for my dog. I did last night." Dr. Peletier's heart leaped into her throat.

"In your video game?" she asked.

"In the forest," he said. "I killed a raccoon. At first, I thought it was an evil clown, but it wasn't."

He sang: *"Blood on my feet, Walking the street, four in the morning, Done with the shit, Clutching the knife, Taking the life, Of the messed up, Call me messed up? At least I'm something, Monster's better than nothing."*

"That's a Trip B song. A Trip B song. It's a good one—good one."

Woot woot! Best-seller guaranteed! she thought.

They came to a fork in the road and looked west at the expanse of kelly green careening toward the edge of the sea. The Pebble Beach Pines Golf Course had been renamed Spyglass Hill many years before in honor of the fictional place in *Treasure Island*.

Bridgette Peletier breathed in her future and quoted Stevenson to herself.

I climbed a thousand times to that tall hill they call the Spyglass, and from the top enjoyed the most wonderful and changing prospects.

WOMAN MURDERED

CHAPTER 7

Aimee waited in the sun-filled atrium by the koi pond in the hospital lobby. Daniel went with a radiology technician for a magnetoencephelography (MEG) scan. MEG scans were the first biological test to diagnose PTSD, autism, Alzheimer's and other psychiatric disturbances. According to Dr. Peletier, MEG correctly identified 97% of patients with PTSD in a study published in the *Journal of Neural Engineering*.

Aimee worried about Daniel having the scan without Puppy there to comfort him, but he had had an MRI before and said the sensory deprivation felt good. He told her not to worry. She was trying not to when she heard familiar music and recognized the Argentine tango, *El Choclo*. A rakish man walked past, attempting to silence his cellphone.

"My apologies," he said.

"Oh, please don't apologize, I love to tango."

Aimee and the tango man looked at each other for an awkward second.

"I mean I love *the* tango," she said.

"I'll turn it back on if you'll dance with me."

Aimee's eyes dropped to an orange and black carp. When she looked up he was gone. She flopped herself back into the chair and picked up her book.

The tango music went off again, but fainter.

On the other side of the koi pond she saw the man spin a nurse in an impromptu tango.

She opened her book and read.

"Usually at the weekly hops, Maggie kept a spot on the

wall warm with her back. She felt and showed so much gratitude whenever a self-sacrificing partner invited her to dance, that his pleasure was cheapened and diminished."

Her nose was in the short stories of O. Henry, but she was distracted by the nagging feeling of something she hadn't done.

Cherries, she thought.

There was that stretch of highway between San Jose and Monterey, a plethora of variegated fields and frilly orchards with hand-written signs: *Artichokes, 8 for a Dollar. Elephant Garlic by the Trunk. Sweet Cherries by the Flat.*

That's it, cherries! She thought.

She had never stopped to buy any roadside cherries, and she'd always meant to.

She looked across the top of *The Four Million* and saw Daniel being led back from the radiology department by a dark-haired, muscular man in scrubs.

"He did fine."

"See, I'm fine," Daniel said. "I'm fine."

"That's not what I said," the tech said.

"You said fine," Daniel said. "Fine."

"I said you did fine. You look fine, but your doctor will get the results."

"Oh shit," Daniel said.

"Daniel!" said his mom.

"I swear too much. Will that show?" he said. "Will that show?"

The tech looked from Daniel to his mother and back again.

"On your brain scan?" he said.

Aimee stepped in to answer the question that, from the look on the tech's face, was lame. "Of course not," she said.

"Actually, anger, rage, autism, even PTSD can be picked up by the MEG. Its purpose is research," the tech said.

"What do you mean, research?"

"Information-gathering."

"I know what research is."

"Healthy people have similar patterns of neural communication, but people with Alzheimer's, schizophrenia, stuff like that, they have disease-specific patterns. Only like thirty facilities in the country have the MEG. It's a $2 million machine. Once the research pans out, the treatments will follow. That's the way it works."

"Research," Aimee said again. "She said it was for treatment."

"In the future it will be," the tech said. "Unless he's on some sort of trial now. Some Alzheimer's patients are on a fast-track experimental thing because they're on the fast-track to … well. Alzheimer's doesn't have a cure, you know. It's progressive."

"Progressive? Toward what? Death?" Daniel said. "Death?"

The tech raised his bushy brow.

"You could say that," he said. "But I wish you wouldn't."

He turned and walked away, shaking his head.

Aimee turned to her son. "You mind if we stop at the market on the way home? I'll just be a couple of minutes."

#

Bixby's Market in Carmel-by-the-Sea was vibrant and alluring for tourists and for Aimee. Baskets of flowers sat outside the open doors beside beds of color-coordinated produce, luring visitors to feel transported to the Côte D'Azure. The cashier fit the scene. He was tall and sturdy, with a shock of Cary Grant hair that threatened to fall in front of his eyes should he have to shake his head.

Judy, Judy, Judy, she imagined him saying. *We don't carry that brand. Give me that box of crackers now. Have you seen the type-face used on this product? For goodness' sake, that label's printed in Comic Sans. Don't you know it takes five-hundred small details to add up to one favorable impression?*

"How ya doin' today, Miss?" the real clerk said. He wore a name tag that said, "Hi, I'm Albert."

She placed her basket on the counter.

"I guess I'm... I guess I'm..." she was searching for the right words, to sum up, her feelings.

"Bored?" he asked.

"How did you know?"

"Laundry soap and magazines," he said.

The word bored made her think of the residents of the Whispering Cypress. She remembered Mrs. Collier, with her stroke.

Such a sweetheart.

"Everyone loves a sweetheart," her mother used to say. "Why don't you be a sweetheart and *insert task*."

When she was in college, she went on vacation to Europe with her parents, but she didn't feel like going shopping with her mother in Paris or gambling with her father in Monte Carlo. Her parents said it was a shame she couldn't just be a sweetheart like she used to be.

What she wanted was to be left alone to sail through the Straights of Delos, stumble upon the Cocteau Chapel in Villefranche, and maybe, just maybe, sip Chartreuse in the 18th arrondissement.

Albert placed her change in the center of her palm, cupping her hand as he did. His touch felt so different from the hands of the people at the nursing home. It was firm and warm, not weak and cold.

Driving back through the Carmel Gate, up the Seventeen Mile Drive past the golf greens and the Lodge at Pebble Beach, she thought about the man from the market. She tried to picture his face, but she couldn't.

Neatly trimmed facial hair? A dimple? Eyes?

WOMAN MURDERED

She drove off into the sunset with little more than an impression of the man who had brightened her day.

They continued along the pine-forested road, rising upward until they crested a ridge and a cinemascope panorama stretched out in front of them. The sun reached in ribbons through the clouds to touch the silver plane of water.

"Look. It's Beauty," Daniel said.

Hot tears splashed on Aimee's cheek.

Back at their rented cottage, which would have had a view if the forest hadn't impinged upon it years ago, she tossed her bag onto the sideboard. A magazine flopped out. The cover promised *Twenty-Nine Tricks to Drive A Man Wild*. Aimee wiped her face with the back of her hand. *Oh, brother.*

#

After dinner, Aimee and Daniel took Puppy to visit the folks at The Whispering Cypress. They were starting to enjoy the now familiar faces that welcomed them so kindly. Being nice to Daniel was, practically, a civic duty for some of the residents. It was a good fit.

Aimee knocked and opened a door the way the volunteer coordinator had instructed.

"Hey, I know you. Come in," said Bob M.

Aimee wondered how he lost his legs. *It's not right to ask.*

"Didn't you grow up on a farm in Salinas—Salinas?" Daniel said.

"You remember that? Yeah, a little farm in Prunedale, north Salinas. But that was later. My dad was in the military, so we moved around a lot."

"Is he dead?" Daniel said. "He dead?"

"Yeah, he's dead."

"Was he killed? Killed?"

Beri Balistreri

"Nah, he didn't die fighting in the war."

"Neither did my dad," Daniel said. "My dad."

"No? Well, I fought in two wars, but they didn't get me either."

Aimee, who was holding Puppy, unconsciously tightened her grip on the dog until it let out a yelp.

"I just remembered we've gotta go do a thing. It was nice to see you again. Take care."

Bob's face wore a question mark.

"Well kid, thanks for coming to see me."

"We brought Puppy to see you," Daniel said, "Puppy to see you."

"Oh, yeah. I know. Well, stay in school."

#

Back at the cottage, Aimee read her book and dozed off, while Daniel played *Grand Theft Naughty* with Puppy at his side. She woke to the sound of the telephone. It was her old boyfriend Norman calling, wanting to know if life had turned out the way she'd hoped.

Trying to answer his questions, she awoke for real. The phone hadn't rung. In her groggy haze, she concluded that Norman was dead. That's what the dream meant. It was an *immemorium*. She didn't like knowing things like this.

Years ago, Aimee had given Norman a present and he'd called it a *gift of the Magi*. He explained the expression as a gift of sacrifice that turns out to be a mistake but is perfect because of the love that made it possible. After that, he went out and found her a rare first edition of *The Four Million*. She wondered if he'd sold something precious to buy it.

Holding the volume open to a short story called "Memoirs of a Yellow Dog," she read: *Hoodlum, doodle, hoodlum, hoodlum, bitsy-witsy skoodlums? A genuine Pomeranian-Hambletonian-Red Irish-Cochin-China-Stoke-*

WOMAN MURDERED

Pogis fox terrier.

Pooches on the beach—pooches in restaurants—pooches in purses, people are like that, pretty much; the same about their pets as they were a hundred years ago. She read on.

Peanut brittle, a little almond cream on the neck muscles, dishes unwashed, half an hour's talk with the iceman, reading a package of old letters, a couple of pickles and two bottles of malt extract, one-hour peeking through a hole in the window shade, into the flat across the air shaft—that's about all there is to it.

It's like a women's magazine! Aimee thought.

She closed her eyes and let the book slip. She began to dream that a dog was licking her hand.

CHAPTER 8

It was morning again and Aimee was fixing her instant coffee, looking out the kitchen window to the fog-blanketed slope and its blackberry brambles upon which no blackberries ever grew. The deer ate all the buds before they fruited.

I wonder if they would wait if they knew?

Along the curved driveway ascending to the dilapidated cottage, a family of black-tailed coastal deer munched on Spanish moss hanging from fog-shrouded evergreens. They could reach only as far as the bottom of the lacy, pale-green parasitic plants, and wanted more.

Someone's gotta help them.

She wondered if she might find a ladder in the shed.

The beeping of the microwave reminded her of coffee. *The richest kind.* As she stirred the Folger's crystals she saw the canister of Milk Bones, and took out a treat for Puppy, who usually trotted in at the sound of the jar opening.

"Puppy! Come on Puppy! Cookie! I got a cookie! Puppy!"

She went to the glass door, but she didn't see Puppy anywhere. The dog must have squeezed under the wire to take herself on an adventure. She hunted raccoons to scare away. At night, when she heard a noise, she'd strain at the door until someone took pity on her. Then she'd go to the deer fence and bark like crazy.

Pulling on her boots, Aimee shoved a Milk Bone into her pocket and went outside.

"Puppy!" she called, "Puppy, where are you? Come

here, Puppy! Come here!"

She walked to the end of the property, but she didn't see Puppy anywhere. Doubling back, she caught sight of a black patch in the brush near the high perimeter fence. She threw her mug onto the weeds and ran toward it, screaming.

"*No!*"

She lifted the lifeless dog, cold as the morning. Holding the beloved creature to her chest, she rocked back and forth. Her heart was racing. She was in a cold sweat. She could see Todd's dead body in his apartment in San Francisco.

This is my fault.

She tried to put together the reasons. She couldn't remember letting the dog out. She couldn't remember finding Todd either.

I know it's my fault.

A surge of anger rose in her. She beat at it, to keep it down.

If you can't remember, how can it be your fault?

Her dead ex-husband was still before her eyes.

What are you going to do about this dog you've killed? she thought.

She slapped at her cheeks, willing herself into the present.

I don't understand.

She moved her face close to the dead dog, smearing her tears on Puppy's soft fur, wailing for the better part of an hour. When she regained her composure, she carried the body to the house and wrapped it in a beach towel.

She opened her laptop and Googled: *What to do for an inconsolable child who doesn't have the power to cry?*

She found advice on how to tell a child their pet has died.

For many, their first experience with loss is when a pet dies, she read.

Beri Balistreri

This is by no means his first experience, she thought.
When a pet dies, children need consolation, love, support, and affection, not complicated medical or scientific explanations, she read.
What if the child is autistic, and he needs scientific explanations? she thought.
Children's reactions to the death of a pet will depend upon their age and developmental level, she read.
What if he's different? she thought.
There are many ways parents can tell their children that a pet has died. It is often helpful to make children as comfortable as possible, using a soothing voice, hold their hand or put an arm around them, she read.
What if he can't tolerate being touched? she thought.
Tell them in a familiar setting, she read.
So, he can hate that place forever? she thought.
It's important to be honest when telling children that a pet has died, she read.
When is it not important to be honest? she thought.
Trying to protect children with vague or inaccurate explanations can create anxiety, confusion, and mistrust, she read.
What if the child already has those things? she thought.
Children may experience sadness, anger, fear, denial, and guilt, she read.
Or stop talking, and spend the rest of their life in prison, she thought.
They may also be jealous of friends with pets, she read.
He doesn't have any friends to be jealous of, she thought.
There is no best way for children to mourn their pets. They need to be given time to remember their pets. It helps to talk about the pet with friends and family, she read.
If he'll talk. God, please let him talk, she thought.
Mourning a pet has to be done in a child's own way, she read.

WOMAN MURDERED

His own way. I can help with that, she thought.
After a pet has died, children may want to bury the pet, make a memorial, or have a ceremony, she read.
We're gonna have to bury her, she thought.
Her face screwed up.
It's best not to replace the pet immediately, she read.
He'll never accept another one, she thought.
The death of a pet may cause a child to remember other painful losses or upsetting events, she read.
That's what I'm worried about, she thought.
A child who appears overwhelmed by their grief, and not able to function in their normal routine may benefit from an evaluation by a child psychiatrist or other qualified mental health professional, she read.
Thank God for Dr. Peletier.
Aimee feared Daniel would stop speaking. He would go to prison. He would die there at the hands of a prison bully or by his own hand. She prayed Dr. Peletier would know what to do. God wasn't her genie, but she desperately rubbed the lamp.
Please help. Please help. Please help.

#

Over at Fanshell Beach, Dr. Bridgette Peletier walked beside her new young charge and her old pet horse—a therapeutic presence during her own teen years. She'd cared for Califia until she went away to school, then reclaimed her, after her efforts to join a prestigious research team tanked. After years of grueling study, setbacks and rejection, struggling for advancement that didn't pan out, she was going to get noticed by using her very own pet. People were beginning to take notice of horses and she was going to ride that wave.
Califia on the cutting edge.
She was finally one hundred percent in the right place at

the right time doing the right thing. Her whole life had boiled down to time spent with this autistic boy and his history of trauma—and murder.

"Today we're going to start the most important part of the work we'll be doing together. I need your full cooperation for this to be a success. Do you understand?"

"Success. Success."

"No sarcasm today, kid. Cooperate, or else."

Daniel sat astride Califia, anxious to leave the equestrian center. The doctor had promised him a ride on the beach. They had something else special to do too. While they headed down the dusty road to a small spit of a beach below the spot called Fanshell Overlook, Dr. Peletier worked to prepare Daniel for what she was planning.

"We're going to use something called Narrative Exposure Therapy to create a story that will help you make sense of your experiences."

"How can the senseless make sense? He asked.

"Trust me. It will."

"You keep saying that. Keep saying that."

Daniel shook the reins for speed, but Dr. Peletier held the bridle in her hand so nothing changed.

Avoid challenging him, for now, she thought.

"Memories can feel like a jumbled mess. They can be an unbearable wash of images, sounds, and feelings. Sharing your story will help them become organized. They'll be more manageable," she said.

"I don't want to be managed. I don't want to be managed."

"It might feel good in the moment to avoid reminders of trauma, but it will cause your symptoms to be worse over time."

Dr. Peletier's cell phone rang and she took it out of her pocket to see who it was. She smiled and silenced the ringer.

"It's going to take several sessions to complete a first

draft. You will be exploring new territory."

"Thought this was about old stuff. About old stuff."

"You see Daniel, NET, or Narrative Exposure Therapy, usually works when someone's back-story is written down; but, since we're combining it with Equine Therapy, I'm going to record what you say. Let's just talk through the facts now for the recorder I have here with me."

"Already told it to the judge. Told it to the judge."

"I'm going to ask you to share your worst memory. I know it's not easy, but it's the best place to start, and it will all be downhill from there. What was your worst moment?"

"You're going to ask me to share? To share?" he said.

"What were you thinking and feeling after your father died?" she pushed.

"Fuck you shit-head—Fuck you shit-head—Fuck you shit-head—You eat shit. Fuck you shit-head—Fuck you shit-head—Fuck you shit-head—I'm sick and tired of it. Fuck you shit-head—Fuck you shit-head—Fuck you shit-head—Best let me be. Fuck you shit-head—Fuck you shit-head—Fuck you shit-head—You're no friend to me."

"Did you just make that up?" Dr. Peletier asked.

"It's Trip B—Trip B the rapper."

"That's another group like ICP, right?"

"It's my thoughts. I was thinking it. That's what I was thinking. You asked what was I thinking after my father died? It's what you asked."

His voice was higher, and his hands were clenching and unclenching.

Decompression, she thought.

"After enough exposure to your painful memories their potency will diminish, and your discomfort will too," she said. "It will be good for you."

"Because you will tell the judge that it was a success? It was a success?"

It will be a success. No matter what happens, it will be a success, she thought.

"Come on, try to focus."

Daniel shook his head.

"If you won't talk about the hard things, at least tell me about your happy memories being with your dad?"

"All done! All done!" Daniel said.

"It's not up to you! You don't end sessions," the doctor said.

Just lives.

"I want Puppy! I want Puppy! I want Puppy now!"

"You can't have your dog now, and besides, it doesn't matter what you want! You have to do this. The judge ordered it. If you don't, you'll go to jail. Trust me, you don't want to go to jail."

Dr. Peletier searched the boy's face, but he was staring beyond her.

What if he stops speaking?

She began to cajole. She pleaded and then she threatened.

"You have to start thinking of Califia as your savior, because guess what? That's what she is."

Daniel, who had been staring at the horse's mane, slid off Califia and fell onto the sand.

Oh shit, she thought.

"Are you hurt?" she asked.

"I hate you! I hate you, you, fucking, horse ho!"

The doctor was not prepared for the force of his rage and lost her temper.

"You can't have Puppy! That dog isn't a therapy animal! It's a pet! And, guess what? Your pet can't keep you safe! Only I can do that!"

Daniel made a high-pitched squeal that pierced her ears.

"No one else can keep you out of jail besides me! Do you understand?"

He plugged his ears with his fingers.

"You don't understand anything, do you?" she said. "You just don't get it."

Daniel scrambled to his feet and ran as fast as he could into the cold, churning waves.

Now, what have I done? she thought.

"Come back here Daniel! You can go home and find your dog!"

Daniel came out of the water sopping and shivering.

Bridgette Peletier took three deep breaths.

"I'm sorry this was so hard on you … but, I'm not a horse ho, and I can't let you talk to me like that, you little … you little …"

Daniel was standing with Califia, trying to dry himself against her coat. "Little what? Little what?"

She was not going to take the bait. "You little *punim*!" she said.

Daniel took a lengthy pause before speaking. "Oh. I get it. I'm Aladdin, and you're the genie. You're the genie."

"That's right. I'm the genie."

"Because you're going to save me? Save me?"

"Daniel, you ain't never had a friend like me," she said.

"Joke's on you. I ain't never had a friend," he said. "Never had a friend."

CHAPTER 9

The next morning Aimee sat holding a book to her chest. Her eyes were closed, but she sensed a presence hovering.

"Get up," Daniel said.

She opened her eyes. Inches from her face, wearing black and white Kabuki makeup, painted like the rap singer Violent J from Insane Clown Posse, Daniel wore camouflage and carried a shovel.

"It's funeral time—funeral time."

Her stomach did a fatidic flip. It was no time to argue with or disrespect the grieving. She jumped up.

Daniel led Aimee to the untamed portion of the fenced-in rental property, pushing a wheelbarrow with a small blanket-wrapped bundle atop its rattling load. They walked among scattered deer bones and raccoon skulls. It was an animal graveyard. Perhaps, it was a bobcat's domain. Daniel kicked at what looked like a femur.

"Cat ate that—cat ate that," he said matter-of-factly.

"But a bobcat won't... I mean... they don't dig up carrion," his mother said.

"Some birds are meat-eaters—meat-eaters," Daniel said, as he busied himself with the paraphernalia he'd brought.

"Puppy isn't going in the ground. She's going in a tree. In a tree."

"What about *No noose*? You always say *No noose*. No hanging!"

He was quickly tying the blanketed bundle in a sort of hammock. She watched him string up his dog's dead body between two high branches, like Rock-A-Bye Baby. She tried to make sense of the ritual.

"Puppy will live on in the birds that eat her?" she asked.

"Ever see a turkey vulture? Turkey vulture?"

"You want vultures to eat Puppy?" Her voice broke.

"Turkey vultures will come and pull her apart into little pieces. Little pieces."

She stared at the boy who stood trial for the murder of his father and saw what the prosecutors had tried to show to the jury.

"I heard about a guy who cut off his own flesh and fed it to vultures. To vultures," he said.

What sort of lycanthropy is this? She thought.

"Where did you hear about that?" she asked.

"On Discovery tv. His name was Sakyamuni. I want to be like him. Be like him."

Daniel lifted an ax from the wheelbarrow and swung it in circles.

"Oh my God, Daniel," she said, her face turning ashen.

"Please don't do that Daniel."

"Body breakers use hatchets," he said. "ICP has a hatchet-man logo. A hatchet-man logo."

Swing that hatchet—off with their head—looney batshit, once it's gone, you can't reattach it, he sang.

"I can't watch," Aimee said.

"I'm not chopping her up. Not chopping her up," Daniel said.

"Thank God."

She turned and looked back and forth between her painted-up son and the body of his dead dog strung between the trees. She wondered if the experts who gave advice on how to help a child cope with the death of a pet would recommend this ritual.

"Look. It's done. It's done," Daniel said. He stood up panting.

"Should we say a word?" Aimee asked.

"A word? What word? To who?"

"To God, I guess. You say a word to God."

"Did God love Puppy? Love Puppy?"

"Who couldn't love Puppy?" Aimee said.

They both fell silent.

After a moment, Daniel closed his eyes and raised his hands to the sky.

"God punish the killer. Punish the killer, please. Amen."

"Forgive us our sins," Aimee added.

Daniel collected his things and put them in the wheelbarrow. They started back toward the house.

"Do you think he's rotting in the ground? Rotting in the ground?"

Aimee stopped.

He's asking about Todd.

Her mind was spinning.

He wants to know if his dead father is putrefying under the ground.

She wanted to tell him she couldn't calculate the rate of human decomposition after embalming, in a sealed subterranean environment.

"Honestly, I have no idea. We could look it up, I guess," she said.

"I hope he's rotting. I hope he's rotting. He'll feed the worms someday. He'll feed the worms someday. They'll die from all the chemicals in him. The chemicals in him. He's not organic."

"Please, Daniel. That's enough!" She walked faster to get ahead of him.

"You want to eat food fertilized by him? Food fertilized by him?" he called after her.

Aimee whirled on him.

"Why do you want to feed Puppy to turkey vultures? Some people might say that's really sick. They might say that you're really sick."

"Do you think I'm sick?"

"Sometimes I feel like I don't know anymore. I just

don't know."

"It's irony. Turkey vultures are irony," he said, with his voice rising.

"You mean ironic?"

"It's Thanksgiving and we're feeding turkey vultures!"

Daniel started to scream. "Irony! Ironic! You tell me! Tell me! *You* tell me what it is! You always tell me because I don't know stuff! I don't know stuff!"

"I'm just trying to teach you things."

"You tell me I'm sick. You tell me I'm innocent. Whatever you say!"

"I'm sorry."

"You tell me how things are because I don't know anything. The only things I know are what you say. What you say."

He picked up a clod of dirt and smashed it against his chest.

"You know about Sakyamuni. I didn't teach you that stuff."

"But you don't like it. It's Thanksgiving and you don't like turkey vultures."

It is *Thanksgiving.*

How had she lost touch? Gotten so detached as to forget a holiday? And how had Daniel conflated eating turkey on Thanksgiving with feeding turkey vultures on Thanksgiving?

They walked back to the house in silence.

Aimee went to the kitchen and opened the cupboards, searching for something to prepare that would make it seem like Thanksgiving. All she could find was half a box of spaghetti. She put water on the stove and went to her bedroom to cry, but she couldn't.

Maybe, my lifetime allotment of tears is all used up?

She went back into the kitchen and turned off the boiling water. Daniel's avatar was shooting up on Grand Theft.

"Come on. We're going to The Whispering Cypress."

"Why?"
"Because it's a good thing to do."
"What's good about it?"
"We're doing it. We're going to say goodbye to the people who expect us to come with Puppy. We'll tell them not to expect us anymore. It's the right thing, and it's good to do the right thing."
"Can I stay here?"
"No. You can't."
Daniel shrugged.
"Go take off that face paint."
"It's *The Mighty Death Pop*."
"Can't you be normal for once?"
What have I said? she thought. "I didn't mean that," she said aloud.
He started to walk away.
"Please look at me," she said.
He stopped but wouldn't turn around.
"I didn't mean ..."
"It doesn't matter what you mean! What you mean!" he said.
"But sweetheart ..."
"The road to hell is paved with good intentions. Good intentions."
It was a phrase Aimee's mother used to use. She choked back a scream.

#

An hour later, Aimee and Daniel were at the Whispering Cypress for the last time. They stopped in at Mrs. Collier's room first. Aimee broke the news of Puppy's death to the fragile stroke victim. She grunted her sadness. Aimee touched the woman's hand one more time, but with no soft Puppy to share between them, she let go of the cold, bony hand quickly.

WOMAN MURDERED

Bob W., who was a double amputee, took the news of Puppy's death hard, burying his face in his hands. Aimee tried to shoo Daniel out of the room, but he resisted. He was interested in this man.

"Did you lose your legs in a war? In a war?" Daniel asked.

Bob lifted his face.

"No, camo-man. I fought in a war, but it wasn't a war that did this to me."

His face screwed up again.

"I did this to myself. I hate myself so damn much sometimes, I about wish I was dead already. I'd like to stop taking up space in this world."

"The world is big. There's a lot of space. A lot of space," Daniel said.

Bob shook his head.

"I wouldn't stop drinking. They said I'd lose my legs to diabetes, but I didn't care. Maybe it made me want to drink even more."

Aimee tried to look sympathetic.

"You ever have like a movie of the war play in your eyes when nothing is really there? Plays in your eyes when nothing is really there?" Daniel asked, eyes on the baseball cap, still on the nightstand.

"Hell yes," Bob said. "Sorry for the swearing, Ma'am."

"Did you ever wake up in the middle of the night ... heart pounding ... pounding because of a dream ... a dream?"

"Yeah," Bob said. "I have PTSD. It's called Post-Traumatic Stress Disorder."

"I know. I know," Daniel said.

"You can't imagine how bad it is," Bob said.

"I have it."

"What happened to you to make you get PTSD?"

Aimee squirmed.

"I saw a dead body."

She motioned to Daniel to wrap it up.
"Yeah," Bob said, "I've seen lots of those."
Daniel seemed lost in thought.
"But did you ever kill someone?"
"Come on guys," Aimee said, getting anxious. "Let's talk about happy stuff." Breathing fast, she sat on a chair and put her head down as far as she could between her knees.
There's no homecoming for most women.
"Looks like your mama has it too," Bob whispered.
"I used to think I was going crazy, and that I was gonna kill someone. When that happened, I'd go to the nearest pet store and walk around till I calmed down," Bob said. "Some people with PTSD go crazy because they keep remembering stuff. Some numb out to avoid stuff. Some are always nervous. They see danger around every corner."
"What kind are you? Kind are you?" Daniel asked.
"I'm a little bit of all of those types. It doesn't go away. It just morphs. What about you, kiddo?"
"I have Asperger's Syndrome."
"What does that mean?"
"Something bad," Daniel said.
"Are you a criminal?" Bob laughed.
"I'm not normal. Not normal."
"Ha!" Bob scoffed. "Who is?"
"My mom is."
"Are you sure about that?"
Now Daniel laughed.
Aimee tried to usher him out the door.
Bob winked and saluted Daniel, then told him to stay in school.
"Come back and see me, when you get another dog."
"We will," Aimee said.
That will never happen, she thought.

#

WOMAN MURDERED

Aimee and Daniel were about to leave The Whispering Cypress Skilled Nursing Facility for the last time, when they heard the commanding voice of the volunteer coordinator.

"You're not supposed to be here today," Roberta Wagner bellowed. "There are no Pet Friends visits on holidays."

"We're not making a Pet Friend visit," Aimee said. We're here to say goodbye."

Roberta's mouth dropped open. "When I train people, I expect a six-month commitment at the very least. It was against my better judgment to let a teenaged boy volunteer..."

"Puppy is dead! Dead!" Daniel blurted out.

Roberta stopped mid-tirade.

"Then you must resign from Pet Friends." She bent over to take a pumpkin pie from a rolling food cart parked in the hallway.

"Was he an old dog?" she asked, placing the pie in a box.

"No," Aimee said. "She wasn't old at all."

"Was he ill?" Roberta asked.

"No, she wasn't."

"Attacked by an animal then?"

"No." Aimee tried to put an end to the intrusive questioning.

"We don't know how she died."

"Do you live near Cypress Point?"

Roberta was busy tying a string around a second pie box.

"Why?" Aimee asked.

"You do. You live in that rental house with the acreage."

"How do you know?"

"Pebble Beach is a big place, but the community is small. I heard that a dog died on that property."

"Are we neighbors?" Aimee asked.

"I'm sure you'll find a suitable situation elsewhere. There is a homeless women's shelter in Salinas."

"Excuse me?"

"Call Dorothy's Place. They may need volunteers like yourself."

She walked out with a boxed pie in each hand and drove away in her seafoam Jaguar XJ7.

"Did you tell anyone that Puppy died?" Aimee asked Daniel.

"That lady is bad," Daniel said, slapping himself in the face.

Here we go again, Aimee thought.

"What makes you say that?" she asked.

"Because I think it. That's what makes me say it."

My boy speaks his mind.

"Would that be irony?"

"It would be language. Language," he said.

"But what makes you think it?"

"My brain makes me think it."

"You said that lady is bad."

"Fuck her!"

Aimee flinched.

"She didn't say she was sorry about Puppy. Everyone else said they were sorry."

"She didn't express sympathy. Maybe she lacks empathy."

They say autistic children lack empathy. That's why people fear them.

"What's the difference?"

"Difference?"

"Between sympathy and empathy? Sympathy and empathy?"

"I don't have the answer to that," she said, not wanting to try anymore.

"You're kidding, right?" Daniel said. "Kidding?"

WOMAN MURDERED

#

It was Thanksgiving Day, and Dr. Bridgette Peletier was sitting in her office trailer, listening to a recording of Daniel singing a song by his idol, Trip B.

"East Bay got me bloody, Everyday I leave my house, Representing horror, Like Disney with Mickey Mouse, My shirt's already bloody and it doesn't show under a red sky, Right now I'm feeling evil, Gonna risk whether I live or die."

She walked to the mini-fridge and looked at its contents. *I hate eating.*

In school, there was little time for food, and being slender had earned her compliments and saved money for buying nice clothes. Back then, the only real meals she ate were the ones bought by men: medical students took her for pizza, professors sprung for steak, and trustees lobster.

Today was Thanksgiving and there was a lot to be thankful for. Bridgette pulled out a bag of frozen M&Ms and poured them into her mouth.

She picked up a pharmaceutical reference book. She was going to give Daniel something, but what? She didn't want to cause psychosis, or worse, catatonia, and she didn't want him having suicidal thoughts. She reviewed the lesser known psychotropics and off-market uses. She needed him functioning… like a normal psychopath.

Putting on another song by Trip B, she glanced at her messages. The only new one was that she won a pair of MiuMiu shoes on an E-Bay auction.

There's nowhere around here I can wear you gorgeous things. She thought about her appearances on Ellen, Jimmy, Dr. Phil and Oprah.

An encouraging meme popped up on her phone.

Once you make a decision the Universe conspires to make it happen. —Paulo Coelho

"Good one. Thumb up." *But Emerson said it first.*

CHAPTER 10

As the forest sky lightened and the birds chattered outside, Aimee heard her phone ring. She knew it was Michael. She hadn't seen him since he came over in the wee hours of the morning—the hour of the pearl—but he was contacting her with regularity now, calling, Snapchatting, and posting memes. After six months of ghosting, he was back, if from a distance of 120 miles.

The line shows you've not arrived at this place in life without bad luck. And there's more to come, she had just read in her O. Henry book.

"Hey stranger," she said. "I see you have a win in your future."

"Huh?" Michael said. "There's always a win in my future. It's what I do."

"I'm reading a story about Irish immigrants who visit a gypsy in Coney Island. She steals information from them and pretends she knows things."

"Did you see what I posted on your Facebook page?" he asked.

"Let me look. Who did you quote this time?" she said, scrolling through her phone.

"How do you know I posted a quote? Are you psychic?"

"Have you ever posted anything original?"

"There's no such thing as original," he said. "Besides, I don't post my own words."

"That's what I was trying to say."

"I can never tell what you're trying to say."

"Here it is," she said. "*Only the hand that erases can write the true thing.* I don't get it. Is that supposed to be something deep?"

"It means keep summarizing those depositions," he said.

"Erase things? Shorten them? Make them truth?"

"That's Eckhart Tolle, baby," he said.

"I'm pretty sure that's Meister Eckhart."

"So. What's the difference?"

"About seven hundred years."

"That was then, this is now. You've got to get with the program."

Six months ago, Michael posted a slurry of encouraging memes. *I love this guy already,* she had thought.

She told him in a Snapchat that she was looking for someone honest, brave, and loyal like an Eagle Scout; but they never comprehended each other. They only traded in effort and mistake.

"Do you remember when you told me you were a stand-up guy?" she said.

"I *am* a stand-up guy!"

"How are you a stand-up guy?"

"I'm funny. I'm a regular comedian. Haven't you noticed?"

Is he pulling my leg or is he being serious? she thought.

It was a mental *roshambo* she lost every time.

She Googled the expression *stand-up guy.*

"It means someone who steps forward; a volunteer to help. *The phrase is American, the earliest citation from a newspaper,* The Charleroi Mail, April 1935."

"That was then," Michael said. "This is now. Nobody thinks that way."

Wanting to point out he just called her a nobody, she realized that an argument about words was pointless with Michael.

"Hold on," she said.

Daniel was pounding on her bedroom door. He burst into her room and threw himself on the floor, writhing.

Aimee's heart sank.

"Whoever killed Puppy I hate them! They should be killed! They should be killed!"

He slapped the floor repeatedly.

Better than slapping himself, Aimee thought.

"Why did Puppy die? Why did Puppy die?"

"I don't know," Aimee said. "Dogs don't live as long as people do."

"But what made her die? What made her die?"

"I don't know. I wish I could tell you what happened."

"You could! You could!" he said.

"But I don't know. How could I possibly tell you if I don't know?" she asked.

"You can know things when you want to. Michael said you saw a guy's picture a long time ago and you knew he killed a girl. He said you knew who the killer was before the police knew. Before the police knew."

Michael had asked Aimee for her gut feeling about a crime, then tipped the FBI. A suspect was arrested but hung himself before his trial. Aimee refused to use her so-called psychic ability ever again.

"He shouldn't have told you about that."

"It was at my trial. People said I was a murderer. Michael said you'd know if I really was because you're psychic. You're psychic."

"He said that?"

"You can tell me what happened to Puppy, but you won't, because you don't care. You don't care!"

"Look, Puppy's gone! She's gone like your father! Okay?"

"Not okay! If you don't tell me what happened, I'm never going to talk to you again! Talk to you again!"

Daniel ran out, slamming the door.

Aimee slumped onto the dingy beige carpet.

It was a powerful threat coming from an autistic boy who once stopped talking for a whole year.

"Aimee! Aimee!"

She heard her name being called by Michael, who was still on the phone.

"Listen to me. You've gotta keep him out of the public eye."

"I'm trying to, but why are you telling me that?"

"He just has to stay under the radar, do you hear me? I know what I'm talking about. Remember, I'm a high-paid lawyer."

"Is there any way you could come down?"

"I can't."

"Okay then," she said. "Hey, did I tell you how the story ends? The gypsy lady predicted the truth without her tricks."

"What story?"

"Goodbye Michael," Aimee said, hanging up the phone.

She held herself very still on the bed like she didn't want it to know she was there.

Everything is broken, and nothing is mending.

She closed her eyes and tried to think happy thoughts.

She saw the quail and bunnies rushing in and out of the brush along the trails of Carmel Meadows. She imagined Mrs. Collier's spirit flying out over the ocean on a warm sunny day with the waves crashing against Point Lobos. She relaxed, if infinitesimally.

She heard her grandmother's voice.

Aimee.

"Grandma is that you?"

Yes, it's me, Dear.

"Is Daddy with you?"

There are so many people here. Kenny is here, Della is here ...

"Grandma are you young again, or are you the age you were when you died, or some other age in between?"

All of them.

Aimee felt a warm vibration in her chest.

"Grandma, I'm so worried about Daniel."

That's why I'm here.
"Is there something that can be done for him?"
It's already been done.
"What?" Aimee asked.
The apparition slipped away before she could say thank you.
Just after dawn, Aimee dreamt that she was nursing Daniel as a baby. He took more than he could hold, and everything came out in a stream of projectile vomit.
She woke up and bolted for the bathroom, retching out the contents of her last meal.
As she clung to the toilet bowl she heard pounding on the door.
"Mama! Mama! I didn't mean it! I didn't mean it!"
Daniel's face was pressed against the painted wooden door and he was making strange animal noises.
He's crying.
Aimee wiped her mouth and took a sip of water. When she opened the door, Daniel fell into her arms.
"I didn't mean to! I didn't mean to make you sick! Make you sick!" he said, between gulps.
"But you didn't make me sick," she said.
"What made you throw up? Throw up?"
"I had a dream. It was a good dream at first. But then it turned bad."
"Was it about Puppy? Was it about Puppy?"
"I think, in a way, it was."
"What happened to her?"
"She ate something very bad."
"Was it poison? Was it poison?"
"It was."

#

At Casablanca, Judith Rodewald sat nursing a Manhattan while she waited for her best friend to meet her for lunch. Tall, thin, glamorous for her age, she had thick platinum hair that had been auburn before changing.

People always compared her to Jackie Kennedy, and her husband Lang, with his sandy hair, tanned-skin, and sky-blue eyes, to Jack. When they met he was only a handsome mechanic working on small airplanes. By the time she had her way, he was part owner of a 1948 Luscombe Silvaire Sedan; the Cadillac of airplanes.

Judith saw her friend making her way through the greenhouse room to their table.

"Tell me I'm not late!" Roberta said, with exaggerated distress.

"You're not late," the waiter said, as he passed by.

"I don't need your sarcasm, thank you very much," Roberta said.

"It's not sarcasm, Hon. She's early." The waiter nodded toward Judith. "She's always early."

"We don't need your lies either," Judith said. "Now shoo!"

"What lies?"

"Go away, kid, you bother me." Judith waved at him.

She held out her Lady Rolex for Roberta to see.

"Twenty minutes! Dammit to hell! I checked my watch against the house clock right before I left, but you can't just dial Popcorn anymore, can you?"

"Sit down, dear, you look tired," Judith said.

"I am. I'm so damned tired. You wouldn't believe how tired I am." Roberta flopped into her seat.

"Kip's not keeping you up, is he?" Judith asked, in an overly intimate voice.

"Ha! He sleeps like a baby."

"*Quelle coincidence.* I sleep like a baby too."

"Well, maybe you wouldn't if you had to put up with what I do."

"Maybe I should introduce you to my friend Hal, he's a doll."

"Did someone say Haldol?" the waiter said, in passing.
"Did you order yet?" Roberta asked.
"Of course, I did."
"What am I having?"
"Salmon."
"To drink?"
"A Fuzzy Navel."
"Be serious."
"Honey, after all these years..."
"Don't call me honey. You know that story!"
"Ancient history, darling."
"Just like us..."
"Bite your tongue! We're mere girls."
"Speak for yourself."
"I am, darling, I am," Judith said.
"I'm too tired to be a golden girl," Roberta complained.
"I know you are, God damn it, I know."
"Here's to us, damn it." Roberta raised her glass.

The two old friends sipped their cocktails, a tonic to their nagging discomfort.

Judith looked for the waiter. "My God, the service is slow. You have to be on Valium to enjoy this place. Lang won't even eat here anymore."

Her animated demeanor vanished.

"Oh God. Listen to me. I'm talking about my late husband as if he were still here."

"It's perfectly understandable," Roberta said.

"God damn it, it's not perfectly anything,"

They fell silent. A group of golfers came in for a table. Judith and Roberta followed them with their eyes as they were seated in the Cezanne Room.

How pretentious, Judith thought. "You're not golfing anymore, are you?" she asked.

"Of course not! My hips."

"What a pity you can't keep Kip company on the greens anymore. It's a shame you never got a chance to play at

Cypress Point Club, living across from it all these years."

"I have played there, as a matter of fact," Roberta said.

"As whose guest?" Judith asked, raising an eyebrow.

"Kip's."

"How could Kip be a member of that club? I thought it was only for royalty."

"His family were Duchies or Dukies or something. They, basically, invented golf back in Scotland. Cypress practically begged him to be a member there."

"Let me get this straight, Kip is a member of The Cypress Point Club?"

"No. He resigned."

"But that's crazy!" Judith said. "Why would he do a thing like that?"

"There was a reason, but I forget what it was now."

"But he could reactivate it if he wanted to, right?"

Roberta was studying her faulty watch. "Damn it, I've got to run."

"Not again in this lifetime," Judith said, chuckling.

"I have a job, you know."

"Oh yes. Your nursing home gig." Judith said. "How you set foot in those kinds of places I'll never understand."

"I *volunteer* at a SNiF. I'll never live in one," Roberta said. She faltered as she rose. The waiter tried to steady her, but she batted him away. "By the by, I took your advice."

"You didn't," Judith said.

"I most certainly did. And, I might add, I'm pleased."

"Jesus Christ. I didn't think you had it in you."

"What one person can do, another can."

"More power to you."

Judith raised her glass. "It was your idea."

"Hardly," Judith said.

"You said I should take care of things for myself."

"My dear, I was only joking."

"Now you tell me." Roberta took the moment to exit.

Stupid woman, Judith thought.

CHAPTER 11

Persuaded by her husband, Roberta strolled arm-in-arm with Kip along Pescadero Point. The old married couple took their morning constitutional on the paths topping the granite cliffs overlooking Ghost Trees.

Stone benches dotted the well-maintained pathways at regular intervals, convenient for a walker like Roberta who had to stop and rest with regularity.

The fog generated by the Indian summer was no longer blanketing the coastline in billowy rolls. It was a crisp December morning; ceiling open, visibility unlimited.

Kip held Stubby by the leash although he was quite safe. The tour buses wouldn't arrive until noon. They were all alone under the bright gray sky.

"Just a moment, Dear, I need to take this call," Kip said, pulling his phone from his pocket.

"This is Kip Wagner."

Roberta knew he was about to leave her.

He said he had to meet someone on a job nearby.

She was tired anyway, and her hips hurt. "Take me home."

"It's just a little thing with the painter over at the new listing on Sombria Lane. It won't take a minute. Trust me."

"That was my first mistake! Trusting you!" Roberta said.

"But Stubby hasn't even done his business yet. It wouldn't be fair to leave."

"Fair to whom? I don't have to be fair to a dog." He went silent.

"Go on. Just go. I'll watch the damn dog. But don't

leave me here on this bench all day."

"If I forget you can always call me," Kip said.

"Don't forget," she said. "I will not be left."

He gave her a peck on the cheek and walked away.

But he *had* left her. He had left her *many* times; always when things got bad. She didn't care to recall those times, but sitting by herself the memories started flooding in.

The time she felt most abandoned by her husband—the one she could never forgive him for—was when he was overseas and their only child, Stephanie, died.

"She's in a coma. She may have brain damage if she comes out of it," a doctor said.

"*When* she comes out ..." Roberta said.

"I said IF she comes out of it. It's very unlikely that there will not be damage to the brain."

Stupid woman, she imagined him saying to her.

But she was not stupid. He had no idea who he was talking to. She sat all night by Stephanie's bed in the ICU. "Please don't leave. Please don't leave," she said, over and over.

On the chance that Stephanie might be able to hear her voice from inside the coma, she talked nonstop. She spoke to her daughter about anything and everything. She told her the story of how she met her daddy, and of what life had been like when she was a little girl. She told all of her stories one by one until they were done. Then she recited the Psalms.

"Though I walk through the valley of the shadow of death..."

Love is never easy, she thought. *It's damned inconvenient, in fact.*

Five days later, she was making funeral arrangements for her only child while her husband Kip was heading home on a transport plane to be there in time.

In time for what? Death?

Willing herself back to the present, Roberta looked to

her faulty watch, but it wasn't on her wrist. *Damn him.* She didn't enjoy time alone. She didn't want to think or remember things that could never have a different outcome.

Her arm shot up in the air, pulled by the leash she was holding. "Stubby! Get back here!" He was pulling so hard she had to get up. "Damn dog!"

#

Aimee James was standing at the kitchen sink of her little rental cottage, trying to scrub dirt off a pair of gloves, when she saw Daniel coming up the driveway. His cheeks were pink, and his hair was mussed. It was nice to see him enjoying the fresh air.

She felt sorry he didn't have Puppy at his side. She looked again. There *was* a dog with him. A tan bulldog was following him up the long, curved driveway.

Aimee stepped outside. "Where did this little buddy come from?" she asked.

"Don't know. Maybe, its owner died? Its owner died?" Daniel said, looking at the dog.

"Come here, puppy," Aimee said.

"That's not Puppy! That's not Puppy!" Daniel shouted.

"You're right, it isn't Puppy, but it is *a* puppy," his mother said.

"No, it's not. No, it's not. It's just a dog. Just a dog."

Aimee looked closer. "You're right."

He calls them like he sees them, she thought.

She got on her knees, making sure the dog was friendly, and grabbed his collar to read the tag.

"Sergeant Stubby. Heaven's Edge."

"The house next door. House next door," Daniel said.

She took out her phone and dialed the number.

You've reached the voicemail of Roberta Wagner, she heard.

Aimee hung up.

WOMAN MURDERED

The volunteer coordinator lives next door?

"You gonna take this dog over to that house? That house?" Daniel asked.

"No," Aimee said. "I'll take it to the animal shelter. Do you understand why?"

Daniel nodded, but he didn't. "It's time I gotta go see Califia. Go see Califia."

"That reminds me, Dr. Peletier said not to come until later. She's got something she has to do."

"Did you tell her I don't adjust well to change in routine? Change in routine?"

It was one of those things about kids with Asperger's Syndrome that Daniel had heard all his life. He wasn't sure if it was true, but sometimes it was convenient.

Aimee opened her eyes wide.

"Made you look. Made you look," he said.

She laughed at the oldie but goodie.

"Dr. Peletier said you can bring Califia a lump of sugar every Friday. She also said that you're doing a great job caring for Califia."

"Do you believe everything she says? he asked.

"Um, yes. Shouldn't I?"

"Trust but verify. Verify."

"Did she tell you that?"

"No. I read it on Facebook."

"You're not supposed to have a Facebook account!"

"I don't. Michael posted it to your wall, and you left it open. You left it open."

"Oops."

#

Driving to the animal shelter way over in Salinas, Aimee let the little bulldog sit on her lap. He was a cute little guy. He snuggled down between the steering wheel and her knees. Aimee looked at the marble eyes gazing up at her.

"You're a sweetheart, aren't you? How can you belong to that volunteer coordinator?" She patted Sergeant Stubby on the head.

The clerk at the shelter asked for Aimee's name, address, and phone number. "We must have it," the woman said. "We get the contact information of every person who brings an animal to this shelter."

Aimee considered giving a false name, but the idea didn't sit well. She gave the required information, including the time and location she found the dog.

It was very hot in the room, and the walls started to spin around her.

"Are you okay? Do you need to sit down?" the clerk said.

"*No se que le pasa*," Aimee answered.

"Why are you talking in Spanish? I speak perfect English."

"Um, I don't know. To practice?"

The clerk handed Aimee a Dixie cup full of water.

"*Gracias. Siento mejor. Ya me voy.*"

She got up to leave. "I'm sorry about the Spanish. I didn't mean anything rude by it."

"It was just weird," the clerk said.

"It's a weird day," Aimee said.

"You gonna be okay to drive?"

"I have to be. My son needs me."

"*Niños,*" the woman said.

#

Driving back from Salinas, Aimee passed the wide-ribbon fields of lettuce, cabbage, broccoli, and asparagus, as far as the eye could see. It was Steinbeck's *salad bowl of the world*. She drove across the low dunes of Old Fort Ord that were covered with fragrant coastal brush.

She thought about the man Faulkner accused of never

WOMAN MURDERED

using a word his readers had to look up.

Is that a good thing? Or is that a bad thing? Is that even a true thing?

She looked up a lot of words when she read *The Grapes of Wrath*. She couldn't find most of them because they were all dialect.

What was that thing Jim Casy talked about ... a speret*?*

As she got closer to Carmel-by-the-Sea she headed the Jeep toward Bixby's Market. The big supermarket by the highway was cheaper, but where was the romance in that? She pictured herself in a white sundress on a bicycle with a loaf of French bread and a bottle of wine.

She embarrassed herself in front of herself. *Why don't you let yourself live, at least in your imagination?*

She kept an eye out for Prince Albert of Bixby, and when she didn't find him she was more disheartened than she wanted to admit, even to herself.

She picked up a cheap bottle of red wine and some chips and guac. *It doesn't matter if he's here or not. It's just a fantasy. I was only looking for a moment's reprieve; a moment, that's all.*

Behind the cash register was Cody, the cute kid with the mop of beach hair. He was talking with his hands to a couple of high-schoolers, describing something amazing that happened to him earlier that morning.

Of course, he didn't place the change in Aimee's hand the way Albert did. That would've been too weird. But he missed her hands completely, letting the change fall to the floor, too engrossed in his story-telling to notice.

"I almost died. Dude! I was pinned under this *gigantor* maverick! Outta nowhere, something rams me and pushes me up. I thought it was like a shark, then a dolphin. But it was a freakin' dead body! A dead body that saved my life! For real. Check out YouTube. You gotta check it out."

Aimee left, disappointed.

Beri Balistreri

CHAPTER 12

Cenobio Hernandez sat overlooking the expanse of Pacific Ocean. He listened to the crashing waves and screaming birds as he ate his deli sandwich. He was a twenty-year-old housepainter on a break for lunch at Pescadero Point. The place reminded him of when he was a kid in Guerrero watching the famed Acapulco cliff-divers every day.

Coming to California with his parents, he had worked picking strawberries. He passed for older, but an inspector said he'd better go to school or else, so he went to school, and he worked. On the weekends he helped his parents at the local farmer's market until his father died from swine flu and his grief-stricken mother went to work in a nursing home. Cenobio was now old enough to work in construction, where the money was better.

A snatch of a ringtone from a cell phone jarred him. He looked around and saw a woman's purse on a bench, but there was no one in sight. He continued eating the barbequed tri-tip from Bixby's Market. When it was time to head back to the job on a nearby house, he grabbed the purse no one had claimed, tossed it into his truck through the cab window, and drove back to the nearby job site to finish the day's work.

Cenobio finished cleaning the last paintbrush and tamping down the last lid as twilight in Pebble Beach deepened. He was in a hurry to get home to Seaside and talk with his mama. He had something to share with her that would change both their lives.

He headed north on Highway 1, where he was always a

little uncomfortable without valid registration and updated insurance. He knew he could get arrested any day and have his truck impounded.

The flashers in his mirror said today was the day.

Cenobio handed his license and expired registration to Officer Kelly of the California Highway Patrol. Kelly leaned into the cab. "Proof of insurance?" Cenobio handed him the expired card. "You married?"

"No, sir."

"Got a girlfriend?"

"No, sir."

"Whose purse is that?"

"I don't know. I found it."

Next thing he knew, Cenobio was bent face down over a patrol car on the shoulder of the highway. Everything was happening too fast.

"Are you *Norteño* or *Sureño*?" Kelly asked.

Cenobio was neither, but he didn't answer. "You're going to jail," Kelly said.

Cenobio was too afraid to speak. He'd never been to jail. He was terrified of the place, and the characters that he knew were there.

He felt his head lowered by force into the patrol car. He would've crossed himself, but his hands were zip-tied together.

#

If Kip Wagner hadn't taken such good care of himself by working out each and every day at the Beach Club, his heart might have given out when the call came from the Coroner's office. Roberta, his wife of over fifty years, had drowned.

Kip filled a Baccarat snifter with cognac and sat down in his wife's cream-colored silk wing-back. Everything looked strange. He could hardly believe Roberta wouldn't walk in from the garden at any minute and deride him for having his muddy shoes on the white rug.

A wave of euphoria swept over him.

His moment was interrupted by the noise of the phone. A detective was calling to tell him that Roberta's purse was found. Inside of it was her cell phone.

The detective informed him that there were five calls to Mrs. Wagner's cell phone that day: one from an Aimee James, one from Kip himself, and three from an animal shelter in Salinas.

"Is that where my dog is? Why Salinas?"

"That's what I'd like to know," the detective said.

"I'll go pick him up," Kip said, rising.

"I don't think you should drive tonight sir, and besides, they're closed. Wait until tomorrow and I'll bring your dog back to you myself."

"Thank you," Kip said.

"One more thing, Mr. Wagner: Do you have any ideas why a house painter would have your wife's handbag?"

"Not a one," Kip said.

#

Aimee set her bag of stuff on the pine sideboard in the rental's kitchen. She couldn't find a corkscrew, so she put the bottle of wine in the cupboard. *Some other time.*

She joined Daniel on the stained living room carpet. He was singing along with his idol, Trip B.

"Nightly I kill! I roam the city, murder without trying, more than strange! Oh God, it's happening right now, my bones will shift, time for a change! I toss and turn and scream in agony, here in sweat and blood I lie."

"What? Did you just say you want to die?" his mother asked.

He sang on.

"'Til it's complete, and frankly in the mood, for some

WOMAN MURDERED

people to die. I walk the night in search of blood under the moon's sinister glow. To shred some carcasses to pieces and bathe in the red spray. Carnivorous canine instincts, through the night until the day."

"Not die, kill," Daniel said. "Kill."

Aimee sat on the distressed gray sofa behind her son. Daniel switched on the video game *Grand Theft Auto Number 4*. It was about modern-day gangsters called *gangstas*. It was full of murdering, swearing, and role-playing, including simulated drug use that distorted graphics and intensified colors. It had the ironic rating of *M for Mature,* which may have been why Daniel called it *Grand Theft Naughty*. She watched him work the controller as his avatar's girlfriend phoned him during a mission to complain that she was lonely.

Oh, brother.

An on-screen friend said to kill her if she got too annoying. *Buy her a dildo and use it to beat people up,* the guy said. "The misogyny portrayed in this game is horrific," said Aimee. *He has a girlfriend?* she thought.

"Is that when men are mean to women? Mean to women?" Daniel asked.

"It's more than mean, it's hatred. It's contempt and disregard. Women are just objects. Such a violent game!"

"No, it's not. No, it's not," Daniel said.

"What are you talking about?" his mother asked.

"Football is a violent game," he said. "A violent game."

Daniel pulled hard to the right with the controller, knocking into some pedestrians with a garbage truck. "See, it's fake. It's fake," he said.

"But the ideas are violent," she said. "Fake could lead to real …"

"Are football players violent in real life?" he asked.

"Actually, some of them are. A few have beaten their girlfriends, shot people in bars, run dog fights, used drugs …"

"Why do they do that bad stuff when they're already famous? They're already famous?"

"Why does anybody do bad stuff, ever?"

"Video games make them? Video games make them?"

"Is that supposed to be sarcasm?"

"You tell me," he said. "You tell me."

"I've heard that they play the same video games in Japan, but they don't go around killing people the way we do here," she said.

"Go around killing people? What do you mean, we go around killing people?"

"Not you and me," she said.

Daniel started yelling. "We go around killing people! Go around killing people!"

"I didn't mean it the way it sounded," she said.

"Not we? Just *me*?" he shouted.

"That's not what I meant."

"What did you mean? Did you mean?"

"Maybe it's all perception."

"What's that?"

"It's kind of like prejudice. Football players are perceived as heroes. Japanese are perceived as polite. People with autism are …"

"Psychopaths?"

"People are gonna see what they want to see."

"People like Dr. Peletier? Like Dr. Peletier?"

"She's on our side," Aimee said. *She is, isn't she?*

Daniel unplugged the PlayStation, and the television reverted to the local channel. Mother and son sat through an agonizing commercial for erectile dysfunction pills.

You'd think this was polite conversation in a civilized world.

"It looks like Carmel Beach, where the dysfunctional go …"

Aimee thought of explaining the commercial, but that would require more than she could handle tonight. She wasn't sure Daniel's pun was unintentional, anyhow.

He's a smart boy.

The next commercial showed a man and woman at a sports arena. *When you don't want to wait,* said the voice.

At a sporting event? Aimee thought.

She knew that on Super Bowl Sundays there was always a spike in calls to the police for domestic violence occurrences. She'd also heard that major sporting events lured human traffickers. *I guess that's why men need their ED pills at the big game. When you don't want to wait, big pharma is there to provide for all your male ...* She had to take several deep breaths.

"Good evening, I'm Alexandra Sundstrom," intoned the local news reporter on the tv. "A woman walking her dog near the famous Ghost Tree at Pescadero Point in Pebble Beach plunged to her death today. When we come back: Should the trails at Pescadero Point have guardrails? Join us tonight for Action News at 8!"

Aimee jumped up. "Ghost Tree! That's close. Like a mile, right? That's really close."

"I know it is. It is," Daniel said.

"Have you been that far on your walks?"

"I wanted to see the big waves. See the big waves."

"It's okay. I just didn't know."

"I went there today. Went there today."

"Do the trails seem dangerous?"

"No."

"I wonder what happened."

"She had to die," Daniel said.

The commercial break was over.

"Good evening, seventy-six-year-old Pebble Beach resident Roberta Wagner fell to her death this morning while walking her dog on the trails at Pescadero Point."

Aimee shrieked. Daniel jumped up and down and began pacing back and forth, hitting himself in the face. "You're scaring me. Why did you say she had to die?"

"Because it's true," he said.
"But that sounds bad, Daniel, really bad."
"She's the bad one! She's the bad one!" he screamed.
Aimee grabbed a paper bag and held it to her mouth. She was gulping air too fast.

#

Kip was still sitting in Roberta's chair, feeling the shock of all that happened in the last 24 hours, when Judith called. "Hello," he said, in a weakened voice.

"Is Roberta there?" Judith asked.

"I'm sorry," he said.

"Kip, I was sitting here in Lang's leather easy-chair with this mohair throw draped around my shoulders. I was eating a piece of chicken with my vodka gimlet when I clicked on the tv. That weatherman is bald as a billiard. He really should get a decent toupee.

"Anyhow, that attractive blonde said a woman walking a dog plunged to her death in Pebble Beach today."

"I know," Kip said.

"And I said, 'Oh God, I hope it's no one I know.'"

"Roberta *never* walks your dog, but I picked up the phone and dialed your number to see if I could talk to her. Is she still awake?"

"Judith, dear, is that you?" Kip asked, bewildered.

"I hate how old people go to bed too early. The older a person gets, the earlier they go to bed, until one day they don't get up at all. You have to fight against that."

"We lost our best friend today."

"What are you saying, Kip?"

"Roberta is gone."

"What do you mean, she's gone?"

"She fell. She's drowned."

"Oh my God," Judith said. "First Lang, now Roberta."

"I'm sorry, Judith. We'll get through this."

"I know what you're going through. It was less than a year ago when Lang died. I'll never be over that."

"I know, dear," Kip said.

"We have to be strong for each other. Just say the word. You know I'm here to help."

Kip recounted what he knew of the accident and how Roberta's body was found. "I came back to fetch her after a quick meeting with a painter at a listing. When she wasn't there, I assumed that she left out of anger with me."

"She does get terribly angry with you," Judith said.

"Walking back to Heaven's Edge from the Ghost Tree was too far for someone like Roberta, but sometimes she surprises me."

"Is that so? When was the last time Roberta surprised you?"

"I thought maybe she took off because she was mad at me when I went to meet the painter, although the listing was just nearby."

"That *is* the kind of thing she would do," Judith said.

"When she wasn't at the house, I called Pebble Beach Security to keep a lookout for her. You know how they'll search for wandering seniors."

"I remember that old man who went unfound for a year until teenagers spotted his body a mere fifty feet off Macomber road."

"My God, Judith, they found her floating in the Pacific Ocean!"

Judith didn't say anything.

"There's something else," Kip said. "They've arrested a man, a house painter."

"God damn it!" Judith shouted.

Kip wished Roberta were there to take the phone.

CHAPTER 13

Kip Wagner opened the front door of Heaven's Edge the next morning to find his beloved Sergeant Stubby squirming out of Detective Frank LaTorella's arms.

"There you are, Stubbs! No worse for the *where* I see." Kip patted his favorite companion on the head. "I appreciate your retrieving him. What do I owe you for the service?"

"May I step in?"

Kip waved him in and motioned to a wingback chair. "Have a seat," he said.

"I'll stand. But, I think you might want to sit," the detective said.

"If you're standing, I'm, standing. Say whatever it is you have to say, but please do it quickly." Kip said, leaning on a side table.

"Your wife didn't fall accidentally."

Kip's face didn't change from its bothered expression.

"According to the preliminary forensic investigation, your wife was pushed off the cliff. We can tell that she was prodded with an object, backed along the ground, and forced over the edge."

The color left Kip's face. "Why don't you just say that she was murdered?"

"Your wife was murdered."

"I was expecting this when you told me about the man who was arrested with her handbag. Robbery and a murder go together."

"Unfortunately, Mr. Wagner, *you* were the last person to see your wife alive."

"Really? Are you here to arrest *me*?" Kip laughed.
"I'm here to talk with you."
"I'll give you five minutes. Five quick minutes."
"Mr. Wagner, you do know that husbands kill their wives every day. It's so common that it hardly makes the news. They kill them when they get mad at them, or tired of them, or when there's someone else in the picture."
"Are you going to arrest me?" Kip asked.
"Do you know Cenobio Hernandez?"
"Not at all."
"He was working as a painter on the house you went to when you left your wife by the Ghost Tree. Did you have any sort of arrangement with him?"
"Like what? Here's fifty dollars, now go push my wife off a cliff while I select crown molding?"
"Something like that."
"I told you I don't know that Mexican and he doesn't know who I am, so he isn't going to be implicating me in my wife's murder."
"What did you do when you didn't find your wife sitting on a bench at Pescadero Point?"
"I called Pebble Beach Security."
"And then?"
"Then I went to the Beach Club."
"Did you think your wife might be there?"
"No."
"What did you do at the Beach Club?"
"I walked on the treadmill."
"Anything else?"
"I ate lunch."
"Did you eat by yourself?"
"Yes. Actually, no."
"Who did you have lunch with at the Beach Club?"
"Judith Rodewald."
"Is she another member?"
"Yes. She came over and sat at my table."

"How would you characterize your relationship?"

The color left Kip's face. "I wasn't having an affair, if that's what you're getting at! Judith is my wife's best friend. I mean, she *was* my wife's best friend."

"Do you know what's become of your wife's jewelry?"

"I do not," Kip said, adjusting his wristwatch.

"You reported quite a list of valuables that she was wearing yesterday."

"I assume they're in the possession of the man who mugged her, or somewhere at the bottom of the ocean; possibly in the belly of a Great White Shark."

"Your wife might not have been found if it weren't for a bunch of crazy tow-surfers out there yesterday. When her body popped up to the surface it actually saved a kid from drowning."

Kip grabbed his stomach.

"That was thoughtless of me," the detective said.

"You need to leave now."

The detective didn't budge.

"Get out!"

As soon as the door closed behind the detective, Kip ran for the bathroom, the one Roberta had recently re-decorated in taupe. Alone on his knees at the commode, the old sailor vomited and wept; vomited and wept.

#

Aimee steered her J40 into the equestrian center to pick up Daniel. She saw him astride Califia, walking circles in the dusty corral. The sight warmed her heart.

Dr. Peletier ushered her into a portable office near the front corral. "Tell me about the music Daniel listens to," the doctor said.

"He listens to rap music, mostly; the famous Insane Clown Posse that you've heard so much about, and that Trip B he worships."

"Worships?" the doctor asked.

"A standard choice of words for music lovers and fans," Aimee said.

"Would you say the music he listens to is hate-filled?"

"I'd say it's cathartic."

"Did anyone ever tell you that some major law enforcement considers Insane Clown Posse fans called *Juggalos* to be a gang? Sometimes they get stiffer sentences and harsher penalties than those who commit non-gang affiliated crimes."

"Daniel's not in a gang."

"The judge wasn't aware that he calls himself a *Juggalo*, was he?"

"Look, what's the harm in letting him listen to songs about murdering and stuff? Isn't it just like letting him watch *Nightmare on Elm Street* or something? I think most teens watch those slasher movies, at least they did when I was working in schools," Aimee said.

It is *my fault for indulging him,* she thought.

"You yourself admit he practically worships that underground rapper Trip B, and he's totally obsessed with the Insane Clown Posse," the doctor said.

"But he's not in a gang."

"He even calls himself a *Juggalo*."

"It's a fan club, not a gang," Aimee said.

"Not according to the FBI."

"He has an Official Secret Ninja Decoder from ICP for God's sake!"

"Really, Aimee, calm down, you're scaring me."

"*Me*? I'm scaring *you*?" All the bravado left Aimee's voice. "You want him to listen to *O Susanna!* after someone killed his dog?"

"So, you think *someone* killed his dog?"

"Someone *did* kill his dog," Aimee said. "She was poisoned."

Dr. Peletier stopped in her tracks. "Look, Aimee,

children like Daniel *do* kill their own pets."

"Daniel would never kill an animal."

"Are you sure about that?"

"Yes," Aimee said.

"Not even a raccoon?"

There was a long silence.

"Just a person, hmmm?"

"Do you really think he's a cold-blooded killer?"

"Listen to this…"

The doctor switched on a recording of Daniel that she made with her iPhone.

"Fuck you, shithead, fuck you, shithead, fuck you, shithead. You eat shit and die."

She switched it off.

"How does that make you feel?" the doctor asked.

"Scared." Aimee bit her lip to keep it from twitching.

"To anyone with half a heart this is devastating stuff," Bridgette Peletier said.

"You're right. I'll start putting my foot down right away."

"Calm down."

"I'll take his music away. The video games too."

"You don't have to take his music away. Just get me his playlist."

It was a confusing request, but Aimee agreed. *Without this woman, I'd be visiting Daniel in prison.*

#

Aimee watched through the kitchen window as a white Ford Crown Vic crept up the driveway like a slow shark. It parked on the asphalt landing outside the little bungalow. Aimee hurried out to meet the plainclothes detective from the Monterey County Sheriff's Office before he could come to the door.

"Are you lost?" she asked.

WOMAN MURDERED

"Are you Aimee James?"

Here we go again, she thought. "I am," she said aloud.

The detective climbed out of his car and brushed off his jacket. "I'm Detective LaTorella, from the Sheriff's Department. This place looks original. Been making repairs or doing some painting?"

"It's a rental. *As is.* I think the owner's waiting for it to collapse."

"Did you drop off a dog at the animal shelter in Salinas yesterday?"

"Was that your dog?" she asked.

"The dog belongs to your neighbor. Were you aware of that?"

"How could I be?" Aimee asked.

"You called the woman's cell phone yesterday. You must know her."

"I called the number on the dog's tag. There was no answer."

"The tag said, Heaven's Edge. It's the house next door. You can't miss the scrollwork on the gate."

Aimee looked at the detective, waiting for more.

"Are you aware that your neighbor is newly deceased?"

Staring through a tunnel of fear, she had to say something.

"I wondered about that. It was on the tv news last night."

"Did you know Mrs. Wagner?"

"We volunteered under her at a nursing home," Aimee said.

"We?"

Aimee wanted to stop talking but clamming up now would only make him more suspicious. She knew that from Daniel's ordeal in San Francisco.

"My son. My son and me."

The detective was watching her face closely.

"Do you know Cenobio Hernandez?" he asked.

"No."

That came out of nowhere, she thought.

"Did you have a conversation in Spanish at the shelter?"

"Yes. I wasn't feeling well. The girl asked if I needed to sit down."

"The girl? Why weren't you feeling well?"

So, this is how the cat and mouse questions go? It's like when the police came after Todd's death. It is all leading up to something. There's a snare somewhere, she thought.

"Excuse me, what are you trying to get at?" she said.

"For starters, why did you take the dog to Salinas when you could have taken it to its home right next door?"

"Sometimes it's just better not to know your neighbors."

"You said that you knew Mrs. Wagner."

"I didn't know that she was the person who lived next door."

"You worked for her, but you didn't know she was your neighbor?"

"Yes. But I didn't work for her, we were volunteers."

"You and your son."

"My son and I."

I sure walked into that.

"Did you quit?"

"Um, yes. No."

The detective smiled. Aimee thought he looked pleased with himself.

It was the um *that gave me away. I've got to be more careful.*

"So, you *did* quit?"

"We had to stop because our dog died."

Aimee wanted to run and hide, but she kept talking. "We volunteered as Pet Friends at The Whispering Cypress. Without a dog to take with us, we couldn't be Pet Friend volunteers anymore."

"I see."

"You said that Mrs. Wagner was killed. I thought she slipped."

WOMAN MURDERED

"She was pushed off a cliff at Pescadero Point."
Aimee's eyes widened.
"The reporter said she fell."
"You heard the news?"
"I told you I did."
"But you heard it carefully," he said.
The trap is about to snap, she thought.
"We're holding a person of interest."
"Cenobio Hernandez?"
"You speak Spanish?"
"I trained to be a school teacher."
"Trained? But you didn't become one?"
"I stayed home with my son. He has a disability."
"All that training. Too bad you didn't become a teacher."
"You think I haven't been a teacher?" she said.
"I didn't mean that. I'm sorry," he said, backing off.
"What kind of disability does your son have?" he asked.
"Autistic spectrum. It's not what you think. It's never what anyone thinks."
"What do you mean, what anyone thinks?"
"I love him. That's all."
"I'm sure you do, ma'am."
She glared at him with fire and ice.
"They can bring you helplessly to your knees, can't they?"
"Who?"
"Children."
"Oh."
"My son has cerebral palsy. He's the purest soul on God's earth. I'd do anything for that kid."
Aimee resisted rolling her eyes.
"I bet you'd do anything for your son, too."
And there snaps the trap, she thought.
He tried a different tack. "I guess it kinda unmakes you and puts you back together differently," he said. He was

looking at the gnarled trunk of a gray Cypress tree, half dead.

"What does?" Aimee asked.

"Love." They were both silent for a moment.

"Are we finished?" Aimee said, breaking the peace.

"For now, but I may need to talk to you again. Can I have your number?"

Hell no! she thought. "Yes," she said.

#

When the detective had gone, Aimee made a cup of chamomile tea to calm her nerves, like Peter Rabbit after he almost got baked into a pie. She'd read that story to Daniel so many times she could see the poor little bunny hiding in a watering can, shivering.

She wished she'd never seen that bulldog.

That man was relentless. He'll find out about Daniel. I have a bad feeling.

Aimee took her tea and sat down with her laptop.

What does he mean anyway? Undone and remade?

She Googled the word love.

Love is a strong positive emotion of regard and affection, according to Princeton wordnetweb.

That's weird, she thought, *I would have sworn it was a verb.*

Walk, run, love. Love is holding on. Love is letting go. Love is everything. Love is… I don't know. Love is for singing about. Love is a many splendor'd thing. Love is like a song. Love is a rainbow, a river, a rose.

If God is love, does that mean love is God?

Apparently love is an emotion.

You can't argue with Princeton wordnetweb.

What's love got to do with it?

Who loves you, baby?

Norman had loved her, but she hadn't stayed with him.

WOMAN MURDERED

He was a binge drinker who could go months without a drop, but when he did imbibe, it scared her.

He was irresponsible, she thought.

He missed work, and he never saved a dime. She had an almost pathological desire for security.

He promised to quit drinking. She promised to cut him loose if he didn't. He made it three months without a drop; but when he didn't show up for Thanksgiving, she knew he'd gone on a bender. He called her three days later.

"You know what this means?" she'd said.

"You're not really going through with that?" he'd asked.

"I told you I would."

"I'm coming over, so we can talk."

"The time for talking is over. You did this to us, not me," she'd said.

"You could give me another chance. There's always a choice, you know."

"I don't know what's the right thing or the wrong thing. I just know what I can and can't live with."

"You can't live with me?" he'd asked.

"I can't live with your choice."

"I'll always love you, Aimee."

"Do you even know what love is?" she'd asked, not at all sure herself.

"No one will ever love you as much I do," he'd said. Those were his last words to her, and there was truth in them.

She had her telephone number changed, and she set about changing her life too.

Sadly, Norman, the man she felt certain was now dead, had predicted correctly.

Beri Balistreri

CHAPTER 14

Cenobio Hernandez was booked by computer for transmission of his fingerprints to the Department of Justice. Dressed in the pink striped pants of the Salinas jail, he completed his video arraignment. He would be sent the bill for the cost.

"You can go home now," a deputy said.

Cenobio looked at him with thankfulness.

"As soon as you make your bail," the man added. "You've got to phone someone for help."

Cenobio called his boss from the painting job. The boss gave him an earful. "Listen, Chico, do you have any idea how many guys ask me to put up bail money for them? I even did it a few times. I always got screwed. Sorry, Chico, no way," and the boss hung up on him.

He had worked steadily for the guy for the last eight months, starting as a day laborer, waiting like the others outside Home Depot in the mornings. The boss called them all by nicknames like *Chiaparo, Huero, Flaco,* and *Gordo,* in other words, Shorty, Whitey, Skinny, and Chubby, because the nicknames were easy, interchangeable, and anonymous. Cenobio was *Chico*, a good painter, and a reliable worker. The boss said he was the guy he could always count on.

El Jefe is a one-way street, Cenobio thought. He wracked his brain for how to come up with the bail. He was owed money, big money, but he couldn't collect it; not from in jail. He was furious with himself for trusting that everything would work out.

Back in the dayroom, filled with the diaspora of

WOMAN MURDERED

Monterey County, the men could tell he hadn't gotten his bond money. The jail was over crowded: built to hold eight hundred men, there were nine hundred convicted felons in the tank, and it was impossible to segregate rival gang members.

I have to declare affiliation soon, or else.

He stood out as fresh meat because he was wearing a plain gray t-shirt. It was to distinguish him from prisoners who were already convicted and serving time.

Surrounded by hectoring felons, it was: *Be scary or be scary.* He was scared.

He walked through the crowd of men. There were gangs to the left of him, gangs to the right. As he made his way to the bunk beds stacked three high, he watched where he was going. He tried not to make eye contact.

At the bunk he'd been assigned, he began to climb up to the third level. A hand shot out from the middle bunk and grabbed his ankle, knocking him to the floor. He felt warm blood trickle down his leg, and saw it drip onto his shoe.

A big man was leaning his head out of the bunk. He seemed to smile at first; but then, Cenobio saw the razor blade held between his lips, just before it disappeared back into his mouth.

Cenobio crawled into the open area of the floor. There were guards in the common room, and video surveillance, but between the bunks was a blind spot. It was the place for violence and illicit activity.

Cenobio pulled his sock up over his bleeding ankle.

"He's establishing power. Going for admiration and fear," he heard. He looked up and saw a guy with a shaved head and a lot of tattoos. The guy handed him a rag. He moved in on Cenobio, talking low and fast. "They're messing with you because you're a virgin." Cenobio didn't respond. "You got no tats. They can tell you ain't in no gang. You don't belong to anyone."

"I don't belong here," Cenobio said.

"You gotta belong to someone," the guy said. You can't not be a part of some group."

"I don't want to be in a gang."

"Well, who you gonna go with?"

"I heard that if I join a gang, and later want out, I'll get killed," Cenobio said.

"If you don't choose, you'll get claimed."

"Who would claim me?"

"You could end up Mara Salvatrucha. MS13 controls prisons all the way from South America," the guy said.

"I'm not South American."

"Don't matter. They organized. They violent as fuck."

"How do I get out of here?"

"You might wanna go with the Norteños, bro."

"I can't be in a gang. I promised..."

"You could run with us if you want."

"Be a skinhead?" Cenobio asked.

"Hell no! I'm no skinhead! I'm a *Juggalo*! We hate those racist motherfuckers. We hate them and pedophiles. We down with the clown!" He pointed to a tattoo on his arm, a silhouette of a man running with a hatchet.

"What kind of gang is that?"

"We ain't no gang. We music fans. Insane Clown Posse. Detroit since the 90s."

"Is that like Trip B?" Cenobio asked.

"We say woop woop. We flash the Wicked Clown hand sign. Ain't no gang, but if it keeps us out of the Aryan Brotherhood, thassalright."

A guard interrupted them and called Cenobio to step out from the common room.

"Come see me if you need something," the guy called. "*Juggalos* ain't no gang, but we family."

Cenobio was relieved to be taken out of the common room for a third round of questioning. Detective LaTorella had had two fruitless interviews with him already, but he was back for more. *I don't care what he wants, he got me out of that room.*

Cenobio told the detective again that he found the handbag on a bench. He noticed it when he heard a cell phone ringing. No one came for the phone, so he took the purse.

He didn't know what he meant to do with it, maybe he was going to turn it in. He hadn't looked inside, and he had no idea who it belonged to.

The detective flipped through the notebook he carried in his pocket. He read aloud. "The victim was wearing a diamond pendant, diamond earring, a diamond bracelet, and a large diamond wedding set. That would be some real money for you, huh? People kill for less."

"I don't know anyone who would do that."

"An addict might kill for fifty cents toward his next score if he was desperate, but you're no drug user. The jail always knows who is and who isn't."

"I'm glad they know something real about me," Cenobio said.

Whatever I say he won't believe it, so it doesn't matter what I say.

"There's one more person I want to ask you about. I have a feeling there's a connection between you two. In fact, I know there is."

Cenobio looked at the ceiling.

The detective watched him closely. "Do you know a woman named Aimee James?"

"No," he said, with no discernable reaction.

"Did you see a dog when you were at Ghost Trees?"

"Ghost Trees?"

"Pescadero Point."

"No, I didn't see any dogs."

The detective stood up to leave. Cenobio pleaded with his eyes. "I can't release you," LaTorella said, shaking his head. "There are too many unanswered questions."

"Can you a get message to my mother at least. Her name

is Maria Madelena Alejo Reynoso."

The detective stopped his leaving. "Does she work at The Whispering Cypress?"

Cenobio stiffened. *They questioned my mother?*

He thought it would kill her to find out that her only child was in jail, but apparently she already knew. He tried to hold onto a few good thoughts, but the only ones that would stay with him were the bad ones.

He thought of his mama walking down a dusty road after they first came to *El Norte*. A pit bull attacked her while two men yelled: *Fuck that bitch, fuck that bitch!*

She thought they were trying to help her, so she yelled it too.

No one ever really tries to help anyone else.

"Does she work there?" the detective asked again.

"Yes, she does. You talked to my mother?"

"Um, sort of," the detective said. "I haven't questioned her about you though."

Cenobio's eyes were searching the detective's.

"What message should I give her?"

"Tell her I'm sorry I didn't call. They wouldn't let me call her. Tell her I'm doing my best to keep my promise, but I don't know how much longer I can hold out. Just tell her those things, please." Cenobio wiped his cheek with the back of his hand.

"Wait a minute. They didn't let you call your mother?"

"Look, I can't let you go, but there might be a way I can protect you for a while. How many calls did you say they let you make?"

"Only one."

#

It was almost 1 a.m. when Aimee let Michael Mizol into her bedroom by way of the sliding glass door from the patio. He sat on the edge of the bed and kicked off his shoes.

"I need your help," she said.

"You have to at least let me get under the covers first. I just drove two hours for this."

Aimee's lip quivered.

"Calm down."

"I can't calm down. I can't get a handle on things," she said.

"Let me see if I can," he grabbed her butt.

She slapped his hand away like a mosquito.

"Wow," he said. "Just wow."

"Please Michael, please. I really need to talk with you."

"Can't we talk after?" he said. He gave her his smoldering eye look.

"Help me," she said.

"I pride myself on being helpful, especially to women."

"You do? Yes, of course, you do," Aimee said.

"Okay. What do you need?"

"They've arrested someone, and I have a terrible feeling about it."

"Do they know about Daniel and his past?"

"No."

"Do they even know he exists?"

"The detective who came here... He came because I'm the one who took the lady's dog to the shelter... somehow that makes me look bad because I drove a long way instead of going next door ... then I talked to the clerk in Spanish, so maybe I know the Spanish-speaking guy who found the lady's purse. I don't know how they connect the dots; but yeah, I accidentally told him about my son."

"You've got to learn to keep your mouth shut."

"I've heard that before," she said.

"I'm not kidding, Aimee. You need to shut up and do what I tell you. I know a lot more about Daniel's situation than you think. Don't let this detective know anything about him. He'll ruin everything. That's the best thing that you can do for now."

She nodded and burst into tears.

"Now what's the matter?"

"The guy they're holding in jail... the guy they picked up with the lady's purse ... the Spanish speaking guy ... I'm afraid he might ... you know ..."

"Hang himself?" he asked.

She nodded.

"I can't get it out of my mind," she said.

"What happened before is ancient history," he said.

"History has a way of repeating itself."

"They won't take him to trial without a case."

"Are you kidding me? A Mexican day laborer with a dead woman's purse?"

"That sounds prejudicial," Michael said.

"That's how people are," she said.

"Same as how they thought Daniel was a little freak or whatever."

"They'll convict him. That is, if he even stays alive in jail."

"It would be worse if they convicted your son, though."

"What if ..." Aimee couldn't get the words out.

"The bottom line, Aims, is: Do you want Daniel to be the one to die in jail?"

"Of course I don't!"

"Then keep him off the radar like I told you and listen to me. They have someone in jail already, and that makes Daniel relatively safe."

"This poor guy in jail might just be a scapegoat?"

"That depends. Do you think Daniel killed again?"

"Again?" she said, her voice rising to a screech.

"I thought you just put that stuff on for the court."

Lowering her voice, she said firmly, "Daniel didn't kill anyone,"

"Can you say that for certain?"

"I... I don't know anything anymore," she sighed.

"I feel things, but I can't be sure."

"What's changed?" he asked.

"Me," she said.

Michael sat up. Aimee was shaking all over.

"Help me not feel so horrible," she said.

"I'll swing by the jail on my way out of town and see what they're charging the guy with."

"Thank you," she said.

"By the way, this bedspread looks like it came from a brothel in Cannery Row."

"Thanks, Mizol. I'd respond, but I got nothin'."

#

Aimee was pacing the kitchen floor the next morning when Mizol called from the jail.

"The only thing I could find out about Cenobio Hernandez is that nobody has been charged with the murder of Roberta Wagner."

"Hmm. Maybe you could ask that Detective LaTorella if he can tell you what's going on."

"La Tortilla? Isn't that the guy who came to your house questioning you?"

"Oh, yeah."

"Because if that's the guy you mean, then sending your boyfriend to ask about a guy you claim to have never met is a really stupid idea."

"First of all, ex-boyfriend. Secondly, I *have* never met Hernandez."

"Prove it," Michael said.

Aimee realized her foolishness. "Oh, wow. How stupid of me. Thank you for saving me yet again."

"You can pay me later," he said.

"Do you think they'll figure out who knocked off that woman?" she asked.

"Did you just say knocked off?"

"I meant pushed. Do you think they'll ever figure out who pushed her off that cliff?"

"Say knocked off again. It's hot."

"Please, Michael, I know that you're trying to help, and I really appreciate it; but, you do understand why I'm so stressed out about this, right?"

"You think Daniel is really the one who should be in jail instead of this guy."

"No. That's crazy. He can't …"

Michael interrupted her.

"There's one more piece of information you'll want to know. I found it out from a clerk who likes my haircut."

"Oh, brother."

"Are you ready for this?"

"Yes? Tell me. What is it?"

"Hernandez is on suicide watch."

"No!" Aimee let out a small scream. "Please tell me this is one of your jokes."

"I kid a lot, Aims, but not now. Your intuition was right."

"If only it were." She tossed her coffee into the sink.

#

Cenobio Hernandez was called out of the common room to meet the Reverend Burns, who was waiting to visit him.

"Hello son," said the spry white haired man wearing a clerical collar. "I came here hoping to set the captive free, metaphorically speaking."

Cenobio said nothing.

"You see, as a Christian, I'm charged by St. Paul to *remember those who are in prison as though in prison with them, and those who are mistreated since you also are in the body.*"

"Saint Paul?" Cenobio asked.

"Do you know why I came here to see you today?" the

Reverend asked.

"You want me to make my confession?"

"Ach, no! Heavens!"

Cenobio wondered about the reverend's real reason for being there. *This man doesn't know me,* he thought. "Why are you here?" he asked.

"Part of my duty as a minister is to remind people that we are all human beings made in the image of God, probably all suffering from loneliness and fear, just when we need each other's empathy most."

Cenobio's face wore a question mark.

"I'm here because I thought you might have need."

"Oh. I do."

Maybe this is the person who can help me get my money.

"I need help," he said.

He needed someone to make an important call for him. He needed someone to help him get money that was owed.

This priest may be the person to help take care of business. They won't mess with a priest.

The Reverend Burns listened closely to the details, jotting them in the little notebook that he carried in his pocket.

"Maybe I can really help set the captive free, and not just not metaphorically this time," he said. Finished, he stood up and shook Cenobio Hernandez' hand.

"I'll be back next week to tell you how it went. Please, if you'll just put my name on the list of visitors."

Cenobio decided to tell him one more thing. "Padre," he said.

"Yes, my child?"

"I don't want to die."

"I don't want you to either."

"But I'm scared."

"I know, son. Me too."

CHAPTER 15

Aimee walked into the little chapel in the forest of Pebble Beach where the funeral of Roberta Wagner was about to take place, Daniel at her side. They looked at the glass wall framing a cluster of cathedral pines behind the altar. Columns of light filtered through the trees. A harpist was playing *Tres Gymnopedes* by Eric Satie.

Aimee thought of angels ascending and descending, as she watched two acolytes with candles. The sanctuary was abuzz. The Pebble Beach elite was chattering. Who among them hadn't walked a dog along the scenic cliffs? That one of their own had been pushed to death by a day laborer was too close. Hundreds of day laborers went in and out through the Pebble Beach gates every day.

It could happen to any of us, swirled through the chapel air on this gray Tuesday afternoon.

A handful of surfers were there to pay their respects to the body they retrieved from the maverick swells at Ghost Trees that day. Their hair was long and they wore corded necklaces in place of ties, but other than that, they fit.

A contralto sang.

I come to the garden alone, While the dew is still on the roses, And the voice I hear falling on my ear, The Son of God discloses. And He walks with me, and He talks with me, And He tells me I am His own; And the joy we share, as we tarry there, None other has ever known.

None other? Aimee thought.

A striking older woman in a black mink coat and white kid gloves caught her eye. The tall platinum-haired woman with the large tortoise-framed glasses and choker of

WOMAN MURDERED

Tahitian pearls made her think of a glamorous film star living out her old age in this anonymous enclave.

As if she felt Aimee's eyes on her, the woman turned and held her gaze. Aimee felt a stabbing pain in her chest and looked away. She was overcome by the same physical sensation she'd had at another funeral many years before.

She had seen a photo of a young girl in the *San Jose Mercury News* and felt both an uncanny prescience and a compulsion to meet the child, only to learn it was too late. This sweet-faced adolescent had been raped, shot in the head, and left for dead, in a deserted schoolyard near the BART tracks in San Leandro. The assailant was unknown.

The next day, Aimee drove to the Williams Chapel Baptist Church on Tenth Avenue in Oakland to attend the funeral of the girl she'd never met. The large brick church was packed. The girl's whole school and the church had turned out to mourn the murder of one of their own.

Aimee sat in the sea of strangers, dandling her baby on her lap to a hymn sung by an African American choir dressed in red and gold robes.

This is my story, this is my song, praising my savior, all the day long. Perfect submission, perfect delight, visions of rapture now burst on my sight; Angels descending bring from above, echoes of mercy, whispers of love.

When Aimee passed the catafalque, she had an urge to throw her arms around the girl's lifeless body and tell her that no one would ever hurt her again. She might have done it if she hadn't been carrying Daniel.

Watching the crowd make their way forward, her eyes fell on a young man who walked in a tight group of teens. That's when the sudden stabbing pain hit her.

This kid is the rapist and murderer who put this beautiful girl in her casket. There wasn't a doubt in her mind.

Now, sitting at the funeral of the volunteer coordinator, she marveled that a murderer would have the gall to show up at the funeral of the person they killed; and yet, here she was attending Roberta Wagner's funeral with her son Daniel, precisely to cast doubt on the possibility of their own involvement.

It was maddening to conjecture, and crazy to try to head something off that hadn't happened yet. But it was all about perceptions. Smoke and mirrors got Daniel convicted. Maybe, smoke and mirrors could save him?

I'm going to be the one in control of things this time.

Reverend Burns, a gentleman Scot with a mellow brogue, was reading From Ecclesiastes.

"To everything, there is a season, and a time to every purpose under the heaven: A time to be born, and a time to die; a time to plant, and a time to pluck up that which is planted; A time to kill..."

"To kill?" Daniel said. "To kill?" he said again.

He elbowed his mother, but she shook him off.

"...and a time to heal; a time to break down, and a time to build up; a time to weep, and a time to laugh; a time to mourn, and a time to dance; a time to cast away stones, and a time to gather stones together; a time to embrace, and a time to refrain from embracing; a time to get, and a time to lose; a time to keep, and a time to cast away; a time to rend, and a time to sew; a time to keep silence—"

A time to keep silent, you mean, Aimee thought.

"—and a time to speak; A time to love, and a time to hate; a time of war, and a time of peace. He hath made everything beautiful in his time," the Reverend read.

Everything beautiful, she repeated in her mind.

"Today is our time to weep, mourn, embrace, speak, and love. Kip Wagner, you've done your best for Roberta, your gentle wife of fifty years. You were attentive to her needs. You cared for her. You sacrificed your days and nights, and your own needs, so that you could offer your love to her."

Kip's face turned red. He swiped his forehead with a handkerchief.

WOMAN MURDERED

"Death is certain for all of us. Rich or poor, strong or weak, death comes to us all. We are all walking along that same path. Roberta has now walked it to its completion. Death may come to some of us after a long illness, or suddenly in a freak accident."

The surfers exchanged glances.

"Cody French, the young man who sits here before us, was not ready for death on that day when God used Roberta's last breath to raise him up. I'm sure you all know by now of the miraculous and strange rescue that occurred off Pescadero Point, between the newly deceased and the nearly drowned."

Whispers were heard throughout the sanctuary.

"Remember that death is not all there is. It is not the end. Dwight Moody, on his deathbed, said that he saw the earth receding, and heaven coming down."

"Heaven on earth?" Daniel said. "On earth?"

Aimee ignored him.

"In closing, I'll share a poem."

"We read of a place that's called Heaven, It's made for the pure and the free; These truths in God's word He hath given, How beautiful Heaven must be. In Heaven no drooping or pining, No wishing for elsewhere to be; God's light is forever there shining, How beautiful Heaven must be. Pure waters of life there are flowing, And all who will drink may be free; Rare jewels of splendor are glowing, How beautiful Heaven must be. The angels so sweetly are singing, Up there by the beautiful sea—"

"Heaven is by the sea? By the sea?" Daniel asked, in a whisper.

"Sweet chords from their gold harps are ringing, How beautiful Heaven must be."

"That was by Mrs. A. S. Bridgewater, care of John Hobbs from the Forsythe Church of Christ in Monroe, Louisiana."

Beautiful, Aimee thought.

"Let us conclude by singing the hymn on Page 3 of your program," Reverend Burns said.

The congregation stood, each at their own speed and ability, and began to sing feebly, unsure of the words and tune.

"And let this feeble body fail, And, let it droop and die; My soul shall quit the mournful vale, And, soar to worlds on high; Shall join the disembodied saints, And, find its long-sought rest, That only bliss for which it pants, In my Redeemer's breast. Where the waters brightly sparkle, In the golden city's light, Will, no shadow ever darkle—"

"Darkle?" Daniel said, frowning. "Darkle? Is that even a word? A word?" he asked.

His mother shrugged.

"And no changing seasons blight; Trees of fadeless beauty quiver, Where the blossoms kiss the tide, As along the shining river, Songs of welcome sweetly glide."

On their way out of the chapel, Aimee felt a tug on her arm. Among those attending who also didn't personally know the deceased was a tall striking blonde in black crepe-de-Chine. With high cheekbones and large crystal-blue eyes, she could have been the sister of the woman in the mink coat, if their ages weren't so far apart.

She looks like she belongs here too, Aimee thought.

"Let's talk," Bridgette Peletier said, "Daniel, you go wait in the car."

"What car? We have a Jeep," he said. "Do you want me to wait in your car? In your car?" Dr. Peletier shot him a look. Daniel headed off to the J40 and the two women stepped off the path.

"Look, I need Daniel to talk to me about the circumstances of his father's death," Dr. Peletier said. "He's got to stop resisting me. I need you to convince him to tell me everything. I know he'll do whatever you tell him to."

Aimee stepped back onto the cobblestone.

"Where did you get that idea? From the prosecutor's notes?"

"Whoa," the doctor said. "Calm down You're good with him. He, seems to, trust you more than he trusts me. I guess that's because you gave birth to him, and I didn't."

"Isn't that normal?"

"A lot of kids don't trust their parents at all. Many would rather confide in a professional therapist. The fact that he's so glued to you, well, it makes me wonder."

"Wonder about what?"

"Whether it's healthy for him, I guess," the doctor said.

Aimee took another step back, widening her distance from the doctor.

"Healthy? Is it healthy for you to make him talk about something that's going to trigger his Post Traumatic Stress Disorder? Because that's what'll happen if you make him talk to you about his father's death."

"But I'm not going to make him talk about his father's death, you are," the doctor said. "You are, because I can't do what I need to do unless you do it for me. And if I can't do what I need to do, then he doesn't get to be here. Remember that part of our little bargain?"

"I'm trusting you with my son," Aimee said to the doctor.

"Wrong! The *court* is trusting me with your son."

"But you're helping him to get over his PTSD," Aimee said.

"What do you think this study is about?" Dr. Peletier asked.

"You're treating him for PTSD with his Asperger's Syndrome."

"It's a study about behavior. It involves PTSD in a youth with Asperger's Syndrome only because it involves Daniel," the doctor said.

"You mean you don't care if his PTSD gets triggered?"

"The study measures responses and looks at behaviors,"

Dr. Peletier said.

"You're not treating him? You're just studying him?" Aimee asked, rattled.

"We learn by studying," Dr. Peletier said.

"You're studying him, but you're not helping him," Aimee said, incredulous.

"To tell you the truth…"

Aimee interrupted the doctor.

"*To tell you the truth?* What do you usually tell me? Lies? Do you usually tell me lies? You know, because I'm really starting to wonder."

"You are?" Dr. Peletier snapped back. "Because from where I stand, it looks like you're worried that your son pushed this woman off a cliff, and now you came to her funeral to make it look like he didn't."

"I'm not worried," Aimee said, trying not to look worried.

"Really?" said Dr. Peletier. "Because the day laborer will be cleared soon enough, and when he is, they'll look at Daniel, and they'll find out."

"Find out what? What will they find?" Aimee said.

"His profile."

"What profile?" Aimee asked, with indignation.

"The profile of a criminal psychopath," the doctor said.

"What are you talking about?" Aimee asked, voice rising.

"The profile that was presented at his first arraignment," Peletier said, grinning.

"You mean his *only* arraignment?" Aimee corrected.

"Right. Think about what I've said. I'll see Daniel tomorrow."

The heels of the doctor's red-soled black patent leather Christian Louboutins clicked down the stone pathway as she left Aimee in her proverbial dust.

#

WOMAN MURDERED

Aimee sat on the floor of the rental cottage doing something she had never wanted to do before. She had to prove to herself, once and for all, that her son Daniel was not like the criminal psychopaths who mowed down their classmates, teachers, and children. She Googled the word Columbine and found an article by a guy named Michael Fitzgerald. Her pulse raced.

They're just words on a page, she thought, trying to steel herself.

Dylan was interested in classical philosophers and renaissance literature. He was into polarities and felt himself to be split in his mind. One of the polarities that fascinated him was 'good and bad.' This was a major focus for him, she read.

That sounds familiar, she thought.

Dylan believed in God. He cried out to God, and cursed at God, for making him a modern-day Job. He demanded an explanation for the divine brutality of his faithful servant, she read.

Everyone feels a little like Job now and then, don't they? she thought.

Dylan wrote that God had chosen him as someone in search of answers, never finding them, yet in hopelessness, understanding things. He seeks knowledge of the unthinkable, of the indefinable, of the unknown. He explores everything, using his mind, the most powerful tool known to him, she read.

Just like my cursed intuition, she thought.

She slammed the laptop shut. She wanted to swear at the top of her lungs and collapse into a heap on the floor.

She ran outside and jumped in the Jeep, driving with the sense of barely hanging onto the edge of the world. The part of the turn where *This is the best thing that could have happened* had not yet arrived.

High breakers surged the inlets. The hairpin road followed the outline of the cliffs, low then high, with small passes that momentarily seemed like they would run off into the ocean. Just before she huryled into the brine, the J40's tires, directed by the plan of some long-dead civil engineer, swerved around a giant tree, and back onto the path.

Aimee maneuvered the crazy-course of a roadway. She drove the turns and surprises around the golf course called Spyglass, where the roads were all named after places in the Robert Louis Stevenson story because he'd once stayed in that area for a few months while he was sick. When she got to Fanshell Overlook, she climbed out onto a rock outcropping and listened to the white noise until her ears buzzed.

She tried to think happy thoughts; becoming a mother, her son's first tooth, his first word, and his first day of school. Not all the firsts were happy.

When Daniel was in kindergarten, the teacher called on him to solve a problem. "If your mom has a nickel and a dime… one is for her, and one is for you, which one do you want her to give to you?"

Daniel wanted the nickel, but the teacher said that his answer was wrong. "The dime is worth more," she told him. She asked again. "Which one do you want?" He told her again. The nickel.

"No Daniel, you're not getting it. The dime is smaller, but it's worth more. The nickel is bigger, but it's worth less." She insisted that the only right answer was the nickel. She sent Daniel to the principal's office for being difficult with her.

Aimee was called to come pick up her son from school. The principal informed her of his bad behavior.

"I don't understand why you're doing this, Daniel. Why do you keep telling your teacher that the nickel is the right answer?" she had asked him.

Remembering his response always killed her. "*I* don't need money, Mama. *You* do—you do," he'd said, staring at the floor.

That was the moment she decided to always believe him, always believe *in* him, and always have his back, no matter what. The world would be hard enough and cruel enough. She would be the one person who would never say that she doubted him.

Squinting at the blinding gray-white sky above the churning Pacific, everything she saw was washed out like the colors in an overexposed photo. She did recognize the things that she read about Dylan Klebold, but she didn't recognize them in Daniel. She saw them in herself. "I'm not the bad guy!" she yelled at the waves.

CHAPTER 16

Aimee was putting on her boots and coat, gathering the courage to walk down one driveway and up another.

There's no such thing as situational ethics. It's an oxymoron, she thought.

She believed what she was taught: right and wrong, black and white, absolute. But now she was putting her child's welfare ahead of everything she knew. Her intuition was all she had to go on, and she was going to use it to protect Daniel. Chips fall where they may.

She didn't bother closing the gate on the rental. There was no Puppy to wander off.

She strode up the driveway of her neighbor's home, with its privacy gate and large stone sculptures, past the manicured lawn and hedge, past the scrollwork *Heaven's Edge*.

Kip opened the door and took stock of the person before him. He vaguely recalled her being at Roberta's funeral, but he had no idea who she was.

Aimee introduced herself and explained that she knew Mrs. Wagner from The Whispering Cypress.

"That's lovely," Kip said, unmoved.

"And I live in the house next door."

His face fell. "You're the renter."

He thinks renters are unstable pretenders, at the same spot, but not the same station, she thought.

"Guilty as charged," she said.

"Would you like to come in?" he asked. Aimee stepped into the vaulted entry. "Please, have a seat." Kip motioned to one of a pair of wingback chairs. Aimee sat on the cream-colored silk. "Would you like something to drink?"

"Thank you," she said.

Kip produced a Baccarat snifter of Napoleon X.

"Your home is beautiful."

"My wife loved to … I was in the military," he said, voice trailing.

"Mrs. Wagner's memorial service was lovely."

"Was it?" Kip asked, with a blank face.

"I'm sorry to bother you, but could you tell me, who was the woman in the mink coat?"

Kip flushed. "Which one?" he asked.

There had *been more than one.* "It was long and black, very shiny, and she wore white kid gloves," she said.

"Oh. The *Blackglamma.* That's Mrs. Rodewald, my wife's best friend."

"Oh dear," Aimee said.

"Oh dear, what?" Kip asked.

"Was she with your wife at Ghost Trees when she fell?"

"My wife didn't fall. She was pushed."

"I'm sorry about that," Aimee said.

Sorrier than you could, possibly, know, she thought.

"They've arrested the man who pushed her, or haven't you heard?"

"I just wonder if they have the right person. My son was out walking…"

"Aha," Kip said. "I know who you are. You're the one who took my dog to the shelter in Salinas."

"I am. I did," Aimee said. "He's such a cute little guy. Where is he?"

"At the groomers," Kip said. "Did you see the man who stole her purse?"

"No. It wasn't—"

"It was your son!" Kip said, interrupting her. "Your son walks his dog."

"He *did* walk his dog, before she was poisoned."

Kip's face turned pale. "The barking dog in the night.

My wife begged me to do something about your dog," he said without inflection.

Aimee's chin set.

"*Somebody* did something about it, didn't they?" Kip said.

"With respect, Mr. Wagner, I'm pretty sure it was your wife who poisoned my son's dog, his therapy dog, for his autism."

Kip's face changed back to red.

"Really, then? That would make him the prime suspect in my wife's murder, wouldn't it?"

She was not expecting this volley, but she gave chase. "I think you know exactly who pushed your wife." She surprised even herself, sounding like the confident badass she wasn't.

Kip reached for his phone. "I'm calling the police now."

"To confess?" Aimee said.

"To tell them about your son," he said.

Aimee panicked. "But he's just a kid! Please don't!"

"A kid with a very strong motive."

"You're really blaming my son for your wife's death?"

"That's what needs to be investigated. A proper investigation will clear up everything," Kip said.

"But it won't! He can't be investigated! Please!"

"Anyone can be investigated, my dear," Kip said.

Aimee jumped to her feet.

"Including you and your girlfriend Mrs. Rodewald! She's the one who should be questioned—about her relationship with you!"

Kip put down the phone.

"We're both chasing wild hares here," he said.

"You're right. It was stupid of me to come here," she said.

She could see he was trembling. So was she.

#

WOMAN MURDERED

Leaving Kip's place, Aimee felt more than ever that her son would be dragged into a murder investigation. She knew he would be judged unfairly because of his Asperger's Syndrome, and his past. The death of his father would be brought to light for sure. He would be convicted by a kangaroo court and spend the rest of his life in prison if he survived.

She headed back to her lonely home, but instead of going in, she jumped into the J40 and swung over to Carmel.

She wandered with her mini-cart up the narrow aisles of Bixby's Market, looking at the vacuum-sealed artichoke hearts, but she couldn't decide on garlic-flavored or balsamic. Local-grown berry pies and secret-recipe Italian cookies called out to her, but they also weren't the treat that would satisfy.

"I have to run out to Pebble Beach for a delivery," she heard the handsome Albert say.

"You gonna be long? It's gonna get busy real soon with all the tourists in town," Cody said, complaining.

"It's Mrs. Rodewald, so, you know—about that long," Albert said.

Aimee, casually listening to the innocuous exchange, suddenly realized her chance was at hand.

Mrs. Rodewald, the woman in the mink coat, Wagner's best friend! To confront her, I have to find her. She abandoned her cart in the aisle and rushed outside to follow Albert as he drove away in the Bixby's Market delivery van.

She trailed along behind the van as it passed through the Carmel Gate. Albert drove the winding roads faster than she was used to. The van took a screeching turn into an open gate, with a pair of stone lions snarling on the posts.

He's either in a hurry to get there, or to get back, Aimee thought. She couldn't go inside the gate, so she parked the Jeep unobtrusively behind a maintenance truck and waited to see Albert leave.

That's when I'll make my move.

Her heart was beating furiously, and she was out of breath. She didn't know what she would say to *the other woman*, though she'd been losing sleep over it. She had a few minutes to formulate her attack. *I can't just walk up and say, "Hi, my name is Aimee. I know you're having an affair with your best friend's husband."*

She was still deep in thought when Albert himself appeared beside her open window. "Did you follow me here because you're lonely?" he asked, with a grin.

Aimee sat up and straightened herself. "I came to see Mrs. Rodewald," she said, in a shaky voice.

"She's a lonely lady too. I'm sure she'll appreciate the company," Albert said.

"I was just waiting until she wasn't busy," said Aimee.

"You're in luck. She hasn't been busy since 1969."

Aimee looked up at the house beyond the gate. "Such a lovely place," she said.

"Such a lovely face," he said.

They smiled at each other. Albert got back in the van and drove off. Aimee was left to carry out her plan.

She walked up the long faux cobblestone driveway of the woman in the mink coat, the *Blackglamma*, as Mr. Wagner called it.

How does he know what brand of coat she wears? He must be the one who bought it for her! she thought.

She sucked in her breath and rang the doorbell. In a minute, the woman she feared and sought to bring to justice was standing before her.

Judith Rodewald didn't look the way Aimee remembered her from the funeral. Her platinum hair was combed in thick waves, her large black-framed glasses were on, and she was as tall and thin as remembered; but she also looked frail, in a way Aimee hadn't noticed before.

WOMAN MURDERED

She looks ancient, Aimee thought.

"My name is Aimee James, I'm a friend of Kip Wagner's. I mean, I was a friend of Mrs. Wagner's. May I speak with you for a moment?"

Judith looked her over, then stepped back to let her in. "Have a seat," she said, pointing to a mauve sofa.

Aimee sat on one end. Judith sat on the other and locked eyes with her visitor.

"You lied to me."

Aimee gulped.

"You're *not* a friend of Roberta's. I know that."

Aimee's heart pounded faster.

"I know it because *I* was her only friend," Judith said.

Aimee exhaled with relief.

"You may be a friend of Kip's now. That man will be friends with, practically, anyone. It's his weakness."

"I just came from his home," Aimee said, omitting her trip to the market.

"Did you?" Judith asked, with irritation.

"He seems to be doing well. I mean, he seems almost relieved that his wife is gone. Can you imagine that?" Aimee asked.

"She was a burden, in more than one way," Judith said, caught off guard.

"He's a very handsome man, Mr. Wagner," Aimee said.

"I suppose so, but have you seen that Albert from Bixby's? Now, *there's* a handsome specimen!"

Aimee's face felt hot.

"Sometimes I call up and order groceries to be delivered even when I don't really need anything, just so I can take a look at him for a few minutes! Can you imagine!"

Aimee shifted in her seat. "Maybe," she said.

"What did you come here for? Making comfort calls to the bereaved?" Judith asked.

Aimee latched onto the idea. "Actually, that *is* why I came."

"Well, I don't need your comfort, thank you very much."

"I'm sorry," Aimee said.

"Where were you when my husband Lang died? Why didn't you come then? Or are you just concerned with the men who lose their wives, and not the other way around?" Judith asked, seeming to slip off into some long-held grievance. "You're not a widow, are you? Of course, you're not. I know things," Judith said, staring into Aimee's eyes, scrutinizing every last detail of her visitor.

"That's true," Aimee said. "I'm not a widow."

"But your husband is dead, isn't he?" Judith asked.

Aimee didn't know how to respond. "How would you know a thing like that?" she asked.

"I told you, I know things. You know things too, don't you?" Judith said.

"Sometimes," Aimee said.

"Aha! I knew I could get you to confess." She laughed and broke her horrid eye contact. "You and I are very much alike. Not that we've had similar lives. But you *are* sharp, aren't you? Mad, too?"

"I suppose I'm mad about a few things," Aimee said.

"That's not what I meant," Judith said. "But then, you know that."

"What are you mad about?" Aimee asked. "I mean, why are you mad?"

"Men," Judith said. "I'm mad about men! Can't you tell?"

"Never quite goes away, huh?" Aimee said.

"They take the best of you and leave the rest of you. They screw you over and think they're better," Judith said.

"I guess I know what you mean," Aimee said.

"You guess?" Judith said. "Have you ever been raped?"

Judith stared intensely at Aimee, her pupils fully dilated behind the big-framed glasses.

"I have to go, Mrs. Rodewald," Aimee said, rising to

take her leave.

"Of course, you do. Just when you were getting interesting."

She offered her hand. Aimee was about to shake the thin elegant paw, but impulsively leaned forward and embraced the older woman instead.

#

That night, staring at the red and gold acanthus leaf comforter, with its heaps of books, clutter, and unpacked boxes, Aimee wondered if things would ever be normal.

It was hard to muster the effort to make a home real. She wished for a hot bath, but the cramped bathroom had only a shower stall. She thought about ironing a vintage silk nightgown, but she didn't own one, and she hated ironing. A shower and a short story by O. Henry would have to do.

She was reading when Michael called at eleven. "I got him freed," he said over the phone.

"Are you kidding?" Aimee said. "That's wonderful!"

"You're welcome," he said.

"Do you think they have any idea who the real killer is?"

"Don't you know who the real killer is?" he asked.

Aimee was silent for a moment. She finally said, "Tell me how you got the guy out of jail,"

"Easily. A writ of *habeas corpus*. He was being held in remand, but no one had ever filed the vehicle charges, or the stolen property charge—so it was an arbitrary arrest and detention."

"Arbitrary? Don't you mean profiled?" she asked.

"The Sixth Amendment gives him the right to be informed of the accusation, which he wasn't, and the Bill of Rights grants him some protections, which he didn't get. As a remanded prisoner, he's supposed to be held separately from sentenced prisoners, which he wasn't, at least until they put him on suicide watch, I guess, which was a good thing. On top of that, he was held incommunicado. I simply asked for the *amparo de libertad*, his protection of freedom, and I got it."

"You don't know how glad I am," Aimee said.

"It doesn't do much for Daniel. It could even come back to hurt him."

"But ever since that guy was arrested because of my tip—the tip you gave to the FBI—and then he killed himself in jail, I've hated myself. I can't have that happen again. I couldn't survive it. If it hadn't been for me, he'd still be alive."

"Aimee, he was a murderer."

"Maybe. But now I'm one too," she said. Dead silence on the line, and then Michael said, "Look, you didn't tie the sheet around his neck."

"But I meddled in something that wasn't my business, and the result was death. It was my fault. I pushed him over the edge," she said.

"Like the old lady?" Michael asked, with a laugh.

"Please don't joke," Aimee said, begging, near tears.

"Well, this day laborer guy is out of jail now, so if he does go and kill someone, I suppose that will be your fault, too. You'll have to flagellate yourself for it."

"You did a good thing, Michael. You gave a prisoner his freedom."

"Is that really a good thing?" Michael asked.

"It may not be good for us, but I think it's a good thing," she said.

"Speaking of flagellation, I'll be right over, just you and me and a certain kind of special freedom."

"What are you talking about?" she said.

"I wanna come over now," he said.

"No, Michael, I can't," she said.

"What!?" he said, incredulous. "What about quid pro quo? You know I'm a stand-up guy. We could do it standing up. You like that, right?"

WOMAN MURDERED

"We can't be like that anymore Michael," she said, soberly.

"You're kidding, right?"

"Am I a kidder?" She could hear his anger rising.

"You know what? You're gonna end up all alone on the sidelines."

"I know that," she said.

"You're the loser, Aims."

"I know that too."

"Then this is the ending for you and me, you realize that, right?"

"Yes," she said.

The line went dead. *I deserved that*, she thought.

She settled back down under the old acanthus-leaf duvet and reached for O. Henry.

In this story, a man at the Pearly Gates was talking to St. Peter. He knew he'd done terrible things. He admitted to being the guy who set fire to an asylum and murdered a blind man for his pennies.

He said, though, that what he'd done was nothing compared to what the prosperous New York businessmen did when they hired young girls to work as secretaries or clerks, and only paid them six dollars a week. Those men were the real demons.

Aimee read how the little shop girl's story played out; the girl with the furnished room, who could only count her pleasures by the years. On page 183 she found out why it was called 'An Unfinished Story.'

"The rest of it comes later—sometime when Piggy asks Dulcie to dine with him, and she is feeling lonelier than usual—"

It doesn't have to end that way, Aimee thought. She snapped the book shut and kicked one of the boxes on her bed. It fell to the floor.

CHAPTER 17

Frank LaTorella didn't think Aimee James looked like a murderer, but who does? *Actors, that's who*, he thought.

This wasn't a movie or a television crime show, and he didn't plan to solve the case by noticing a cold-blooded gleam in someone's eyes. Anyway, Aimee James didn't have a gleam. She was pretty ordinary. He couldn't remember. *Probably pretty.*

He was careful to remember details unless they became a distraction, then he blocked them out. He wouldn't be blinded by love or beauty, and especially not by a woman.

Reading Aimee James' handwritten notes at the Whispering Cypress, the detective wanted to speak with patients who remembered the boy with the speech impediment, and his dog named Puppy, who always came there with his mother.

He plopped down on a chair in the hallway and stared at the woman's cursive writing. The first thing he noticed was that each line traveled slightly upward.

A sign of optimism, he thought.

The capital letters were all the same size as the lower case. *That signifies humility.*

The flow of the writing was connected sometimes, but not always. *That's like my writing,* he thought. *She gets hunches.*

He had learned how to read handwriting from his grandmother, an old *zingara* from Italy.

He took a stack of pages between his fingers and held them while they fell into a sort of flip book.

There it is. That's a pattern.

WOMAN MURDERED

Some of the notes were a lot longer, and they were from the same room numbers every week.

Detective LaTorella knocked on Room 27. Opening the door, he asked, "Can I come in?"

"You got a dog with you?" asked the old man sitting in a wheelchair beside his bed.

"I just wanna ask a few questions about a lady and a boy with a dog."

"Come on in. See if I can help."

From Bob, Frank learned that Aimee James knew a lot about Post Traumatic Stress Disorder.

"She was a real funny lady. Funny haha, not funny weird," Bob said.

"Was she inappropriate?" the detective asked, raising an eyebrow.

"Naw. She liked to joke though. One time she said, *How is the game of baseball like a girl's night out?*"

"Oh yeah?" the detective said. "How?"

"She said it was because you gotta be able to hit hard, be a good runner, and get home safe."

"Sounds like she knows a lot about life," the detective said.

"She knew a lot about baseball too, and that's almost the same."

"I never thought of it like that," the detective said.

"She's a real clever lady. That boy's clever too," Bob said.

"Can you give me an example?"

"He told me a funny story about mixing up turkey vultures with turkeys on Thanksgiving Day. What a character," Bob said.

The detective wasn't sure it was meant to be a funny story.

"Anything else?" he asked.

"He told me he liked scary music. He didn't think I'd like it. He thought it might shock me if I heard it. He played me some songs by some rapper named Trip B, and I told him the guy didn't have nothin' on some of that old music from the 1920s. My own mother used to sing the Mad Mama's Blues by Josie Miles."

"I don't know that one," the detective said.

"I'm a devil in disguise, Got murder in my eyes, Now I could see blood runnin', Through the streets, Could be everybody, Layin' dead right at my feet, Now man, who invented war, Sure is my friend, Don't believe that I'm kiddin', Just look what a hole I am in, Give me gunpowder, Give me dynamite, Give me gunpowder, Wanna blow it up tonight, Down off the shelf, When I get through shoot', There won't be nobody left."

"Did the kid like that song?" the detective asked.

"I don't remember," Bob said. "But, his mother sure did. She said it should be her theme song."

"Well, I'll be damned," LaTorella said.

He returned the clipboard to the nurses' station and asked to speak with the charge nurse. He wanted to get her take on the volunteer coordinator.

"You mean the old lady who got knocked off?" the charge nurse asked, rolling her eyes.

The detective was taking notes. "You were on a first name basis?" he asked.

"No, we weren't. Not unless her first name was Queen, her last name was Otch, and her middle initial was B."

"Oh. I get it," he said.

Queen B. Otch, he scribbled.

"She was so damn full of herself. For what reason, I don't know. I'm sorry if I sound mean, but *she* was the really mean one. You wanted the truth, right?"

"I think I can handle the truth," he said, in his best Jack Nicholson voice.

The nurse didn't get the joke.

"Did other people notice that she was full of herself?" he asked.

WOMAN MURDERED

"Of course, they did. No one could miss it," she said.

"In what way was she full of herself?" he asked.

"She was a terrible snob. She thought she was better than everyone," she said. She went on describing the martinet that was Roberta Wagner.

"Can you give me an example?" the detective asked.

"Well, for one thing, she didn't allow the volunteers to wear jeans. I mean, they were just volunteers. They worked for free! I'm sorry, but I really hated her. I mean, I didn't kill her or anything like that."

"Don't worry, you're not a suspect," the detective said, smiling. "Unless you confess, of course."

"Most of the patients weren't going to remember any of the rules she was so strict about."

"Was she hard on anyone else? The patients, for instance?" he asked.

"I never really saw her interact with patients. I mean, that was beneath her. She thought of herself like a CEO or something."

"So, it was just the volunteers that she was hard on?"

"Not exactly. She was rude to the staff too. I mean, she was so bossy. She was rotten to the aides," the charge nurse said.

"The aides?" he said.

"Yeah. One time she was standing in the hallway after a patient slipped into a coma. She was looking kinda dazed, and this little Mexican aide tried to tell her that everything was going to be alright."

"She looked like she would kill her, and she practically shouted, *You stupid woman!* I mean, the poor thing was just trying to be nice by comforting her."

"Was that racially motivated, do you think?" he asked.

"Maybe, but she thought she was better than *everyone*."

"Even men? Or was it just women she felt superior to?"

"Come to think of it, she did throw some respect to the doctors; they're all male here, so I can't really say if it was the position or the sex that she was deferential to. But you know, I actually felt sorry for her," the charge nurse said.

"Why would you feel sorry for a person like that?" LaTorella asked.

"Well, because of her mind. It was obviously slipping."

"How obvious, would you say?"

"Sometimes it starts out with rudeness, repeating the rules, trying to look like they're still in charge. It's a big cover-up, a big cheat. Every mistake is your fault, not theirs."

"You think trying to hide a weakness is cheating?" the detective asked.

"It's cheating, and it's dangerous. We always find out about it eventually, but a lot of times we only discover it after someone gets hurt."

Detective LaTorella thanked her and went to his son's room. Frankie Jr. was staring at *Wheel of Fortune.* Frank tussled the kid's hair and kissed him on the cheek.

Frankie Jr.'s eyes smiled.

There was a dinner tray on the bed table. The detective picked up a spoon and smashed some peas.

"I'm sorry I'm late. I hope you didn't get too hungry waiting. I'm on a case. I get a little excited working on a case."

"The Whimpering Cypress Murder," his son said.

Frank Sr. laughed. *Always worth waiting for,* he thought.

"She was pushed off a cliff near the Ghost Tree," he said.

"Witch Tree," Frankie Jr. said.

"Ghost Tree," the dad answered. "The big surfing break where Pete Davi drowned."

"That was sad," Frankie Jr. said.

"He was a third-generation fisherman. His leash snapped, and he ended up swimming without a board for a couple hundred feet until he disappeared in the whitewash. He was found face down floating in a patch of kelp."

His son stared at him. "What?" the dad asked.

"I said Witch Tree. The Witch Tree fell in," Frankie said.

"Oh yeah. There was a witch tree to go with the ghost tree, wasn't there? I think that was back in the 60s. You know?

"The Witch Tree fell into the ocean after a storm. No one remembers her. But she lived."

"You remember her. That's good enough," the dad said.

"Good enough for a dead tree all alone at the bottom of the ocean," Frankie said.

"I doubt if she's alone." The dad looked around the room because the conversation was getting creepy.

"Hey, there," he called out. "Anybody working around here? My son doesn't want to watch a crummy game show. Who took the remote?"

Maria Madalena came into the room.

"Are you calling for me, Daddy?" she asked.

"Help me out. I know I can count on you to make sure the housecleaners don't take his remote controller away again. He needs his sports and his games. A kid's gotta play."

"You are right, as usual, Daddy. Boys got to have their fighting and kicking. But your boy, he doesn't like football. I ask him to put the Chivos on tv and he says *no way, Jose.*"

She winked at Frankie.

"That's not football," he said, in protest.

"Oh yeah? Which game uses the feet more? Huh? Soccer or your crazy American football?" Maria protested back.

"You win," Frankie Jr. said.

"Touchdown!" Maria Madelena said.

"Goal," Frank Sr. said.

The detective raised his arms like a referee.

"Hey Maria, did you know the volunteer coordinator?" he asked, changing the subject.

Her face went from smelling roses to smelling cabbage.

"She called me a stupid woman, but I'm not a stupid woman."

"I know you're not," he said.

"She doesn't know me, or what I've been through."

"I'm sorry," the detective said. "Which reminds me, I've been meaning to talk to you about your son."

"What do you know about my son? He's being a naughty boy."

"What do you mean?" the detective asked.

Maria shook her head. "I think he left me for another woman. He didn't come home last week," she said.

The detective watched the worry set in.

"*Dios Mio*! Something bad has happened? That's why he didn't call. Is he... Is he..."

"He's not hurt. He was arrested. He's being held as a possible suspect in the murder of the volunteer coordinator."

"No, no, no!" Maria cried out. "Not my son! *I* hated that woman, but my son didn't even know her."

She was rude. She disrespected people.

"Wouldn't a boy who really loved his mother do just about anything for her, especially if he thought she was being mistreated?" he asked.

Maria's eyes narrowed.

"I'm not saying that's what happened. I'm not even talking about your son. I'm just asking you because you're the mother of a son."

"It could happen that way," she said.

"Your son asked me to give you a message before he was released from jail. He must have called you by now, though."

WOMAN MURDERED

He could tell from the expression on her face that she hadn't heard from Cenobio.

"He wouldn't skip town, would he? I mean, if he hasn't come home or called?"

"This was the first time he didn't come home. I really hoped he was just with a girl, but I guess I know my son better than that. He's a good boy. *Ay Dios Mio*, he must be so scared wherever he is now."

"Where do you think he is?" the detective asked.

Maria frowned at him, then she looked at Frankie Jr., whom she'd cared for since he came to the Cypress. "Maybe Guerrero," the mother said, looking down.

CHAPTER 18

Detective LaTorella couldn't shake his hunch that Aimee James was connected to Cenobio Hernandez. Maybe, it was the vibe he got when he mentioned the guy's name or asked why she spoke Spanish at the animal shelter?

He didn't know why she went all the way to Salinas when she could have returned the dog to the house next door. She was hiding something important. He felt it in the DNA of his gypsy grandmother.

When he found out that a lawyer from San Francisco named Michael Mizol filed the writ of habeas corpus on Hernandez' behalf, he had him checked out. He didn't work for an advocacy group. It wasn't even his type of law.

He decided to see where this lawyer went when he came Monterey County. M-i-z-o-l-r-y was a license plate easy to spot. He put the word out.

He got the call from CHP the next night around eleven. The car was heading south on Highway 1 by Seaside.

LaTorella tailed M-i-z-o-l-r-y through the Pebble Beach Gate. He was pleased with his supernatural hunch, right up to the point when M-i-z-o-l-r-y turned off the Seventeen Mile Drive and headed to the equestrian center.

What the hell? he thought.

Michael Mizol parked in front of the small residence and knocked on the door. In the glow of the yellow porch lamp the detective caught a glimpse of the tall blonde woman who answered.

That's not James.

WOMAN MURDERED

His hunch was all wrong. He was mostly disappointed, but not completely.

#

Paying a call to Bridgette Peletier the next morning in her portable office at the equestrian center, Detective LaTorella was prepared.

"I hope you like Pumpkin Spice," he said, handing her a grande latte from the Starbucks kiosk at Safeway. It's popular this time of year."

"I'd rather have the bacon," the doctor said, seating herself on the edge of her desk so that she was a little bit higher than, but very close to the detective, who had taken the guest chair.

He didn't get her joke.

"Do they really make that? A bacon flavored latte?" he said.

She looked at him with curiosity.

"I just get plain espresso and add a drop of cream," she said.

"You like what you like. Am I right, or am I right?"

"I was certain I'd hear from the police," Dr. Peletier said.

"I'm from the sheriff's department, but that's okay. It's an easy mistake."

"Sorry Sheriff," she said.

"I'm not the Sheriff."

"I see. Sounds like a song."

"No, I did not shoot the deputy," he said.

She looked down at her phone and swiped her thumb across the screen.

"Why did you think you would be contacted?" he asked.

"About the boy," she said. "My research."

"What's your research about?" he asked.

"Equine therapy with Asperger's Syndrome; PTSD

thrown in. There are a number of components."

"Something like *The Effectiveness of Horse Therapy with Asperger's Syndrome and PTSD?*" he said.

"Something like that."

"Do you know a San Francisco attorney named Michael Mizol?"

"Um, guilty," she said, looking like her teen crush had just been revealed.

"Do you know why he would have gone to the Monterey County Courthouse to try to free Cenobio Hernandez, the man who was being questioned in the murder of Roberta Wagner?"

"I can take a stab at it," she said.

"Stab away."

"Aimee James probably asked him to. Michael Mizol does whatever she asks. Seems most men do, including her son."

"Let me get this straight, Aimee James is connected to a day laborer, and she wants her business lawyer to secretly intervene? I'd say that's kind of mysterious."

"That's deep," she said.

"You think so?" he asked.

"No."

"Oh. That was sarcasm. I guess I missed it."

"You know about his dog?" she asked. "I believe he poisoned it."

LaTorella's face twisted.

"Why would he do a thing like that?"

"It fits the profile."

"What profile are you talking about?"

"Criminal Autistic Psychopathy. Sometimes it overlaps with Asperger's Syndrome."

"The heck you say?"

"A lot of them start out as animal killers. The scary part is, it can be completely missed in kids with Asperger's, even with all the warning signs."

"Does Daniel James have the warning signs?"

"Are you kidding? I'm even afraid for my horse," she said. "I don't like Daniel being around, but it's the price I pay for helping. I knew what I was getting into, but I'm still scared spending so much time with someone like that."

"Someone like what? A teenager?"

"You can read about it in the work of Michael Fitzgerald. Adam Lanza shot twenty-six people at his school. He had poor eye contact. Classic features of Asperger's. He had problems with social relationships, perseveration, narrow interests, poor communication skills, and sensory issues. These are all what Daniel has. That's why he's working with me."

"But he isn't a mass murderer. He didn't shoot up a school full of kids or a movie theater. I'd have heard about that," the detective responded.

"The individual murderers rarely make the national news, but they're just as psychopathic as the mass killers."

"These Criminal Autistic Psychopaths, do you think Daniel is one?"

"In my opinion, he's very dangerous. He has PTSD like Eddie Ray Routh, the guy who killed Chris Kyle, the American Sniper. He could be triggered by practically anything—a memory, a bad dream, or a flashback. He's an angry young man."

"Can you give me an example?"

"As a matter of fact, I can. Take a listen." She handed the detective a pair of headphones.

He listened. "That's Daniel singing?"

"If you call it that. Listen to the words."

"Sounds like a lot of swearing," the detective said.

"I told you, he's a very angry young man."

"You're absolutely certain," he asked.

"Do those sound like the words of a well-adjusted individual?"

"The world is a pretty crazy place, for anyone sane to be

too well-adjusted to it."

"He plays violent video games too," Dr. Peletier said.

"I suppose that's bad too?" the detective asked.

"Don't mess with me, Detective. There's a very clear link between violent video games and violence."

The detective glanced at the small row of books on the doctor's desk.

Nothing too interesting, he thought.

"I read that Stephen King testified before the State Legislature of Vermont, saying that the economic divide between rich and poor, and the easy availability of guns, were the legitimate causes of violence in this country."

"Stephen King is not qualified to say what the effects of violent video games are on children. He's not an expert."

"Maybe not but he was a high school teacher when he wrote his first novel. He might know something about kids."

"I think the *King of Horror* is disqualified from speaking about what incites violence."

She got up from the desk and opened the screen door for him to leave. The detective took the hint and followed.

"As far as we know, though, Stephen King hasn't murdered anyone, right?" he said, from the door.

"I just wonder if we can say the same about Daniel James, huh, Detective?"

"Oh yeah, the dog," he said.

"And more animals, perhaps," she said.

"Let me know if there are any other murders I should know about." He handed her his card as the screen door was swinging shut.

"I will," she said.

#

Arriving home from Bixby's Market with a box of handmade Italian cookies in the shape of flowers, Aimee saw the white Crown Vic at the top of her driveway.

She rushed in and found Daniel sitting on the floor, pointing his controller at the television, with Detective LaTorella watching. "See—I ran over him with a lawnmower—a lawnmower," Daniel said.

"Oh, Danny, what have you done?" his mother asked, tossing her bag on the table.

"He said he was your friend. Your friend," Daniel said.

Aimee groaned.

"What I said was, I met you before," LaTorella said.

"What you said was, you met her before and you think she's pretty. Pretty as a peach. A peach."

Aimee's eyes narrowed.

"You tried to ingratiate yourself with my son by using false flattery?"

"I didn't mean to. Well, okay, I was trying to do something like that. It was a cheap trick. I see that now. I'm really sorry."

"I wasn't fooled," Daniel said. "I wasn't fooled. I know that peaches aren't pretty. Peaches aren't pretty. They look like butts. Butts."

Detective LaTorella and Aimee James both laughed.

"Why are you laughing?" Daniel asked. "They do look like butts. It's true. It's true. I'm not wrong. Not wrong."

The adults excused themselves to the kitchen. They sat at the table, but the detective declined her offer of coffee.

"Your son is a person of interest in the death of Mrs. Roberta Wagner."

"What?" Aimee slammed her hand on the table.

"I spoke with the psychiatrist who's treating Daniel."

She clenched and unclenched her hand. *Oh my God, no!* she thought. "Oh," she said.

"I hear that he likes to sing."

The detective was laying his groundwork.

"What did she tell you about?" he asked.

He's setting another trap, she thought.

"She thinks that your son is a very angry young man."

"Why shouldn't he be?"

"Why *should* he be?"

Aimee stared holes through the detective.

"Dr. Peletier played a recording of Daniel singing," the detective said.

"He likes to sing."

"He's listening to some violent stuff. These songs have words about killing and gore."

"Well tell me this, Detective, did Beatles fans run out and commit murder when they played Revolution Number 9 backward? Seriously, *I killed a man, groovy*?" she said.

"Do we know what music the Manson family listened to?"

Aimee rolled her eyes.

"What about these songs?" He read, "Lord of The Harvest; The Tree; Smile For Your Neighbor; Can't Clown Me?"

"Those are just dark humor. Horror fantasy," Aimee said.

"He fantasizes about horror?"

"It's a genre."

"Not revenge?" the detective asked. "Does he fantasize about revenge?"

"Some of the songs are about revenge, sure," Aimee said. "Bang Pow Boom is about catching pedophiles. I think it's based on that tv show *To Catch a Predator*. A lot of people watch that show."

"Maybe so, but at the end of the show, they don't kill all the predators," he said.

"Well, maybe they should. Who wouldn't want a few less pedophiles in the world?"

He would have spit out his coffee if he'd accepted it.

Maybe I am the bad guy? she thought.

The detective got up to leave, thanking her for her time. *This didn't go well,* she thought. "She poisoned his dog," she said.

The detective stopped frozen. "I'm sorry about his dog. I heard that it died."

Aimee was quiet. "Thanks," she said, after a thought.

"If Mrs. Wagner didn't poison your son's dog, though, that would mean…"

"… that Dr. Peletier killed his dog."

The detective's mouth fell open.

"That's a very strong assumption for a professional who's working to help him," he said.

"You'd think that, wouldn't you?" Aimee said.

"Yes, of course, I would. Why wouldn't I?"

"Somehow it's like she wants Daniel to get agitated. Like it helps her. It's almost like she wants him to kill again."

They both caught the extra word. "Again?" the detective asked.

"No! Daniel didn't kill anyone. That woman is the murderer. She killed his dog!"

The detective shook off what she was saying. "As bad as killing a dog is, we don't call that murder. And confidentially, she said something about being worried about the safety of her horse around Daniel."

Aimee clenched both fists and made a guttural cry.

Detective LaTorella looked away. "I guess I shouldn't tell you to calm down?"

She rocked in her chair and then sprang to her feet. "People are trying to frame my son! He's being persecuted! Do you have any idea what that's like?"

"I think I might."

CHAPTER 19

Kip sat on the edge of the bed that he and his bride had shared for more than half their lives. He had loved her from the moment he first saw her, maybe, even before?

His first glimpse of her was a photograph at a friend's house when he was a young cadet.

"There's the girl I'm going to marry," he said, or at least that's how he liked to remember the story. He'd been telling it for so many years, it was real, whether it was true or not.

At first, when they were young, he tried to make his wife happy all the time. In midlife, he tried to make her happy some of the time. By the end of life, he tried not to make her too unhappy.

I failed at the one thing that mattered most.

His thoughts turned dark.

He got up and poured himself a double Dewar's.

He sat back down and dialed Judith's number.

She was happy to hear from him and accepted his invitation for lunch. "Listen, Kip, now I've got you on the phone, there's something I've been meaning to ask you."

Kip exhaled heavily.

"Roberta told me something shocking."

He braced himself.

"She said you used to belong to the Cypress Point Club."

"What?" Kip was confused. "Once. Yes. Why?"

"I don't understand why you gave up a membership like that," Judith said, with genuine pain in her voice.

He tried to oblige her with a response.

WOMAN MURDERED

"When I was stationed overseas I had a good friend named Charles. He was a fellow officer. I bragged to him about this place. We joked about whose *back home* was more beautiful. I told him about the 16th hole of the Cypress Point Golf Club; how your shot soars over the ocean, and if you're lucky, it makes it to the green.

"Charles finally came to see this place I'd built up as so grand. We had a 7 a.m. tee time. He had a new set of clubs. They were fantastic, much better than mine. When we pulled up the private road leading to the clubhouse I knew something was wrong, but it was too late."

"For God's sake, Kip, I don't need the long version. Just tell me why you gave up your membership at the most prestigious golf club in the world."

"I'm telling you." His voice dropped to a hush. "We were turned away at the door."

He could hear Judith gasp. "Why would they do that?"

"My friend was African American."

"Oh my God! Kip!"

"It was the most humiliating experience of my life," Kip said. The rims of his eyes filled with tears.

"I can only imagine," Judith said.

"Naturally, I could never go back there."

"How could you? But people do forget. You could have kept your membership anyway."

"It wasn't the club I was humiliated in front of, it was my friend."

"What are you talking about?" Judith asked.

"My stupidity put him in that unforgivable situation. He was a decorated officer and a war hero too."

"Well, my God, Kip! Did you really have to give up your membership over *that*? What did Roberta have to say?"

"It wasn't hers to have any say about. Women aren't allowed to be members of that club. Savvy?"

"I never dreamed you were such a liberal."

"He was my friend."

"What am I?" Judith cooed into the phone.

"Oh, God," Kip said. "I have to go."

"I'll see you tomorrow," she said, with a syrupy tongue. "Noon sharp."

#

Kip was seated in the greenhouse room at Casablanca when his platinum-haired lunch date arrived.

"Hello, dear," she said, patting him on the hand and leaning down to kiss his cheek before she sat.

He didn't stand or pull her chair out. His face was stern. "I've been waiting twenty minutes."

Judith waved a dismissive hand and seated herself.

"You were always here *waiting* for Roberta, weren't you?" Kip shook his head.

"She did run behind, poor dear," Judith said, in her best pitying voice.

"Like her watch?" Kip asked.

Judith's forehead twitched just above her left eye. "Just like that horrid watch!" she said.

"What was it she used to say about it?" Kip asked.

"Your wife said it was driving her bonkers. Her words."

Kip's face flushed.

"She was having a hard time with so many things," Judith said.

Kip reached into his breast pocket and pulled out the Lady Rolex he'd given Roberta for their 30th anniversary.

"Oh my God, is that the broken watch?" Judith asked. "I was sure she was wearing it. She was always wearing that damned thing."

His eyes glared a warning shot. "It was at Hesselbein's, where I'd finally taken it to be repaired."

Judith paused, snickering as softly as she could while still being noticed. "Well done," she said, raising her glass.

"There's nothing wrong with the watch," Kip said, his face expressionless. "It was only wrong when she met you here, wasn't it?"

"What are you saying?"

"You were gas-lighting her."

Judith put her empty cocktail glass to her lips and tried to suck down a last trickle before answering. "How can you suggest such a thing? That's what men do. It's that Charles Boyer/Ingrid Bergman thing."

"Listen, Judith," Kip said. "Listen good. I know that you confused her on purpose. It was part of your little game of one-upsmanship."

"Why, I never …"

"Why you women have to be so petty to each other I will never be able to comprehend." Kip tossed a wadded cocktail napkin across the table at her.

The waiter signaled the bartender to look.

"All I ever did was help her in every conceivable way," Judith said.

Kip took back the crumpled napkin and unfolded it for Judith to see.

"Is this what you were helping her with?"

The bartender and waiter looked at each other.

"Put that away," Judith said, in a stage whisper.

"If Roberta gave that dog rat poison, I hold you responsible."

"That dog was standing between your wife and a good night's sleep, or hadn't you noticed?"

"I hadn't noticed, and that's my fault. I'll live with that until my dying day."

"You're just a man, Kip. Don't punish yourself."

"You killed that dog," he said, with scorn.

"I did nothing of the sort. I never touched it. In fact, I've never even seen it. Wouldn't recognize it if you showed me a photo," Judith said.

"You have your innocence all worked out, don't you? I

think you even believe it yourself."

"I merely gave your wife an idea of how some people get rid of unwanted pests, like rats and such. It's used by millions of people every year. It says so on the label. And may I remind you that *you* are not exactly innocent. In fact, you're the one responsible. She hadn't slept in a week, you stupid bastard."

Kip Wagner rose and walked out of Judith Rodewald's life. The waiter and the bartender bumped fists.

#

Kip wanted to go to the Beach Club and hit the treadmill after walking out on Judith, but he was feeling shaky. Like Roberta, he was just so tired. He wished he could put his arms around her and they could rest for a good long time.

He couldn't remember whether they had kissed goodbye. There was a 50/50 chance they had. Some couples never kissed after a certain point in their marriage, but he and his bride had vowed never to be like that.

Kip drove to Pescadero Point instead of the club. Sitting there watching tourists preen and pose in front of the glowering gnarled cypress trunk, he gathered his courage.

Climbing out of his car, he went to the bench where he left Roberta that day. He tried to remember her last words. He couldn't. He walked to the edge of the cliff. *God, I hope it was quick.* Drowning in salt water was a horrible death. The old sailor—a naval officer—knew that.

The chemical compounds in seawater enter the bloodstream rapidly by way of the lungs, throwing off the body's fluid balance. The body is toxically shocked for a tortuous two minutes. *I never wanted her to suffer.*

Her dependence on him was childlike. She tried to seem grown up, but it was an act. She was lost without him.

Kip Wagner sat down on the stone bench and wept for all the world to see. *What does it matter? She isn't here.*

WOMAN MURDERED

CHAPTER 20

Cody French watched Albert waltz around the store, putting a liquor bottle and a carton of cigarettes into a brown paper bag. The two-item phone-in order was filled for delivery to Mrs. Judith Rodewald.

"Hey Cody, drive this picnic over to Pebble Beach for me," the manager said.

"I thought you had an exclusive on that gig?"

"I like to get out of the office when I can, but not this time," he said.

"You think that chick might come in today?" Cody asked.

"Don't call her a chick, man."

"Well, she's not an old hen like most of the women around here."

"Speaking of hens…" Albert grabbed a couple of women's magazines off the shelf and stuffed them in the bag with the bottle and smokes. "Tell Pebble Beach those are on me."

"What's so special about Ponytail Chick?" Cody asked, grabbing the bag.

"I think her name is Emily. For one thing, she doesn't have fake fingernails. I hate those."

"Any tats?" Cody asked.

"Not that I can see. But you never know. They could be hiding."

"I think you found yourself a love connection," Cody said.

"I wonder if she likes men who stock shelves. A stocker is better than a stalker. Anyway, I'm in a lot better shape than most guys my age." He flexed a bicep.

"Keep telling yourself that, old man," Cody said, laughing as he strolled out of the store. He hopped into his orange surf truck and sped down the hill.

#

Judith Rodewald spoke through the intercom to the front porch. "Come around to the side, through the gate, then the French doors." Cody obliged.

"Just bring them in here, young man." He entered the kitchen of the single-story Pebble Beach home and beheld a living, platinum-haired Yzma, the Disney character from the *Emperor's New Groove*, played by Eartha Kitt.

"Proof that dinosaurs once existed, as Cronk says," he thought.

"Just set them on the counter, young man. I'll get my purse."

"Okay."

Judith left the room and returned with her wallet.

"I felt so cheated when I saw that garish orange truck pass through my stone lions and realized it wasn't Albert coming. But now that I see you up close, you'll do."

"Um, thanks," Cody said.

"Do you smoke?" she asked.

"Smoke what?"

"Well, not marijuana, if that's what you mean."

"Only if I'm really drunk," he said.

"Well, how about I pour you a drink, and you have a cigarette with me?"

"You got any beer?" Cody asked.

"Let me see," Judith said, stooping to look in the back of the refrigerator, swaying her buttocks like maracas underneath her cream-colored double-knit slacks. "Here we are," she said, producing a Heineken. "Voila."

Cody accepted the cold bottle of beer.

"Sit, sit." Judith motioned to a chair. "Come on." She patted the cushion. Cody sat down next to Judith as she broke open the box of Vantage cigarettes.

"I'm just going to light myself a ciggy," she said, taking a long drag with relief. "Do you know what?"

"No."

"I have a secret. A very big secret." She giggled. "Well, it's not actually that big." She giggled some more.

"It's okay. You don't have to tell me," Cody said. Swilling the beer.

"I'm going to tell you my secret. It's risqué. But I think you'll be able to handle it," she said, with a wink.

Cody squirmed a bit.

"Relax. I'm not going to bite you."

He gave an awkward chuckle.

"You want to know my secret?"

"Sure, I guess," he said, taking a long draught of Heineken.

"I shouldn't tell you. You wouldn't believe me," she said.

"Try me," he said, raising his hand to mask a burp.

"Alright then, you asked for it."

"Well, what is it?"

"I'm going to tell you now. Wait for it…"

"Waiting," he said. "Still waiting."

"I'm growing a penis."

Cody choked on his beer.

"I won't show it to you. You're too young."

"Uh, thanks," he said. "Have you, um, seen a doctor?"

"Of course I've seen a doctor! And, that's the last time I'll ever be seeing a doctor in this lifetime too. The idiot didn't even look at it. He wrote out a prescription. That's what they do. Never fix anything. Just pass out pills."

"Oh, yeah? What did he give you?" Cody asked.

"I forget. Thyroid—thyroid—something—zine."

"Thioridazine?" he said.

"Yes. That's it."
"That's no good," Cody said.
He paused to form a thought.
"Got any left?"
"Any left?" she asked, looking confused.
"Just in case."
"I don't have anyone left, and there's no pill out there that can cure that."
"But it's great to be alive," Cody said.
"For you. You're young. You have your whole future ahead."
"True. I hope."
"You don't know what it's like to feel death's hand grasping for you."
"I might," Cody said.
"What do you know about it?"
"I had a near-death experience. Up 'til then, nothing much mattered. Now it does."
"What do *you* care about?" she said, chuckling.
"A lot of things. But mostly people, animals, the environment. The planet, you know? All of it."
"Sometimes I just stare out the window hoping to see the face of the man I've known for half my life."
"Your late husband?"
"No, not my husband. My husband's best friend. But Kip isn't coming. He hates me."
"That sucks," Cody said.
"Kip and Lang were best friends, so naturally we wives followed suit. We were a handsome foursome on the golf courses at the Pebble Beach Links, Spyglass, and even Spanish Bay after it was built."
"There's some good surfing over there," he said.
"We spent every New Year's Eve together, dining and dancing at the Beach Club, or at the big shindig over at Spanish Bay. When it was Hollywood-themed, there were searchlights in the night sky that could be seen from Big

WOMAN MURDERED

Sur. There were gypsy fortune tellers, who would give you the news of the year to come. That was Roberta's favorite part. I preferred the more exclusive party at The Beach Club."

"The Beach Club is cool. I like it over there in Stillwater Cove. I paddle out from there sometimes," Cody said.

"The men didn't care where we went. They let us girls choose. As long as there were brandy and cigars the gentlemen were content. They could associate with others of their ilk, you know, on the patios, under the gas-heated torches."

"Cool," he said.

"Now, Kip's blaming me for the death of a God damned renter's dog."

She took another Vantage from the pack and lit it from of the one she was still smoking.

"You know, I didn't smoke for years, until the day my husband Lang died."

Puffing on the new Vantage, she began to review the injustices of her life.

"My mother, Hilda, was left with two small boys during the Great Depression. When she met Carl, a newly minted civil engineer, she saw her chance to get married again. But when she told him that she was pregnant, he refused."

"I think that happens a lot," Cody said.

"After she tried to drink Drano, he finally agreed to marry her, but it didn't last. Growing up as the resented daughter of a single mother during the Depression, I planned my escape. I told my mother: *When I grow up, I'm going to marry a man who's got a thousand dollars*. And, that's exactly what I did. Unfortunately, I didn't know that wasn't very much money."

"It's not?" Cody asked.

"Langdon Rodewald was handsome and smart, but he didn't have any *real* money. Not finding an heiress, he married the most attractive, clever woman he could find."

She looked for Cody's reaction.

"You know what I did then? I helped that man parlay his tiny bankroll into a small fortune in real estate. I could have made a great partner for Kip, too. We could have helped each other now that we've both lost our spouses. We're all each other has."

"That's too bad," Cody said.

"I was a great friend to Roberta, lunching with her every single week for years, sharing activities, even after she'd started slowing down. Losing her was a terrible loss for me. I was her only real friend for about the last twenty years, but then she changed."

"What changed?"

"My husband died."

"I'm sorry."

"And she got old."

"But not you?"

"Kip should realize that it's better this way. Roberta never wanted him to end up playing nursemaid to her. Do you think he really wanted to be stuck changing her Depends?"

"That sounds gnarly. Not in a good way."

"Kip quit the Cypress Point Club. What an idiot. We could have played there so happily. Who cares if only the husband can be the member? Who'd want to be a member without a husband anyhow?"

"I'm sorry your friend fell off a cliff," Cody said, getting up to leave.

Judith barked, "She didn't fall!"

Cody stopped dead.

"She was pushed," Judith said, glaring.

"Yeah. I know. She saved my life. It just sounded better to say fell."

"Cody, would you believe me if I said that *I* was the one who saved your life?" Judith asked.

"Huh?"

"Of course, you wouldn't! That would be crazy. I'm not crazy!"

"Yeah, that would be crazy," he said.

"My God! She was my best friend. How could anyone think I would hurt her. I tried to help her all the time. As God is my witness, that's all I ever did for Roberta. I helped her whenever I could, right up until the end."

"Poor lady. But you know what? I've got a secret too…"

"Her husband thinks I pushed her over the edge, not literally, but figuratively. He thinks very badly of me right now. He practically accused me of poisoning a dog. I ask you, what kind of person does that?"

"The same kind that would kill a person. Fucking asshole. I love dogs."

Cody got up to leave.

"You gonna be okay?" he asked.

"Sure. If I get too lonely, I'll dial 911," she said, crushing out her Vantage.

"For reals," he said, turning to leave.

"Cody, you forgot your tip." Judith held up a fifty-dollar bill. "I trust you now. Come next time too, you hear?"

But the only thing Cody heard was his surfer's jam by *Sublime*, blasting from the stereo as he tore down the curves in his Chevy truck by Hurley. *I don't practice Santeria. I ain't got no crystal ball,* he sang. *I feel the break, feel the break, feel the break—*

When Cody got back to the store, Albert could smell beer on his breath.

"Don't worry, I know how a customer can insist on entertaining a guy who's just there trying to do his job. But next time …" Albert said.

"… Next time!" Cody said. "There'll be no next time!"

"I get it," Albert nodded. "'Bye, Felicia.'"

CHAPTER 21

"Knock knock," said Detective LaTorella of the Monterey County Sheriff's Department as he peered into Judith Rodewald's room in the hospital's Garden Pavilion wing.

She was taken there on an involuntary psychiatric hold, or 5150, as it's called.

Sitting propped up in a chair with a lot of pillows was a glamorous old woman with mussed white hair, looking up at him with doe eyes behind large tortoise-framed glasses. "Are you here to give me my sponge bath?" she asked, attempting a sultry voice.

"My name is Frank LaTorella. I'm a detective. I was hoping we could talk."

"I *knew* that," Judith said, dismissively. "I was kidding. Doesn't anyone around here have a sense of humor?"

"Not normally," he said.

She waved her hand with an authoritative air. "Sit down. It makes me nervous when a man just hovers."

"I didn't know I was hovering," the detective said.

"For God's sake, sit!" she ordered. The detective sat.

"Better," Judith said, using her voice reserved for males in authority. "My, you have striking features. Are you Italian? You remind me of Dean Martin or Victor Mature. I think they're both dead now." She sighed heavily. "Everyone dies, you know."

"That's what I hear."

"I remember Spaghetti Hill when it was covered with Italians walking up and down to work at the canneries. You look like a fisherman."

"I'm from Old Monterey, a fishing family," he said. "My family was Sicilian."

"Sardines?" Judith asked, confidentially.

"Shrimp," he said.

Judith flopped back against the pillows. "You don't say?"

"I used to help stoke the fire on the boat when I was a kid. I hated getting up so early. Some guys like that brisk morning air. Me, not so much. How about you? Morning person?"

Judith shook her head. "I'd get up for an early tee-time at the right golf course, though," she said.

"Aaah. You're a golfer?"

"Aren't you?"

He wanted to say yes, to keep her going, but he had a rule about not making things up. "I never picked up the game, but it looks like fun."

"You haven't lived! You must play a round at Pebble Beach," she said. "Promise me you will."

"Isn't that kind of pricey?"

"Oh pish! Play one round of golf on the Pebble Beach course before you die. It was revamped when they had the U.S. Open."

"I'll put it on my bucket list," he said. For a moment neither spoke.

"Are you bored?" she asked, at last.

"How could I be bored in the company of such an interesting woman?"

Judith tossed her head back. "Ha! Interesting?" she said. "Is that what I am?"

"Certainly; but tell me, why are you here in the hospital?"

"I don't quite know, myself," she said. "This will be my first New Year's Eve without Lang. I suppose that has something to do with it."

"Your husband? I'm sorry."

"I can't bear knowing I've become a third wheel. People don't want me to feel left out, but I *am* left out. I'm left out of being someone's *wife*, and nothing makes up for that."

"So, that's how you ended up here?"

"They just want to run some tests," she said.

"What kind of tests?"

"Well, they have to rule out whether I had a stroke, and they have to rule out whether I have a brain tumor. Run enough tests and they'll find something, I'm sure. It's what they do. I don't remember everything they said, but I know I'm going to have a very expensive, very exclusive test. It's named after a woman. Meg, I think it's called. They have to rule things out, you know."

"There's a coincidence," the detective said.

"What?"

"I have to rule things out too."

"Like?"

"I was hoping you could help me."

"What do you need?"

"I need to rule out all the people who might have killed your friend, Mrs. Wagner."

"Hmm. Let me think," she said, clearly not thinking.

"Do you know who I can rule out?"

Judith Rodewald cocked her head and furrowed her brow.

"Can I rule out Kip?" he asked.

"Husbands!"

"What about them?"

"They kill their wives all the time, or didn't you know?"

The detective's face lost its friendliness.

"Can you tell me about Roberta's husband?"

"He was a good man ... until he turned bad."

We're getting somewhere, he thought.

"In what way did he turn bad?"

"What's schizophrenia, but a horrifying state where what's in here doesn't match what's out there? The doctor explained that to me," Judith said.

Frank LaTorella scratched his head.

"Kip shouldn't be angry with me. We're all each other has left."

"Why would he be angry with you?" the detective asked, pouncing on a lead.

"Because he's stupid!" she said.

"In what way is he stupid?"

"In the same way that *all* men are stupid."

"Oh, I get it," he said, not getting it. He shook his head.

"Do you know that he accused me of killing a dog. I think that's a very stupid thing to do, didn't you?"

"I don't know. He thinks you killed his dog?"

"Not his dog, a damn renter's dog. But I never touched that dog and I can prove it."

The detective was writing in his notebook for the first time.

"I'm not the bad guy," Judith said.

"Of course, you're not."

No one ever is.

"But Kip hates my guts, and he never wants to see me again." Judith's face twisted, and tears slid over her high cheekbones. The detective handed her a tissue. "Thank you," she said, blotting beneath her eyes as she regained her composure.

"Mrs. Rodewald, I'm going to ask you another question. Please think hard about your answer and give me the truth as best you can."

Judith nodded her accord.

"Who killed your friend?"

"Darling, don't you know? Don't you really know?"

"No, I really don't. Please tell me."

Judith took a dramatic pause.

"*Life* killed Roberta, that's all!"

Oh great, he thought. "I'm afraid I'm not following you."

"She was old. She was feeble. *Fare la mano morta.*" Judith said, waving. "The hand of fate swept her off that cliff."

"You think it was an accident in spite of the evidence?"

"Being born a woman was the accident," Judith said.

"Please try to be a little clearer, Mrs. Rodewald."

"Roberta and I were sisters until the balance was thrown off."

"Balance?" he asked.

"You know the story of Cain and Abel? How many stories are based on it? Steinbeck's *East of Eden* for one. The original sin wasn't Eve and her apple, it was her damn sons killing each other," Judith said.

The detective was writing in his pocket notebook.

"Look at all the wars men bring on. You never see women starting wars."

"I suppose that's true," the detective said. "But, maybe it's because they don't get the chance. Maybe they would if they could."

"No. That's ridiculous," Judith said.

Her face grew somber.

"I'm going to tell you a secret because I like you."

"Why not? Go ahead."

He braced for the bomb.

Judith motioned for him to lean in.

"I'm growing a penis," she said, discreetly.

Detective LaTorella straightened up and ran his fingers through his hair.

If she's pretending to be crazy, she's also got some balls.

WOMAN MURDERED

CHAPTER 22

Aimee was at Bixby's Market waiting to see Albert the clerk. Her heart was racing. When her turn in line came she set dishwashing liquid and a women's magazine onto the counter. He waited for more, but that was all there was.

Albert rang up her meager purchase and cupped her hand as he gave her change. "Could I talk to you in private?" Aimee asked, using all her courage.

"I'm going on break," Albert called to Cody, without hesitation. They walked to the parking lot where an employee stood watching a barbecue grill full of sizzling tri-tip steak. "I'll watch the fire," Albert said. The guy felt for his cigarettes and trotted off.

Aimee and Albert stood warming themselves by the coals. "I want to thank you. This has been a really hard year for me and you've made it a little more bearable," she said. Albert smiled but said nothing.

After a pause, she continued.

"Every time you touch my hands there's a real human connection. It's not just a monetary transaction like a couple of machines or robots."

"That's nice," he said.

He's a guy of fewer words than I expected, she thought.

"You knew somehow that I was lonely," she said.

"Yeah. You seemed like it. Hot though, for a lonely chick."

Aimee's jaw dropped. "What?"

"You bought all those magazines about how to please a man."

Oh my gosh. I did.

Beri Balistreri

"I thought you might wanna please this?" Albert said, outlining his crotch with his hands.

The irony! Tragedy! Fantasy! Comedy!

"No, thanks," she said.

At least we never went on a date.

"I gotta get back to work."

"Bye, then."

"Bye, Felicia," he answered, turning away. "By the way, you're not all that hot, and you're, kind of, a bitch too," he called as he walked out of her fantasies forever.

For once in her life, Aimee knew what to say on the spot. "Just because you've got a soul patch doesn't mean you've got a soul," she yelled after hm.

#

Back at the rental cottage, Aimee set her last bag, ever, from Bixby's Market, on the counter and threw herself onto the sofa, where she could stare at her lone piece of art: a painting of the Bixby Bridge on the way to Big Sur, the one used in all those tv commercials, mostly for cars.

It hangs in the air, doesn't it? She thought. She wondered why Lawrence Ferlinghetti painted it that way. It was abstract expressionism, but what was he expressing?

Within the canyon, under the bridge, there was a rustic cabin owned by the poet, publisher, and painter himself. She knew because he told her about it the day she bought the painting from him.

Allen Ginsberg, Kenneth Rexroth, and Jack Kerouac all visited the cabin in the halcyon days of the beat generation.

After Aimee's high school English teacher read her class *Christ Climbed Down*, a canto on the commercialism of Christmas, she fell hard. She borrowed the book from the teacher's desk, not meaning to steal; but before she returned it, he quit to go work with the Zuni Indians in New Mexico.

Professor Marvin, wherever you are, I have your book.

WOMAN MURDERED

Like a fan whose dream came true, she'd got to meet Lawrence many years later in San Francisco. An art dealer introduced them. He told her not to expect much. Ferlinghetti was a shy man. *Good,* she thought. *We won't overwhelm each other with words.*

She spent a whole afternoon with Lawrence Ferlinghetti in his second-floor studio at Hunter's Point. He wore jeans and a sweatshirt. He was a tall, thin, agile man, sixty years her senior, dancing around his large canvases.

He pulled a handmade pin out of a drawer. He'd painted the words, *Fuck Art, Let's Dance,* on it. It made Aimee giggle, so he gave it to her.

She was remembering how his gray eyes twinkled. *They did, they really did,* she thought. *I didn't imagine that.*

Aimee looked above the bridge into an ochre sky. She could make out the shape of a heart that Lawrence had traced with his finger into the wet paint. "You always have to look for that. It hides in plain sight."

Lawrence had driven her to the 23rd Street BART Station. Riding along Mission Street in his little red pickup, she'd watched another driver flip him off. *How could anyone do that to this gentle peacenik?* she'd thought.

"Everyone you meet is fighting a battle," he had said.

"Is that one of your sayings?" she'd asked him.

"No. That would be . . . Philo … of Alexandria's," he'd said.

"Philo?" she'd asked.

"Yes," he'd answered.

"Then it *could* be from one of your poems, right? You've been known to reference the greats."

"I reference what I love. You know, there's more than enough wisdom in the world already. We should borrow from it all. We're all connected, after all."

"Bleep art! Let's dance!" she'd said, grinning.

"You know, you're allowed to swear, right?"

"I know," she'd said, looking heavenward.

"Remember Ginsberg's Howl?" Lawrence asked. "Allen wrote a line of it: *With mother finally F****d.* It was supposed to say Fucked, but he couldn't bring himself to write it down. It was years before he could say it out loud."

"Why was his mother bleeped?' Aimee'd asked.

"For one thing, she was fucked by a lobotomy."

I saw the best minds of my generation destroyed by madness, she quoted Ginsberg in her head.

Everyone knew that in 1957 Lawrence Ferlinghetti was arrested on obscenity charges for publishing Allen Ginsberg's lament for the *lamb-like youths, preyed upon by industrial civilization.*

And now, once again, she thought, *art has saved me. Ferlinghetti and his friends were there when I needed them.* Insane Clown Posse *and* Trip B *are the same for Daniel.*

She pulled out her book of O. Henry's short stories and re-read *The Caliph, Cupid and the Clock*, about a vagabond in Central Park.

"He could have sat at table with reigning sovereigns. The social world, the world of art, the fellowship of the elect, adulation, imitation, the homage of the fairest, honors from the highest, praise from the wisest, flattery, esteem, credit, pleasure, fame—all the honey of life was waiting in the comb in the hive—

"But his choice was to sit in rags and dinginess on a bench in a park. For he had tasted of the fruit of the tree of life, and, finding it bitter in his mouth, had stepped out of Eden for a time to seek distraction close to the unarmored beating heart of the world."

WOMAN MURDERED

CHAPTER 23

Standing in the checkout line at her new discovery, Mulligan's Market-by-the-Sea, Aimee was surrounded by fresh cut flowers and colorful produce. She noticed Reverend Burns standing there wearing a wide-wale corduroy jacket and a green sweater, buying tea.

She'd seen him several times around town since moving to the area, and now she recognized him as the officiate at Roberta Wagner's funeral. *In this town he's, probably, always, busy with funerals*, she thought. With so many elderly people in Pebble Beach, surely someone's always dying. Then she had a realization. *We're all dying. We just don't think about it.*

Aimee felt the minister's eyes on her as she placed her items on the counter. She was buying soap, cookies, and instant coffee.

He gave her a smile.

"Top of the morning," she said. *I'm such an idiot*, she thought.

A middle-aged woman rang up her items and placed her change squarely into her cupped hand. Picking up her bag, she squeezed past the Reverend Burns, who was loitering.

"*It's a lang road that's no goat a turning*," he said.

What the heck? she thought.

"Excuse me?" she said.

"I was just pondering a thing," he said.

"I see," but she didn't.

"Without life's twists and turns, we might as well all fall asleep at the wheel."

Aimee nodded and wondered. "I'll try to stay awake,"

she assured him.

"That's the spirit." He winked as he left the market.

Aimee slid behind the wheel of her rickety vintage jeep, picturing herself as Linda Hamilton at the end of *The Terminator,* prepared to face the big storm brewing.

As she drove into Pebble Beach through the Carmel gate, she noticed that at the fork the road split right and left. She'd always thought one side continued straight. She and Michael had fought over it.

"Which way?" he'd asked.

"Straight," she'd said.

"There is no straight!" he'd said.

"If you can't go straight go forward, then!" she'd said.

"Why do you always have to be such a bitch?" he'd asked.

Even remembering stung. But, she had to admit, *There IS no straight. Now I see it so clearly.* It was all curves, all twists, all turns. A dip in the road kept her from seeing what was beyond. *Why do I see it now, when it's too late?* she thought.

She heard a loud noise like a gun.

The steering wheel failed to respond in her hands. She could only go straight, but the road curved. Her heart was in her throat.

She slowed the rickety J40 to a stop and gathered her thoughts. Her cell phone was dead, she knew.

She got out and unlatched the jeep's bonnet. She couldn't do anything, but, maybe, she could look not completely helpless.

Within minutes, a classic silver Z28 stopped. The driver got out and walked toward her as she sat in her disabled Jeep. Aimee panicked.

You're not a whore, are you? she heard a man say, in her mind. *I kill whores.* Sounds smells, and tastes suddenly bombarded her senses.

In her mind, she was back with her college roommate at

a dance in San Francisco at the Galleria, a five-story atrium filled with ficus trees and twinkling lights. The place was packed. She saw no one she knew, but her roommate did, and danced away with him.

Somehow Aimee found herself in the passenger seat of a tricked-out silver Z28. Most of the details were padlocked in a corner of her brain. "You're not a whore, are you?" asked the stranger in the driver's seat. She froze. "I killed a whore," he said. "You'd better not be a whore."

That was the moment she realized that they, probably, weren't heading to Denny's for a late-night snack. *He's just trying to scare me,* she told herself, as he drove farther away from everything familiar to her. In a barren scape of rusted warehouses and train tracks, the driver pulled into a gas station. There were no other cars. "Get me a pack of Kools," he said.

Aimee got out of the car and walked to the glass kiosk, lost. She thought about running, but there was nowhere to go where she wouldn't be picked up and tossed back into the car; maybe, killed, like a whore.

She searched the face of the guy behind the counter. *Does he know I'm in trouble? What kind of trouble am I actually in?* She wasn't sure what was really happening. She felt like she was running in a dream. She couldn't feel her limbs. She couldn't make her voice heard. She wanted to mouth the words *help me,* but what if he didn't understand? What if he signaled to the guy in the silver Z28?

Live now. Escape later.

Inside a bright room, a television blared, then gave way to darkness and silence. She felt her arms being squeezed. She felt pushed against a wall; choked. She pleaded in the name of God for mercy.

Please make it stop! She tried to bargain with the rapist. Eventually, she dissociated to a safe place in her mind. *This must be death,* she thought. She felt herself floating in the sky over the San Francisco Bay.

She was listening to the rhythm of the waves. *Chhh—chhh—chhh—chhh—*she heard. It was the sound of her own pulse in her ear.

"Aimee! Aimee!"

Her roommate was screaming her name. She and the guy she'd danced with had noticed Aimee missing and tracked her to the basement of this frat house. Her attacker ran off when he heard voices.

Another co-ed was there, crying hysterically. *Please stop. You're hurting my ears,* Aimee thought.

"Stupid bitch!" the girl yelled at her. "You're going to get him in trouble! You're going to ruin his life! It's all your fault if he gets kicked off the team!"

Aimee tried to understand what was happening. "He's not getting in trouble," she said, finally. The girl stopped crying and straightened up. "Don't you get it? I'm never gonna tell *anyone*."

"Oh. Good," the woman said. "Do you want a glass of water or something?" The only thing Aimee wanted was to keep the whole thing a secret for abso-fucking-lutely ever.

As the sun came up over the Berkeley hills, she waited to be seen at the free clinic. She sat on a cot behind a dirty curtain. It was cold, and the linoleum was wet. She drifted into twilight sleep and felt someone stroking her hair and giving her a soft kiss on the forehead; and yet, she was all alone with herself.

When the policeman finally came, the first question he asked was, "What were you wearing?"

She motioned to a plastic bag. He took out the dress she picked out with her mother while on vacation last summer.

"Were you soliciting?" he asked.

Aimee groaned. She couldn't find words.

"I'll just put it down as a lover's quarrel," the officer said, writing in his handy dandy notebook.

Now, standing on the Seventeen Mile Drive overlooking

WOMAN MURDERED

the vast Pacific that has no memory, Aimee waved off the stranger who stopped to help.

"It's okay," she called out.

"Did you call a tow-truck?" he asked.

She started to hold up her dead phone but thought better. "I would call, but I want to check something first. Can you make the call?" she asked.

"Sure. Is any towing company alright with you?" he asked.

"Yes, thank you," she said.

"Would you like me to wait with you until they get here?"

"No! Please just go!"

#

Back at the cottage, Aimee made chamomile tea for her nerves. She had just sat down with her book when she heard a knock. Looking out the kitchen window, she saw a little dog sniffing at the deer grass from the end of a retractable leash.

That's the dog that rode on my lap all the way to Salinas.

She signaled for Daniel to answer the door.

"Hello, son. I'm your neighbor. I believe you knew my wife, Mrs. Wagner."

"Mr. Wagner and I have met before," Aimee said.

Kip and his dog entered at her bidding.

"This is Sergeant Stubby," Kip said.

"Because his legs are short?" Daniel asked.

"He's named after the most highly decorated dog ever to serve in the armed forces. That Stubby was a hero who saved his regiment from mustard gas attacks. He found wounded soldiers too. He once caught a German spy by the seat of his pants."

"Seat of his pants. Seat of his pants," Daniel said.

"He made the front page of all the papers, and I don't mean by piddling on them," Kip winked.

Daniel scrunched his nose.

"They say in Paris he even saved a little girl from being hit by a car. A French woman made a dog-sized coat to pin his medals to."

"A dog's coat," Daniel said. "A dog's coat."

"The first Sergeant Stubby was a stray that hung around a training field. When it was time to ship out to Europe a corporal smuggled him onboard. He served in the trenches of France and was wounded by a German grenade."

"Did he die? Die?" Daniel asked.

Aimee's shoulders tensed.

"Didn't you have a dog when you first came here?" Kip asked.

Daniel nodded.

"What happened to it, son?"

"She got poisoned. Poisoned."

Kip winced and bowed his head. He had come to suspect that the selfish actions of two spoiled old women had taken the life of this boy's dog. He felt ashamed because he'd looked the other way while it was happening.

He recalled Roberta's complaining about a barking dog, but he'd ignored her. Now, burdened by his own inaction, he castigated himself. "It's a terrible thing not to get a good night's sleep," he said.

"Everybody dies," Daniel said.

Aimee raised an eyebrow.

"Stubby died in the arms of his dear friend Corporal Conroy a long time after the war. In fact, he died the same year I was born. This is going to be *my* year for dying. I've got something called pancreatic cancer."

"I'm so sorry!" Aimee exclaimed.

"I'm just glad Mrs. Wagner went first."

"You are," Daniel said. "You are."

"It would have been too hard for her without me. She

needed help, but she was stubborn. She didn't want help from anyone but me. If we'd had children everything might have been different. We *did* have a daughter, but ... we lost her. Mrs. Wagner never recovered. She buried herself under her grief."

"I had no idea," Aimee said.

"Young man, what I'm trying to say is that I need you to look after Sergeant Stubby. I'm going to the nursing home to receive hospice care."

"I'm truly sorry," Aimee said again.

"I understand they allow therapy dogs to visit The Whispering Cypress."

"I'll bring him. I'll bring him," Daniel said.

Aimee could hardly believe her ears. She looked at the little bulldog, who was her new hero.

"Hey there, fella, do you have a doggie bed?"

"I'm afraid he sleeps in the bed with me," Kip said.

"Well, Sarge, have you ever dreamed of a bed at the Palace of Versailles?"

"He should sleep with me. Sleep with me," Daniel said.

"Does this settle it?" Kip asked.

"I don't know what to say," Aimee said.

"Say thank you. Thank you," Daniel said.

"Thank you."

CHAPTER 24

Bridgette Peletier went to the stall of the horse she had owned since childhood; the horse that was now her business partner, a bona fide equine therapist.

Califia was hobbling from arthritis. The doctor was keeping her going on steroids that were less effective every day. They were taking a toll on her organs. It was only a matter of time before she gave out.

Dr. Peletier only let herself think about the inevitability of the horse's death because she was racing to get enough material for her true-crime book, the one that Oprah would call to talk about personally.

Yes, it's twenty weeks on the New York Times bestseller list, she imagined saying.

"You're the next Ann Rule, the intimate biographer of Ted Bundy," she heard Oprah say in front of her studio audience, in her mind.

I want to be the expert, the one who knows things, the only one privy to it all, the one whose opinions matter. I will be sought after by the celebrity-makers: Dr. Phil, Ellen, Jimmy Fallon.

My true-crime bestseller written from inside the mind of an autistic teen murderer will be straight from the horse's mouth. I'm going to call it that: Straight from the Horse's Mouth, Inside the Mind and Motive of an Asperger's Murderer.

She acceded to the treatment of this criminal with the expectation of financial reward and éclat. *If only he were more interesting. If only he would kill again.* Her gambit was to blandish a bond between the boy and the horse until he spilled all, but things hadn't gone as planned.

The detective pointed out that this kid wasn't like the other mass murderers with Asperger's.

Still, he lacks empathy, like the serial killer Ted Bundy, and he kills animals. Everyone hates a dog killer. Yes, Daniel will be seen as a serial killer if people believe he killed his own father, his therapy dog, that poor old Roberta Wagner, my special horse, and that random raccoon, she thought. *He will be the sensation that puts my book over the top.*

#

It was afternoon and the Jameses were expected at the equestrian center.

"Please hurry," she said to Daniel. "Dr. Peletier wants us to be there for some kind of meeting. Remember, we have to walk everywhere we go now."

Aimee was aware that it was junky when she bought it, but now, finally, the old Brazilian-made Bandeirante J40 Toyota jeep just wouldn't go anymore. It would be a while before she could get it fixed, if it could even be repaired at all, but they wouldn't be starving; not with a cupboard full of instant oatmeal and dried spaghetti.

Daniel started out the door while putting his jacket on, and his mother followed him without hers.

There was a commotion going on as they approached the equestrian center. Two guys were dragging cables from a Channel 8 News van. *Oh God, no!* she thought. "What's going on?" she asked.

The men couldn't answer.

Aimee and Daniel looked over to where Dr. Peletier was standing in the midst of a crowd.

Califia was down on her side on the ground. A veterinarian knelt beside her, brushing dirt from her coat as he attended the horse.

Daniel ran toward her. "She's alive! She's alive!" Two men in uniforms held him from getting closer. Dr. Peletier was standing beside a reporter as a cameraman focused on them.

"We're here at the Phillips Equestrian Center in Pebble Beach with a highly trained therapy horse," said the blonde reporter. "The animal appears to be on the brink of dying from *unnatural* causes. Here with us now, is the anxious owner, Dr. Bridgette Peletier."

"My horse is used to treat the mentally ill," Dr. Peletier said, tears showing in her eyes.

The reporter spoke into the mic. "This amazing animal has been poisoned, allegedly by a mentally disturbed boy, and there's more. When we come back, we'll hear from the Monterey County Sheriff's Detective with new evidence in the murder of Pebble Beach resident Roberta Wagner, who was pushed to her death at Pescadero Point. I'm Alexandra Sundstrom. Back in a minute."

Aimee broke into a sweat. It was hard to breathe. She began to shiver uncontrollably. Everything was dark around the edges of her vision. She could only make out the back of the cameraman's head. She was speaking in word salad.

Daniel, who was watching his mother, broke away to attend to her. "Look at me," he said. "Can you look at me?" She couldn't. "We're gonna talk backward from five—backward from five. Name five things you can see—you can see." His mother didn't answer. He said it again. "Tell me five things you can see right now." Still nothing. "Do you see me?" Aimee nodded her head. "Say, I can see Daniel. Say it. Come on—come on. Say what you see."

"I see Daniel," she said.

WOMAN MURDERED

"That's one. Good. Name four more things you can see," he said, squeezing both of his mother's hands. "Come on, what else do you see?"

"I see—I see—I see my hands," she said.

"Good. Three more to go. Tell me three more things you can see."

"Your hands," she said, hyperventilating.

"Good. Two more. Come on, Mom. Come on, Mom. What else do you see—you see?"

"Your face," she said.

"Last thing. Can you see something that's far away? What can you see that's far away?" Daniel said. Aimee raised her head with an effort.

"I see the corral."

"Woohoo, Mom, you can see the corral," he said.

"Is that? Is that?" Aimee struggled with the words.

"Not sarcasm," he said. "Enthusiasm."

Aimee nodded, and let her head drop against her chest.

"Quick! Name four things you can touch."

"Pants, Shirt," she said.

"Good. Two more. Two more. What can you touch?"

"You and me," she said, squeezing his hands harder.

"Good. Three things you can hear. Three things you can hear. What do you hear?"

"Your voice," she said.

"Two more. What do you hear? C'mon, Mom. Do you want me to tell you what you hear?"

"My pulse. I hear my pulse."

"Too much inside your head. Sorry. Okay, one more thing to go. What else do you hear?" She heard nothing. Her eyes rolled back. Daniel pulled an earbud out of his pocket and put it up to his mother's ear. She let out a laugh.

"I hear ICP," she said, laughing more.

"That's funny?" he asked.

"*Where's God When Shit Goes Down*," she said. It was the name of an Insane Clown Posse song.

"Okay, Mom, stay with me. With me. Say two things you can smell—tell me two things you can smell?"

"I smell horse s-h-i-t," she said.

"Good. You're spelling. That's a good sign—a good sign."

"Is that—?"

"Yes," Daniel said. "That was sarcasm. I'm studying it in school. Give me one more thing you can smell. What's one more thing?"

"Your deodorant," she said.

"Nice," he said.

"Axe," she said.

"Last thing. What can you taste right now? Taste right now?" he asked.

Aimee's breath was slow and steady now, and her field of vision had returned. She pulled her son's hand to her mouth and kissed it.

"Salt," she said, "I taste salt." Daniel wiped the kiss off on his shirt.

"Good," he said. "You're cured—cured."

"Thank you," she said, wiping her sweaty face.

"What's going on here anyhow—going on here anyhow?" he asked.

"It's a big mess," Aimee said. "All these people are here because of you."

"Because something's wrong with Califia?" he asked.

A face appeared in front of Aimee, incongruous from the rest of the crowd.

"Are you going to stand there, or are you going to come find out what's going on?" It was definitely Michael Mizol.

"I don't understand," she said. "What is going on, and why are you here?"

Michael shrugged his shoulders.

"Thank you, I think," she said. "But why are you here? What's happening?"

"You know Bridgette's horse might die, and not from natural causes either."

"Bridgette?"

"It's worse than that," Michael said. "Daniel will be named a suspect in the death of the old lady."

We're doomed, she thought.

"How do you know?" she asked.

"The sheriff is here to announce it," Michael said.

"But how do *you* know?" she asked again.

"It's a press conference."

"How did you know about it?" she asked, ire rising.

"I keep track of things."

"How?"

"The doc keeps me posted," Michael said, after dancing around the question enough.

Aimee shook her head. "What doc? Dr. Peletier?"

"Thing is, I'm the one who told her about Daniel. I met her while I was in Canada. You were so upset that Daniel would be locked up."

"What?"

"She was looking to write a book. She needed a criminal mind to write about."

"Daniel's not a criminal mind!"

"I'm right here," Daniel said.

"Look, Aimee, it was win-win. Daniel didn't get locked up, and she's getting a book deal."

"How is this a win-win situation?"

"Come on Aimee, she didn't know he was gonna end up pushing that old lady off a cliff."

"You keep saying that," she said.

"I didn't hurt Califia!" Daniel said.

"Well, Daniel, that's for the investigators to determine."

"Are you kidding?" Aimee said, raising her voice.

"Aimee, the kid listens to that music about murdering all the time. He plays violent video games 24/7. He was involved in a murder, for Christ's sake! If you think he has a shred of empathy for anyone but himself? You're naïve."

Daniel bolted for Califia, who was still on the ground with the veterinarian. Aimee ran after him. Two deputies barred them from getting any closer. "Everybody dies!" he yelled.

Alexandra Sundstrom stuck the mic in front of Dr. Peletier. "Can you please describe how this autistic young man may be linked with this tragedy?"

"Yes, I can, Alexandra. His therapy dog was poisoned last month, now his therapy horse is poisoned, and there's more …" The cameraman cut back to the reporter.

"Investigators concluded earlier this month, that the death of Pebble Beach resident, Roberta Wagner, was not an accident, but that the victim was forcibly pushed off a cliff to her death at Pescadero Point."

"One suspect has been released. But tonight, Action News has learned that an autistic juvenile male, living at the property next to the deceased woman, has previously been convicted in the poisoning death of his own father."

Michael approached the deputies barring Daniel and Aimee, so he could speak to her.

"Look, the best thing you can do is calmly take Daniel back to the house," he said, with the authoritative air of a lawyer.

She hated him for that.

"Then what will happen?" she asked, thinking she knew.

Michael looked at her with professional pity.

"There will be someone waiting to arrest you both at the house."

"*Both* of us?" She was glad the Jeep was scuttled. She might have driven it off a cliff. Arrest was a terrible thing to wait for.

WOMAN MURDERED

CHAPTER 25

After the ambush at the press conference, Aimee and Daniel walked in silence for the mile or so uphill, to their dingy rented cottage on its plot of forest that didn't belong there, among the houses of the rich. The fog rolled in tufts of white breath over the asphalt.

"Do you know why Califia is sick?" Aimee asked, breaking the silence.

"No," Daniel said.

"You didn't give her anything strange? Nothing in the sugar cubes?"

"Everybody dies. Everybody dies."

"But why Califia? Why now?" the mom asked.

"Why Puppy?" the son asked.

"You're right. I'm sorry."

"Dr. Peletier told me that Califia wasn't going to live long after Puppy died. She said Califia would be youth … she'd be youth …"

"Euthanized?"

"What does that mean?"

"It's what they do when an animal gets too old or too sick, or if they're in a lot of pain. Maybe, they can't get around anymore. Maybe, they don't have too much longer to live, so they put them down; kill them as painlessly as possible? It's a way of putting them out of their misery."

"Like the volunteer coordinator?" he asked.

"What?"

"She was miserable."

"Oh. Yeah. I suppose she was."

"Or that man in the wheelchair at the Whispering Cypress who wanted to get out."

"But people don't get euthanized," Aimee said.

"No. Just *oldenized*."

#

Detective Frank LaTorella was waiting at the top of the curved driveway in his white Crown Vic. There were no federal agents there to haul off James' computer, and no yellow crime scene tape across their front door, but he had enough reasons to arrest the boy for the murder of Roberta Wagner. The kid's own psychiatrist had accused Daniel of being a serial killer of animals, at the least.

A manslaughter conviction? His own father?

With the newly revealed prior, the detective's hunches about who this boy was appeared to have all gone south. *He has a disability. How accountable is he, even if he did do all this stuff?* he thought.

Aimee and Daniel inched up to the car as the detective was getting out. He thought he felt their fear, so he spoke fast to alleviate it. "I'm not putting him in jail until I really know."

"Thank you," she said, with her lip starting to quiver.

"But I will be back," Frank said.

"When?"

"How about the day after Christmas?"

"If you have to," she said, bristling.

"Don't leave Monterey County."

"We can't leave. Can't leave," Daniel said. "Jeep is dead."

The detective looked at the sad old jeep parked above his boring white sedan. "Oh. Sorry," he said.

"It's funeral time again," Daniel said.

"No. Not for a car," Aimee said, exhausted.

"But she was our friend. Our only friend," Daniel said.

WOMAN MURDERED

"One of the best, at least," Aimee said.
"See?"
"*Si.*"

#

Detective LaTorella drove to the little chapel in the forest. He wanted to talk to the man who knew more about the secret lives of Pebble Beach than anyone else: the man who christened, married and buried them.

The Reverend Burns kept confidences like any priest would, but the detective wasn't looking for someone's confession. He wanted to learn something about the dead woman.

"Kip did speak to me about Mrs. Rodewald once, after the death of her husband."

The detective sat up.

"I reminded him that true religion is to care for widows and orphans."

The detective slouched again.

"Mr. Wagner seemed ashamed that he had complained to me, after that."

The detective couldn't help looking past the minister's shoulder at a stained-glass window. In its center was the figure of large black crow.

Crows: The official bird of Carmel-by-the-Sea, he thought.

They were on every street corner: picking through garbage, splashing, cawing. They drove the songbirds away. Only jays, woodpeckers, and certain doves would stay; and of course, the gulls and shorebirds, but their territory was different, and the gulls were just as amusing.

The crow pictured in the window was eating carrion; entrails hanging from its beak.

"It's from the Canticle of St. Francis," the Reverend Burns said.

"Excuse me?"

"Perhaps you've heard of our thirteenth-century nature-loving Italian monk."

"I think so."

"Your given name is Francis, is it not?"

"It is."

The detective read aloud the Italian words on the stained glass, then translated. *"Laudato si mi Signore, per sora nostra Morte corporale, da la quale nullu homo uiuente pò skappare.* Be praised my Lord through our sister Bodily Death, from whose embrace no living person can escape." He shuddered.

"Francis understood the unity of all things," the reverend said to the man beside him.

"I wish I did," LaTorella said, snorting.

"He called the sun his brother and the moon his sister."

"Makes me think of that boy accused of killing Mrs. Wagner."

"To tell the truth, I was quite worried about him too," the reverend said.

What else would you tell, if not the truth? the detective thought.

"I'm glad I was able to help that young man," Reverend Burns said.

"Help him?"

"I visited him in the jail …"

"You saw Daniel James in the San Francisco jail?"

The minister shook his head.

"Cenobio Hernandez, the young man accused of pushing Mrs. Wagner off a cliff. I helped him be freed."

"You don't know what you've done. He fled to Mexico with a huge sum of money."

"Then he's a rich man now?" the reverend asked.

"Millions."

"I'm glad I could help."

"Excuse me?" LaTorella said.

WOMAN MURDERED

"He was having a time getting his bail together. I made calls on his behalf, so he could collect his due."

"His due in payment for a crime?"

"Indeed, a crime against humanity."

"I'll be damned," the detective said. "Hernandez did it."

"That's God's business, not mine," the reverend said.

"If God's business isn't your business, then whose business are you in?"

The minister laughed. "All I did was contact a party for him. I made it clear that he couldn't wait any longer, that he needed to be paid what he was owed, and they obliged."

"I'm sorry Reverend, but this makes you a party to a crime."

"I have the contact information of the person I called. You might speak directly with them."

The detective accepted the phone number. *Well, thanks be to God,* he thought.

CHAPTER 26

Aimee James watched her son roll around on the living room floor with his new friend Sergeant Stubby. *A boy and his dog.*

Rifling through a bag of things left by Kip, Daniel found the dog's wardrobe. "Sergeant Stubby has a Santa hat. He has a Santa hat," Daniel said. "Should we put it on him? On him?"

"Of course, we should!" Aimee said.

Stubby looked bewildered in his Santa disguise, with its fake beard wagging below his doggy grin. Aimee and Daniel rolled on the floor in helpless giggles before the undignified bulldog.

"What have we done to you?" she asked, daubing an eye.

Daniel reached into his pocket to get his headphones out. Music calmed him whenever there was too much stimulation. "Wait," he said. "We need Christmas music."

"Doesn't Insane Clown Posse have a Christmas album?" Aimee asked.

"*Christmassy* music. We need *Christmassy* music."

"I bet that church has *Christmassy* music tonight; Christmas Eve, after all," she says.

"Jesus wouldn't mind a *Juggalo* at his birthday party?" Daniel asked.

Aimee jumped to her feet. "Come on, hurry, we have to get to the church on time," she said.

"Church on time," Daniel said. "Church on time."

"Puts my trust in God and man," Aimee sang.

"What are you singing? I didn't know you sang. Didn't know you sang."

"Just David Bowie songs," she said.

"Is he that clown who sings about ashes? Sings about ashes? *The shrieking of nothing is killing,*" Daniel said. *"The shrieking of nothing is killing."*

"It's Ashes to Ashes," she said. "Ashes to Ashes."

"*We all fall down.* You like that song? That song?"

"I like David Bowie," his mom said.

"But he dressed up like a clown. Like a clown. He could have been a *Juggalo*," Daniel said.

"Seems like you think everyone could be a *Juggalo*."

"It's Christmas," Daniel said, sheepishly.

#

The sanctuary was festooned with garlands. A fifteen-foot Christmas silver tip near the altar looked dwarfed compared to the pine trees outside the windows that showcased the Del Monte Forest.

An organ, cello, and trumpet were playing carols as they walked down the pathway to the entrance.

Greeting them at the door was the Reverend Burns. He shook Daniel's hand and patted him on the back. Aimee winced, but Daniel didn't. *Take* that*! Dr. Peletier,* she thought.

"Say, the Burning of the Greens is in twelve days. Advent Sunday, Three Kings Day, Epiphany, whatever you like to call it. We take our trees and wreaths down to the beach and have a great bonfire. We could use a strong young man like yourself, to help haul the trees down to the beach. Would you do that for us? Will you help?"

Aimee was about to decline on her son's behalf, but he interrupted. "I'll do that. I'll do that," Daniel said. The minister beamed.

#

Back home after the church service, Daniel and Stubby were in their perches. *Dreaming of holiday proverbials.* No one had been arrested, and no one would be arrested, at least not until the day after tomorrow. *It's a good Christmas, after all,* she thought.

Aimee pulled on her *Nick and Nora* Christmas pajamas and climbed under the funky bedspread. She reached for *The Four Million* and opened it to page sixteen. She'd been waiting a long time for *The Gift of The Magi*.

One dollar and eighty-seven cents. And the next day would be Christmas. There was clearly nothing to do but flop down on the shabby little couch and howl. So, Della did it. Which instigates the moral reflection that life is made up of sobs, sniffles, and smiles, with sniffles predominating.

Jim and Della each bought the perfect Christmas gift for the other, but the gifts were useless without the items sold to buy them. Jim sold his watch to buy Della combs for her hair, and Della sold her hair to buy Jim a chain for his watch.

The mistakes people make for love, she thought.

She fell asleep with the book on her chest and dreamed that Norman's head was on the pillow next to hers.

"I wish you could see yourself through my eyes," he said.

"How is it that you're here?" she asked.

"I suspect it has something to do with love," he said.

"Can I call you again?" she asked.

"Love goes wherever you send it."

Norman drifted away.

Aimee was alone, asleep.

#

WOMAN MURDERED

It was *the hour of the pearl* when Daniel slipped out of his bed, sneaked out of the house, and ran down the hill to the building where the horses were. As he went, he watched his breath float before him like a dragon's.

Things happen, he thought.

Things had happened in the middle of the night before, and now he felt scared. He had his face painted so that if anyone saw him, they'd be the one scared.

There's nothing scarier than a clown in the dark.

Everything was locked up at the equestrian center, but he was observant and knew where to find the keys. He unlocked Califia's stable and went to her stall with a flashlight.

She was down on her side, her breathing labored, her eyes glazed. Daniel lay down in the straw next to her and scooted close enough for her to feel him. He didn't know what he could do for her, so he sang her one of his Trip B songs:

"You don't like what you see in the mirror, It don't make sense, You're beautiful. You say you've lived a life that's ugly, Let's make it beautiful."

He rubbed his hand across his wet cheek.

"Let's run into the sun, I'll make you happy again. If I can't, I'll still shelter this flame that you hold within. I'll keep you warm when it's cold, hold you tight in the night, I want to make it all right."

#

Dr. Bridgette Peletier had risen at the same hour, intending to go to the stable where the horse Califia was dying or dead. There wasn't much left to be done. The equestrian center would arrange for the disposition of the body in the morning. She didn't need to be there for the horse's last breath, but she wanted to see if it had happened yet.

This is the end of an era for me, she thought. She was about to embark on a new life, one with doors flung wide open. The past was finally passed. *Animals* do *serve people.*

Califia had served her well to the end. There would be the right kind of controversy and suspicion swirling around Daniel James at last. It would be in all the news cycles for days, maybe, even years to come?

I have the exclusive rights to tell the whole story. He can't talk to anyone but me!

She was about to go back to bed when she heard soft singing. *"Let's run into the sun, I'll make you happy again. If I can't, I'll still shelter this flame that you hold within. I'll keep you warm when it's cold, hold you tight in the night, I want to make it all right."*

She strained her eyes and made out the figure of Daniel on the ground by the horse, with one arm around its neck.

If I don't feel that, how can you? she thought. *You will make my life beautiful, Daniel. Let that be enough.* She looked at the body of the dead horse partly covered with saddle blankets by an insane boy whose twisted problems were about to become her own miracle. She dropped to her knees in gratitude.

#

Daniel sneaked back up the road toward the cottage, his bed, and Sergeant Stubby.

His black and white face paint was streaked with tears. *Califia is dead.*

As he walked in the dark, he was startled by two deer that crossed in front of him. One of those strange rabbits with ears that stuck straight up jumped out. His heart beat faster, and he wondered what would pop out next.

He wondered if the raccoons knew he had killed one of them. He was sorry he did it, but he'd had to protect

WOMAN MURDERED

Puppy. *Some job. Some job,* he thought. As he walked up the long, curved driveway, he heard footsteps behind him.

No! No! His heart pounded so hard his chest hurt. He stopped, and he held his breath. The footsteps stopped. He walked. He heard the footsteps. *I'm not brave enough for this.* He ran toward the cottage. The footsteps ran. He stopped.

Dr. Peletier said I have to face my fears. He peered into the trees, straining his eyes. In the moonlight, he saw a spot of red. There was a figure standing in front of him; tall, thin, and not human. *Holy fuck, it's a clown!*

Daniel screamed at the top of his lungs. "John Wayne Gacy! John Wayne Gacy!" He whirled around. Bright headlights from a car momentarily blinded him.

Michael Mizol sat at the top of the driveway in his Tesla, flashing the car's halogen high beams.

Shaking as though a seizure had taken hold, Daniel could now see the clown facing him in all its terrifying garishness.

Michael jumped out of his car and ran over to the clown standing between the trees. "What the *hell*, Bridgette?" he yelled, pulling her mask off.

Daniel screamed.

"What the hell are you trying to do?" Michael yelled again.

"What does it look like?" she sneered.

"It looks like you're insane!"

Daniel, who had dropped to his knees in the dirt, called out, "Not like the Insane Clown Posse, though!"

"I had to scare him," Bridgette Peletier said.

"Why?" Michael asked.

"To destabilize him, of course. He's got to be scared, and dangerous."

"I *am* scared, but I'm trying to be brave. Trying to be brave!" Daniel called back.

"He's not going to try to kill anyone else unless he's full of fear. Clowns are what he's most afraid of."

"People like you are what he should be most afraid of," Michael snapped.

"What are you doing here, anyhow? I thought you were done with her?" Bridgette said.

"Actually, she's done with me," Michael said. "I was looking for you. I came here on a hunch."

"Oh, thanks," Bridgette said.

"You look ridiculous," he said.

"I hate you!" she said.

"Well, that's almost mutual."

Daniel sensed the atmosphere and tried to comfort Michael. "It's not really a clown, it's Dr. Peletier," he said.

"She's not really a clown, but she *is* evil," Michael said.

Aimee came running out of the cottage in her pajamas, holding Sergeant Stubby.

Daniel ran to the bulldog.

WOMAN MURDERED

CHAPTER 27

Detective LaTorella didn't want to disturb Kip Wagner at the Whispering Cypress any more than he'd wanted to disturb Judith Rodewald at the Garden Pavilion, but a murder had been committed.

It doesn't matter how young or old. He's still a murderer.

From his bed at the nursing home, Kip Wagner looked up, swollen from ascites and yellowed with jaundice, to see the familiar face of his own personal Inspector Javert standing in the doorway.

"You again?" Kip said.

"I'm sorry for coming. I should leave." LaTorella backed out of the doorway. "Please forget that I was ever here," the detective said.

Kip gestured. "Stay," he said.

"I must seem like a complete ass," LaTorella said.

"You've been trying to solve my wife's murder. I respect that."

"Really?"

"Really."

The detective stepped closer to Kip.

"There's a new suspect," he said.

Kips face darkened. "You've talked to my wife's friend Judith?"

"I have," LaTorella said.

Kip bowed his head.

"It looks like the neighbor boy killed your wife."

Kip looked up and began to talk over the detective. "She's a mental case! I know all about her!"

"They're testing Judith Rodewald with something called a MEG," the detective said.

"And the newly rich young Mexican?" Kip asked, strained.

"A class action lawsuit finally settled. A grower exposed a bunch of under-aged kids to dangerous pesticides."

"Oh, poison," Kip said. "Terrible stuff."

"Yes, it is."

"Judith's first choice," Kip said softly, with scorn. The detective's eyes grew wide as he leaned in closer to hear Kip's story. "She told my wife to poison that boy's dog. Wrote the instructions on a napkin."

"I didn't know about that," the detective said.

"Sweet little Judith," Kip said, with all the sarcasm he could muster. "You say she has dementia?"

"That's one possibility," the detective said.

"My wife killed that boy's dog. I'm all torn up about it."

The detective looked genuinely surprised.

"He has a right to be angry, you know," Kip said.

"Yes, he does, but he doesn't have the right to kill another person," LaTorella said. "No one has that right."

Kip raised his eyebrows. "You're talking to a veteran of two wars."

"I'm sorry," LaTorella said. "But wars are different. Police work is different?"

"If that boy had killed my wife, I could understand," Kip said.

"*If?*" the detective said.

"He didn't kill Roberta," Kip said. His eyes were shining.

"There's a psychiatrist who's convinced that he killed your wife," the detective said.

"Really?" Kip asked.

"She has recordings of him talking about murder."

Kip shook his head.

"Talking or singing?" he asked.

"Since you mention it, I believe it was singing," the detective said.

"Yes. I used to hear him out in the yard. It sounded like all kinds of nonsense to me."

"He was singing?"

"Yes. *Ooooh. Scary. Look at me, I'm a werewolf. Shoot 'em up. Pew pew pew.*"

"I think that's called rapping," Frank said. "A lot of the kids are into it these days."

"Do you know I gave him my dog, Sergeant Stubby?"

"No, I didn't know that. Why?" LaTorella said.

"I wanted to atone for the thing Roberta did."

The detective studied the pain on Kip's face. "That kid is about to be charged with murder again," the detective said.

"*Again?*" Kip said.

"He was convicted of manslaughter in the poisoning death of his father. He would have been locked up if that psychiatrist hadn't gotten him released for her study on horse therapy."

"Is she writing a book about him?" Kip asked.

A light went on. "I wonder," the detective said.

"Of course, she is," Kip said.

"One way or another, everyone will know about him. He's got Asperger's Syndrome."

"Asperger's you say?"

"Yes, Asperger's Syndrome. It's …"

"Named after the Nazi doctor Hans Asperger? The guy who was trying to make a name for himself with the Third Reich?" Kip said.

"The kid fills his mind with songs and games about killing."

"Sounds like a war," Kip said.

"It does," the detective said.

"Look, I don't know anything about the boy killing his father, but I know he didn't kill my wife. I'm certain."

"You're not trying to protect him as part of this atonement thing, are you?" the detective asked.

"Did you know this Hans Asperger came up with nonsense about children who were different, in order to feed them into the Nazi eugenics program?"

"No, I didn't know that," La Torella said.

Kip shifted on his pillow, took a sip of water, and spoke gravely. "I understand that most women who are murdered are actually killed by their husbands."

"That's a fact," the detective said.

"I also understand that more women are killed in the war between the sexes, than men are killed in actual wars," Kip said.

"Yes. Those are the numbers," LaTorella said.

"Tell me something. Do you have a wife?" Kip asked.

"No, I don't."

"Why not?"

"She's deceased," Frank LaTorella said.

"I'm sorry."

"Me too."

Both men were silent for a moment, until Kip spoke.

"Well? Did you kill her?"

The detective blanched at first. "I was a suspect," he said.

Detective Frank LaTorella's wife hadn't died in childbirth, the way people supposed. She was slashed on her beautiful face and throat by a home intruder. Her baby was saved by emergency caesarian section. Her husband was the last known person to see her alive.

"Me too," Kip said.

"Yes, the most likely."

"Do you think I killed my wife?"

"Well, the odds are in favor of it."

"Then maybe I can do something about that boy."

"What do you mean?" the detective asked.

"I'm going to dictate my confession," Kip said.

Detective LaTorella's mouth fell open, but he couldn't say a word. A few moments later, Detective LaTorella was preparing a written document and starting a recorder. He handed Kip a pen and held the paper steady. Two deputies had been called in to watch.

"Gentlemen, I'm about to give my autograph for the last time. This one has more value than anything I've ever signed before. In fact, I believe this signature will be priceless." He signed his confession. "Thank you, everyone. I'm very tired now." He closed his eyes, then opened them again. He raised his right hand in the air and made two swooping gestures: one short, one long. His lips formed three silent words, and then his eyes closed for the last time.

The air in the room got suddenly cold. The ceiling light flared for a millisecond.

"What was that he just did with his hand?" a deputy asked.

"He made a check mark," LaTorella said.

"What did that mean? What did he say?"

"He said: *I'm checking out.*"

CHAPTER 28

On the day after Christmas—Boxing Day, the feast of St. Stephen—Detective LaTorella was back at the rental cottage as promised.

Aimee's heart ached at the sound of the doorbell. She opened the door half expecting handcuffs.

The detective stood alone on the step with his hands in the pockets of his jacket.

"Would you like to come in for a cup of coffee," she said, as nervous as she'd ever been.

"Sure."

"It's just instant. I don't have the real stuff."

"I need to tell you something first," LaTorella said.

Aimee twitched.

He rushed the words out of his mouth. "I won't be arresting anyone."

A parking space, Aimee thought. "Thank you," she said. "I know I should let sleeping dogs lie, but I'm confused. Are we still in trouble?"

"You're off the hook," he said. "Someone else is on it. I have a signed confession from Mr. Kip Wagner."

Daniel listened from the living room floor, where he was playing a video game.

Frank came in and sat across the kitchen table from Aimee while she told him about the day she and Daniel first met the volunteer coordinator.

"Mrs. Wagner got so angry with Daniel when he wouldn't make eye contact with her. I tried to explain that it's hard for him, but she wouldn't listen. She said she didn't trust anyone who didn't look her in the eye."

WOMAN MURDERED

"You wanna know something about eye contact?" the detective asked.

"Sure, but I think I already know everything there is to know about eye contact."

"Did you know that it's a myth that people look away because they're hiding something?"

"It is?"

"Research has shown that people who look away are just processing information."

"You know a lot more than the average Joe," Aimee said.

"It's an important factoid in the kind of work I do."

He was staring at her eyes.

"You've got what they used to call *sloe eyes*. They have a kind of purple color to them."

Aimee shook her head.

"They don't?" he asked.

"They do. It's just that nobody ever notices that."

"Excuse me. Did you just call me a nobody?"

She laughed.

"No, Buddy. I called you Buddy," she said.

"Is that sarcasm?"

"She's not sarcastic," Daniel called from the living room. "You have to be her buddy now. Be her buddy now."

"It's just a play on words," Aimee said to Daniel.

"Play *with* words. Play *with* words," he called back.

The detective continued explaining. "Looking at faces is a mentally demanding activity."

"Yeah, it is," Daniel called out.

"Looking away helps a person concentrate."

"If only more people knew that. People believe in a theory as if it's true, and then the effect is that it *becomes* the truth. The real truth is irrelevant," Aimee said.

"The real truth?"

"Absolute truth then."

"I try to pay attention to the words, so I can get a

person's truth," said Frank.

"I hadn't thought of it that way, but I think I do that, too."

"That's right. You summarize legal depositions for work."

"That's me, paid by the page." Aimee made typing motions with her fingers. "A fast worker can make a decent wage," she said.

"That's great!" Frank said.

"I'm not a fast worker," Aimee said.

"I'm sorry. I didn't know." His eyes dropped.

"It's like lumpy sugar," Daniel said, still calling in his contributions from the living room floor.

"Yes, it's like that," Aimee said.

"He didn't kill his father, did he?" the detective asked.

"Why don't you ask him?"

"Okay. Daniel, did you kill your father?"

"They say I did."

"They?"

"The Court. The jury. The experts."

"Oh, so you did?" the detective asked as he got up and went into the living room to be with Daniel.

"My mom tells me I didn't. I didn't."

"What do *you* say?" the detective asked, settling on his haunches beside the boy.

"I don't know," Daniel said. "He was naked on the floor of the closet when I found him. There was a bungee cord around his neck. The other was on the doorknob. The doorknob."

The detective fell back onto his seat.

"His computer was on the floor. There was a movie playing. A movie playing."

Aimee interjected from the kitchen. "It looked like autoerotic asphyxiation, but the toxicology reports said he was poisoned."

Daniel sat up. His face had a vacant expression, different

from his usual flat affect. He began to tell the detective the same stilted testimony he'd memorized for the Court.

"The day before my dad died he picked me up after school. We drove to the tenderloin and he parked in front of a liquor store. He made me get out and give an envelope with money to a man waiting on the corner. The man gave me an envelope too, but it wasn't money. It wasn't money."

"Was it drugs?" LaTorella asked.

Daniel nodded.

"At my dad's apartment I was playing video games while he was making dinner. It wasn't *Grand Theft Naughty*. I wasn't allowed to play that back then. It was Minecraft—Minecraft."

"The envelope the man gave me had powder in it, and I saw my dad pouring it into my bottle of PowerAde. My blue PowerAde. I only drank the blue stuff, so I knew it was mine. But then he poured our drinks into two red solo cups—red solo cups."

"So, you couldn't see which color you had?"

"Not good. Not good. He asked if I wanted to watch a movie, but I knew the movies he liked to watch. The ones with naked ladies screaming. He showed them to me when I was little, when I sat on his lap. Sat on his lap."

"Are you okay to be telling me all this?" the detective asked. He whispered to Aimee. "Couldn't this trigger a PTSD attack or something?"

"I'm fine," Daniel said.

"He's told this story so many times, it doesn't do anything to him anymore. He's told it to the police, to the lawyers, to the judge, to the psychiatrists, and he even told it to Dr. Peletier. It doesn't affect him anymore. It's just a narrative."

"So how did you end up convicted if your dad was the one trying to drug you?"

"I switched the cups," Daniel said. "I switched the cups."

"LaTorella got up from the floor to sit on the couch and Aimee joined him from the kitchen. "The investigation established where the drugs had been purchased and by whom: Daniel," Aimee said. "The prosecutor built the case that he gave his father a lethal combination of drugs, killing him intentionally."

"Did he?"

"They portrayed Daniel as a psychopath. They found more 'evidence.' Then they convicted him of manslaughter."

"I *did* trick him. I saw him put the powder in my PowerAde. I switched our cups. I switched our cups. I'm the bad guy. The bad guy." Daniel's face scrunched.

"He wouldn't have died from what was in that cup if he didn't already have a high level of drugs in his system," his mother said.

"I should have called you to ask before I switched them. I always ask you before I do things. Before I do things."

"You don't need to," Aimee said. "I'm always trying to protect you, but you can do so many things without me now."

"But, what if?" Daniel said.

"Those are some dangerous words: *What if?*" the detective said.

"I could have saved you all this. All this," Daniel said.

"All this? All this *is* my life, and you've already saved it."

"I didn't call you, because the Court said that you were trying to turn me against my father. I didn't want them to think that. To think that," Daniel said.

The detective looked at Daniel's mother. "Parental Alienation Syndrome—PAS," LaTorella said. "It's not even a real thing. It's a made-up pseudo-syndrome that's been completely debunked, but the courts still eat it up like it's the Word of God. It's based on a book by a psychiatrist named Richard Gardner. He started a company called

Creative Therapeutics, back in the 80s. He was a divorced father who made himself into an authority by writing a spiteful book. None of it was ever published in a scholarly journal because it was so unfounded. He had to self-publish it. Later on, he committed suicide."

"Oh, my gosh!" Aimee said. "That's horrible."

"The only horrible thing was what he did to people's lives with his made-up syndrome."

"That's what I meant."

"Making accusations of Parental Alienation Syndrome is standard procedure for high-paid attorneys whenever there are allegations of any kind of abuse. Those guys pull out all the stops."

"All the stops?" Daniel said.

"Like when someone plays the organ at full volume," his mother said. "They pull out all the stops so more air goes through the pipes."

"That's too loud. Too loud," Daniel said.

"You're right. And maybe that's the point."

"I don't like music too loud. Music too loud," Daniel said.

"I thought you were a *Juggalo*?" LaTorella said, craning his neck to see Daniel.

"But I don't listen to my music too loud. I don't want to go deaf," Daniel said.

"Me neither."

"Do you think I'm bad because I'm a *Juggalo*? A *Juggalo*?"

"Let me see, the last time I looked into it, the National Gang Intelligence Center said there were over one million *Juggalos*, and about ninety percent of them were peaceful non-criminal music fans. The FBI investigation states that *Juggalos* practice fan-club type behavior."

"I knew it!" Aimee said.

"They're no longer on the official gang list," the detective said.

"Dr. Peletier scared me. She said his sentence would be increased if the judge found out about him being a *Juggalo*. What a relief. When did you learn about all this?"

"About a week ago," he said. Aimee laughed. "I researched it and listened to some of the music. It's gory, but so is The Walking Dead."

"Do you like that show?" Daniel asked.

"Uh-uh, but my son does. He can also tell you everything there is to know about Freddy and Jason and Chuckie and yadda yadda yadda."

"Aw, man!" Daniel said. "That's cool. That's cool."

"The scary clown thing of the Psychopathic Label is just their original shtick. They started out as backyard wrestlers," the detective said.

"What songs did you listen to? Listen to?"

"Well, let me see. I listened to *Bang Pow Boom* since the experts seem to think songs about killing pedophiles might lead to actually killing pedophiles."

"You don't agree?" Aimee asked.

"If that were true," the detective said, "I think there would be a lot more dead pedophiles."

"Ha!" Daniel said. "Dead pedophiles. That's not a song. Not a song."

"But doesn't listening to the Devil's music make a person evil?" Aimee said.

"T*hat's* sarcasm," Daniel said, "I think. No. I *know* that's sarcasm. Right, Mom? Right, Mom?"

"Yes. That's me practicing for the real world," she said.

"The truth is, Daniel is more likely to be victimized for having Asperger's Syndrome, than he is likely to victimize someone else, no matter what kind of music he listens to," the detective said.

"You're sounding like a protective parent."

"You know my secret then," he said. "That's exactly what I am."

"Can I ask you a serious question?" she said.

"Sure. Of course."

She leaned in and whispered. "Did Kip Wagner really kill his wife?"

The detective exhaled. "He made a confession and signed it. It was witnessed in my presence."

"I don't believe he did it," Daniel said.

"Sometimes you have to play the fool, in order to fool the fool who thinks they're fooling you," Frank LaTorella said.

"What does that even mean?" Aimee asked.

"Is it sarcasm?" Daniel asked. "Sarcasm?"

"It's what you might call a gaslight fixer."

"I know what gaslighting is," Aimee said.

"I don't," Daniel said.

"You know, Detective, there was a moment when I thought I knew who killed Roberta Wagner. I was almost positive. It was like the dead woman herself had whispered it in my ear."

"What happened to your hunch?"

"I was wrong."

"Are you sure about that?"

"It was just a crazy thought."

"What was crazy about it?"

"Do you think people can come to us from beyond when we need them?"

"Like summoning loved ones, when we ask them to come?"

"Because love never dies," she said.

"It just remakes you."

"Why are you guys talking about love?" Daniel asked.

"So, uh, if you ever get another message about a murder here in Monterey County, will you let me know?"

Aimee fidgeted, studying the floor.

"It's normal to be scared," Frank said, followed by an awkward silence.

Daniel broke it. "Can we go to the Whispering Cypress

now?" he asked.

Detective LaTorella perked up at the suggestion.

"I want to take Stubby there. Take Stubby there."

Aimee slumped. "Aren't you tired?" she asked. "I feel like a truck ran over me."

She looked at the sad-dog faces of the two men before her.

"Well, hey, it's been a long time since we stood in that foyer and got dressed down by the volunteer coordinator. We have a new dog. Nobody is getting arrested. It's a great day. Why not?" she said.

"I can introduce you to my son," the detective said to Daniel. "He's a real character. He plays video games all the time—even *Grand Theft Naughty*."

"Smart guy," Daniel said. "Does he like dogs—like dogs?"

"He's never had a dog visit him in his room, as far as, I know. I bet he'd love to meet your dog," Frank said.

Daniel got quiet. "Sergeant Stubby is Mr. Wagner's dog. I'm just taking care of him. Taking care of him."

The detective's face darkened, and he swallowed hard. "I'm sorry, Daniel, I don't want to have to tell you this, but Mr. Wagner passed away today."

Daniel's face screwed up. "Everyone dies!" he said. "Everyone dies!"

"It's true, Daniel," he said. "No one gets out of this place alive."

"That's what people tell me, but it never helps. It never helps."

"I'm sorry. I know it doesn't. I shouldn't have tried to make light of it," Frank said.

Daniel was slapping his legs. "I wanted to tell him that I know he didn't kill his wife," he said.

"But Daniel …" Aimee said.

The detective interrupted quickly. "He would have appreciated that. I'm certain."

WOMAN MURDERED

CHAPTER 29

Aimee placed Sergeant Stubby's little blue kepi low on his wrinkled forehead. "Your hat looks good with your pleather bomber jacket from Kip. You've even got squadron patches!"

She and Daniel were dressed in scarves and gloves for their wintertime walk to Bird Rock. The Reverend Burns had pressed Daniel to help carry Christmas trees down the beach, to be burned in a bonfire for Three King's Day. Daniel had agreed, to Aimee's surprise.

By the time they walked to Fanshell Beach, there was already a large heap of dry evergreens piled beside the parking spaces. Daniel presented himself to the minister.

"Over here son, let's make an assembly line and get these trees down to the water."

Daniel took his place passing the trees down the dune.

Most of the group of about fifty churchgoers stood around sipping hot cider. The ocean was roaring in front of them and the air smelled of salt and kelp. Gulls swirled and dipped their wings close to the waves, catching the spray. A bagpiper played.

Aimee imagined that she was in that mysterious Highland village that only appears once every hundred years.

The minister set fire to the pile of dried conifers and everyone "Ooooohed" as the blazing ball shot into the sky and then slowly settled to the sand. The reverend turned to address the gathering.

"As we say in Scotland, *Lang may yer lum reek*. For all you lowlanders, that is: May your chimney be burning for a long time."

"Lowlanders?" Daniel asked in a whisper.

"I don't know," Aimee said.

"The Burning of the Greens is a symbolic time for each of us to discharge something from our hearts," Reverend Burns continued in his lilting brogue. "Perhaps something has troubled you during this past year. Maybe, you've lost, something, or someone. It's time to say goodbye to the heartaches, the burdens, and the troubles of last year, whatever they may be. What gave you pain, give it now, to God. Release it in the symbol of the burning branch."

He raised a branch from one of the dead Christmas trees.

"Pick up a twig or a branch, whichever you like, from this pile of greens, and think on what it is you want to let go of, then toss it into the fire. Watch it go up in smoke and vanish as it floats away over the ocean and disappears. I'll now read a poem by a great physician and poet. He wasn't a Scotsman, but he had a way with words nonetheless."

The reverend began to recite *Burning the Christmas Green*, by William Carlos Williams.

"Their time past pulled down
cracked and flung to the fire
—go up in a roar

All recognition lost, burnt clean
clean in the flame, the green
dispersed, a living red,
flame red, red as blood wakes
on the ash—

"Great," Daniel said. "More blood."

"...and ebbs to a steady burning
the rekindled bed become
a landscape of flame

WOMAN MURDERED

*At the winter's midnight
we went to the trees, the coarse
holly, the balsam and
the hemlock for their green*

*At the thick of the dark
the moment of the cold's
deepest plunge we brought branches
cut from the green trees*

*to fill our need, and over
doorways, about paper Christmas
bells covered with tinfoil
and fastened by red ribbons*

*we stuck the green prongs
in the windows hung
woven wreaths and above pictures
the living green. On the
mantle we built a green forest
and among those hemlock
sprays put a herd of small
white deer as if they*

*were walking there. All this!
and it seemed gentle and good
to us. Their time past,
relief! The room bare. We*

*stuffed the dead grate
with them upon the half burnt out
log's smoldering eye, opening
red and closing under them*

and we stood there looking down.

Beri Balistreri

"Scary," Daniel whispered.

Green is a solace
a promise of peace, a fort
against the cold (though we

did not say so) a challenge
above the snow's
hard shell. Green (we might
have said) that, where

small birds hide and dodge
and lift their plaintive
rallying cries, blocks for them
and knocks down

the unseeing bullets of
the storm. Green spruce boughs
pulled down by a weight of
snow—Transformed!

Violence leaped and appeared.

"Enough with the violence," Aimee said.

Recreant! roared to life
as the flame rose through and
our eyes recoiled from it.

In the jagged flames green
to red, instant and alive. Green!
those sure abutments . . . Gone!
lost to mind

and quick in the contracting
tunnel of the grate

WOMAN MURDERED

appeared a world! Black
mountains, black and red—as

yet uncolored—and ash white,
an infant landscape of shimmering
ash and flame and we, in
that instant, lost,

breathless to be witnesses,
as if we stood
ourselves refreshed among
the shining fauna of that fire."

As the minister finished his recitation some well-meaning person tucked a spray of pine into Aimee's hand. Her eyes looked at the dry evergreen branch, but all she saw was a palm frond.

In her mind, it was Palm Sunday, the year she had graduated from Cal Berkeley, and she was with her family at Grace Cathedral on California Street in San Francisco. Her eyes were on the red-and-white-robed choir, but all she could see was her attacker from that horrible night.

She could see him and smell him. She could no longer see the inside of the cathedral or hear the choir singing. She was experiencing what had happened to her as if it was happening all over again. She waited, paralyzed until the flashback was over.

After the church service, during brunch at the Sheraton Palace on Third Street, her father was irritated with her for being sullen and untalkative. Two of his law partners were there with their own families. Aimee's father asked, of no one in particular, why he had the only child who couldn't just smile and be happy.

"She'll never find a husband if she doesn't tone down her BP." Aimee remembered that BP was short for *bitch potential*.

Beri Balistreri

She left the Sheraton Palace and drove down 19th Avenue, staying on the Scenic Highway as she went, the city in her rearview mirror. She drove south along Highway 1 past Half Moon Bay, Santa Cruz, Monterey, and San Simeon, crying and screaming the whole way. The flashback was relentless. She screamed as loud as she could, for as long as she could. Over and over she yelled, "Make it stop!"

Exhausted, she pulled into a scenic overlook. After a few minutes of silence, she turned the car around and headed back north.

Standing in front of the roaring fire at Fanshell Beach, on Twelfth Night, she realized a thing. The flashback had never returned, at least not until the day her car broke down on Seventeen Mile Drive. *How did I miss that? I'm like that person who prayed for a parking space and when a spot opened up right in front of them, said, "Nevermind, I found one."*

She tossed the evergreen branch into the fire and watched it sizzle and dance. Another woman tossed her branch in at the same time and they smiled at each other.

"It's really beautiful," the woman said.

"Beautiful," Aimee said.

They looked at the sky, the ocean, the fire, and then down at Sergeant Stubby, who was scratching himself, oblivious, and laughed together.

#

After the service, Daniel went looking for Reverend Burns. He had something on his mind that he wanted to talk to the man of God about. He found him on the beach with a small crowd of people wanting to bend his ear. Reverend Burns noticed the boy and called to him. "Come here, Daniel," he said. Daniel went to the minister's side.

"Thank you for helping with the trees today. You were

as good as your word and better."

Daniel didn't answer. He was staring at the sand.

"Was there something you wanted to ask me?"

"It's about the funeral," Daniel said. "You said Jesus was killed because he chose not to fight back. Not to fight back. You said even though a lot of people would have fought for him, he didn't want anyone getting killed. Getting killed."

"I see you're a great listener," the reverend said.

"You also said God would forgive the person who killed Mrs. Wagner. Forgive the person who killed Mrs. Wagner."

"I did say that. Not everyone likes to hear it. Some people think they'd prefer revenge."

"Would God forgive anybody who killed somebody?"

"There's no doubt about it, son. If we are to believe the Bible, God has already forgiven every bad thing we've ever done, every mistake we've ever made, even before we make it."

"Even before?" Daniel asked. "Before?"

Our task on Earth is to learn to be as forgiving."

Daniel stood, digesting.

"I hope that helps," the minister said.

"It helps."

Daniel went back to his mother's side and picked up a branch. He tossed it onto the pyre, standing as close to the blaze as he could. The smoke wafted out to sea. He ran to the edge of the water, following the gray wisps.

Aimee joined her son beside the real heaven's edge. They stood watching a pillar of light open up in the sky, illuminating the dark water.

"Do you think it's better to live in heaven, or here on the edge of it?" Daniel asked.

"I like it here just fine," Aimee said.

"Yeah," he said. "Yeah. I put a branch on the fire to send the smoke to God. To God," Daniel said, watching his mother's face.

"Cool," she said.

"I let go of something, like the reverend said to do."

"Good," she added.

"If I tell you what I sent on the smoke, does that mean it won't come true?"

"A prayer *is* a sort of wish; but it's not the same as birthday candles, so I doubt it would matter."

"I'm gonna tell you then. Tell you then."

"Please don't. Please just keep it all to yourself for absolutely ever." Aimee's shoulders tightened, and her breathing quickened.

"I want to tell you!" he said, ignoring her plea for silence. "It's about the old lady who killed Puppy."

"Oh my God, no Daniel, please don't say it!"

But he blurted it out anyway. "I forgive her," he said.

Aimee's shoulders slumped and her breathing relaxed. "I thought you were going say you pushed her off the cliff."

"Why would I say that? Say that?"

She turned her face to him. "Because you pushed her off the cliff?"

"But I *didn't*. I *didn't*, Mom!"

Aimee let out the breath she wasn't aware she'd been holding, lightheaded with relief.

"Oh Daniel! Really?"

"Really, really," he said.

Her grin became pensive. "Then who did?" she asked.

Daniel looked sideways at her, trying to judge her meaning. "Huh? I thought *you* did."

"Me?"

"I thought you were mad at her for killing Puppy, so you pushed her on accident. On accident."

"*I* didn't push her off that cliff! I had nothing to do with that woman's death!"

Daniel shrugged his shoulders. "I sure get things all mixed up," he said. "All mixed up."

Aimee shook her head slowly. "If it wasn't me and it wasn't you, who was it?"

"I guess we'll never know. We'll never know. But Mom, if you did kill her, I'd take the blame for you."

Aimee stepped back. "What are you talking about?"

"I'd lay down my life for you," he said. "My life for you."

"That's what *I'm* supposed to do," she said. "Lay down my life for *you*."

"It's okay Mom, I'm good—I'm good."

"I know you are," she said.

"But what am I?" he said.

Together they laughed.

"I *knew* you didn't kill her," Aimee said.

"Earth to Mom. You didn't," he said, in *Zoolander* voice.

"Earth to Daniel. You're pretty smart."

"Is it pretty to be smart, or smart to be pretty?"

Daniel grabbed his mom's knee and tugged.

"Hey, that tickles! What are you doing?"

"It's so obvious—so obvious!"

"Not to me," his mom said.

"I'm pulling your leg."

"Oh! I get it!" She laughed, pulling him in for a rare hug. "That's clever," she said.

"That's an idiom," he said, beaming, with his cheek on her shoulder.

CHAPTER 30

One December morning late last year, Kip Wagner persuaded his wife of more than half a century to stroll with him along Seventeen Mile Drive, to enjoy the view and fresh air.

He promised her they'd find a place to rest by the Ghost Tree, where it was beautiful and safe, with an ocean view, manicured pathways, and benches at regular intervals.

He wanted to know that she was going to be okay without him.

Kip didn't like aging any more than Roberta did, but he was doing it better. He applied every discipline from his days in the military to his approach to life. He arose early, kept fit, dressed clean and sharp, and followed routines. He performed all of his duties competently. He was admired at the social clubs and all over Pebble Beach, where nothing was more coveted than aging well.

Shortly after beginning their stroll, Kip's cell phone rang. He was called away to the nearby property he was flipping for profit. He told Roberta that he felt bad leaving her there alone on a bench at Pescadero Point, but she should try to enjoy it. He'd be back soon.

Kip had seen a doctor recently and received a terminal diagnosis: deadly pancreatic cancer. He was a short-timer. He wasn't ready to tell his wife. It would terrify her.

He loved his honey bride. It was hard to think of hurting her in any way. The poor woman had lost her only child while he was off serving in a war. Everything might have turned out differently if he'd been around then.

He knew that there were people who thought his wife

was harsh, but they didn't know her or what she'd been through. They didn't know each cruel disappointment, each sorrowful loss, each hopeless resignation. Only Kip knew who she really was, and only he loved her, because of who he really was. He couldn't imagine life without her any more than he could imagine not being alive.

#

Roberta Wagner was walking along a pathway at Pescadero Point, waiting for the dog to do its business. Kip had tricked her into going for a walk, and now he'd left her there all alone with her thoughts, and his ridiculous, wrinkled, drooling dog.

She looked east toward Seventeen Mile Drive just in time to see her friend Judith Rodewald round the curve in her late model BMW.

Normally, Roberta would have been delighted to have Judith's company. After all Stubby wasn't going to make conversation. But, this morning she was teetering on the edge of depression. *True sadness belongs to this stage of life,* she thought.

She wasn't at all happy that Judith had arrived. She wished it were Kip. *Why am I always so mean to him? I guess I'm safe if I haven't driven him away by now.*

Judith joined Roberta and they walked together, not saying much, observing the dog, as it snuffled along the verge. Finally, Judith broke their silence. "You're the lucky one, dear," she said. "Kip is so attentive to your needs."

"But I'm not lucky to have so many needs!" Roberta said.

"Those are your cards. Play 'em as they…" Judith said, wagging her head.

"What are you doing here, anyway?" Roberta asked.

"God! I thought you might like my company!"

"Of course. What would I do without you?"

"Well, I know what I would do without you."

Roberta's expression soured at the smell of something feculent. "Damn it! Stubby just did his business over by the sagewort."

"That's not sagewort, Einstein! It's skullcap."

"Don't *we* know everything!?"

"One of us does."

Roberta pulled a plastic bag from her pocket and bent to collect the dog's mess.

No self-respecting resident of Pebble Beach would leave dog poop on a walking path. That's what tourists did.

Tourists everywhere with their stupid dogs, crapping all over the scenery. Dogs living in falling-down rental houses, lowering the property values. Dogs at all hours of the night.

"Damn dog!" she said.

As Roberta stooped to pick up the feces, she lost her balance. Her knees buckled, and she slipped to the ground.

"Oh, God!" she said, groaning. "Damn it to blue blazes!"

She tried to push herself up but slipped again.

"Can you get up?" Judith asked.

"No!" Roberta reached for her friend's hand, but it was too far.

"Help me!" she demanded. "Help me get up!"

Judith was staring blankly.

"Dammit, what's wrong with you?" Roberta was panting.

"I'll be right back," Judith said.

"Well, hurry. I've fallen, and I can't get up! This is not a stupid tv commercial!"

Judith ran to her car and returned with a minatory five iron.

"Hold the thing still so I can grab it," Roberta said. She was exasperated and becoming exhausted.

Judith was moving the golf club with determination.

WOMAN MURDERED

"What the hell are you doing!?"

She was jabbing and poking at Roberta, who couldn't catch hold. With each thrust, the golf club scooted her closer to the edge of the cliff.

"You ... you ... At least have the decency to *look* at me!"

Judith wouldn't make eye contact.

Roberta flopped helplessly as Judith used the golf club as a lever fulcrum. Gravity and the rocks below would do the rest.

"Look at me, you bitch!" Roberta said, gasping.

But Judith wouldn't give her the satisfaction.

"You think you're going to be the next Mrs. Kip Wagner!?"

The last motion seemed rather easy, as Judith Rodewald pushed Roberta Wagner off the cliff.

"You've got to watch out for that decade between seventy and eighty…" Judith called after her friend. "It's a killer."

CHAPTER 31

Cody French was ready in his wetsuit with his surfboard by his side. He held two ten-pound plastic boxes cradled in his arms as he stood in the wet sand of Stillwater Cove. Five people and one dog in a jacket were huddling around him.

One of the boxes held the cremated remains of Roberta Wagner, the woman whose unusual death had saved his life. The other held the cremated remains of Kip Wagner, her faithful husband of many years.

"Everyone please hold-hands," The Reverend Burns said.

"What is this, a séance?" Detective LaTorella whispered to Daniel. "It's cold enough," he said, offering the boy his hand.

Daniel looked at the outstretched palm and placed his own gloved hand in it.

Reverend Burns read from the *Book of Common Prayer*. *"After my awakening, he will raise me up, and in my body, I shall see God. I myself shall see, and my eyes behold him who is my friend and not a stranger."* He closed the book.

"Roberta and Kip Wagner will forevermore belong to the particulate matter of this place; to its substance, and also to its mythos and its mystery."

The minister nodded to Cody. Cody balanced the boxes on the nose of his surfboard and began his long stand-up paddle toward the channel out into open water.

"Cody my boy, you make me wonder if Jesus himself, wasn't the first paddle-boarder," the Reverend Burns said.

Cody dropped his stick and duck-paddled the rest of the

way to the surf break called Ghost Trees, in the shadow of Pescadero Point. The swells weren't gargantuan, like they had been the day his life was saved by the body of the woman whose ashes he carried.

That's a good thing.

This grommet with a gun, bagging groceries and listening to alt-rock for all his born days in this California tourist utopia, positioned himself for the drop: Too extreme for words.

It's the craziest thing, Cody thought, *just to be alive.*

#

The next morning, while stirring her Folgers instant coffee into a plain brown mug, Aimee decided she really wanted a coffee maker. *Maybe, an espresso machine?*

Daniel came into the kitchen and plopped down beside his mother, who was reading from the Internet.

"All women are the star gates to other worlds. Souls enter the world through women. They are the matrix."

"Is that one of those memes Michael sends you?" he asked, pouring a bowl of Chex.

"Ha! No. It's a feminist thing."

"It makes sense," he said. "I mean, I know where babies come from; but, I always wondered how the souls got inside of them—got inside of them."

Aimee's eyes widened. She nodded.

"Last night I dreamed that there was a giant yellow python in the tree outside our kitchen window," she said.

"Snakes! Why'd it have to be snakes?"

"I had a feeling this snake had been near me for my whole life," she said.

"Maybe that's why you're always so scared."

"You think I'm always scared?"

"I *know* you are," he said.

"I know you are, but what am I?" His mother laughed.

"Okay. Tell me. What did the snake mean?"

"Jung said a snake can be a wise bridge connecting two halves through some sort of longing."

"Longing for life and longing for death?" he asked.

"I didn't read that far." Aimee sipped her coffee and grimaced at the flavor.

"Well, last night I dreamed I was under the ocean in a pillar of light, and a manatee was petting me on the arm—was petting me on the arm."

Aimee nearly sprayed her Folgers instant.

"That's uncanny!"

"And by uncanny, you mean completely canny?"

"Uncanny isn't just familiar, it's mysterious!"

"I know. I looked it up. German psychologist, 1906."

"When did you look that up?"

"The last time you said something was uncanny. You use that word at least three times a week. Three times a week," Daniel said.

"Oops," she said. "1906, you say? That was the year *The Four Million* was published!"

"Canny," Daniel said.

"What's uncanny is that you and I had the same dream last night!"

"I didn't dream about a yellow snake."

"But I dreamed of a manatee! You have to believe me!"

"Do I?" he asked.

"You don't believe me?"

"I do, I was just wondering if I *had* to."

"It's an expression."

"I know. I get it," he said.

"Good! By-the-way, I looked up Sakyamuni, the guy who cut off his own flesh to feed the birds," his mother said.

"Oh, yeah?"

"He had another name," she said.

Daniel was looking down, fussing with his phone.

WOMAN MURDERED

"Can I play this song by Trip B for you before you tell me whatever it is you're going to tell me?"

"Yes," she said. "But will you?"

Daniel smiled and switched on his music.

"Here comes the creepy caravan, Hop on! Try and catch it like the ice cream man. Come one, come all, and you know you're not alone. Never alone when you're in the Trip B Zone. Under a dark purple sky, Stars shimmer in green, Everyday is Halloween. The Trip B Zone is kinda weird, strange, awkward and often feared. Would you like to donate a body part? Not the brain, not your eyes, nor the heart? Perhaps a tooth or a thumb? Only jokes, don't play dumb. That kinda shit ain't where I come from. I come from Jack O Lantern tunes and rattle a skeleton bone. Black hoodie, rubber mask and sugar skull on tombstone. But Trip B Zone's 'bout so much more than creepy stuff. It holds the keys to inner peace when life gets tough."

"I think maybe I get it, at least a little bit," his mom said.

Daniel grinned.

"I want you to know that I know that gory stuff isn't really real to me—real to me."

"Thanks. That reminds me of what that detective said. You know, about fooling the fool."

"What about Sakyamuni and the body breakers?" Daniel said.

"He was called Gautama Buddha!"

"Really?" Daniel said. "I've heard of him."

"Siddhartha was his other name."

"*The* Buddha?"

"Mmm hmm."

"I like that guy."

"Me too," Aimee said.

Daniel laughed.

"Do you think the manatee was God?"

Aimee was tired of telling her son what to think. He was growing up, and maybe, he didn't need so much instruction

from her anymore?
"I don't know that kind of stuff. What do you think?"
Daniel stood up to say what he thought.
"I think the manatee was Mrs. Wagner."
Aimee felt a warm sensation buzzing in her chest.
He's wise, she thought.
"Me too," she said.

∞

WOMAN MURDERED

**Thank you for taking a chance on my debut novel <3
I hope you'll please take a moment to leave a review:**
   https://www.amazon.com/author/beribalistreri
The sequel is in progress. Send your e-mail to be notified. You can write to beri.balistreri@gmail.com or visit www.beri-balistreri.com to read short stories and blogs.

ACKNOWLEDGEMENTS

With all the love in my heart I wish to thank:
The beautiful (in every way) Gracie Balistreri, without whose love I can hardly think what life would be; the incomparably talented Trip B, who graciously allowed me to use his amazing lyrics and photo; my first reader and lifelong friend Gregor Mendieta, who even cried; an early and generous champion, Dr. Robin Farley; the very kind readers Timothy McCabe and Holly Harris; the loving and enormously talented, intuitive syndicated radio host Karen Hager; my dear friends Patty Acosta Garcia, Billy B., Roberto Alejo Reynoso, Alison Casciano, Ronda Perea, guitar-man Nick, Robin Jensen, the beautiful artist-author Laynee Silva-Reyna who is also a Korean War Veteran (air medic and pilot); Sonne Reyna, Vietnam Veteran and speaker; the big-hearted Juggalos and Lettes who accept me; my Street Team of 6 including Donna Hudson, cheerleader extraordinaire, Hannah Kirsten Allen, who gave so generously of her time and heart, gracious Juanita Scharnhorst, sweet Kimberly Wiruth, and talented Angelica Zapatin-Solis; also the women's champion, Dr. Carolann Peterson, and my entire MSW cohort at USC; plus everyone who nominated the book and 'liked' the page. Most especially, I thank the beautiful-hearted, talented, Mary Parsons, who had the grace to admit that she *ghosted me* after I sent her the first draft but was eventually moved to become the best reader/proofer ever!

Made in the USA
Columbia, SC
04 March 2019